INSPE
AND THE LOS...   ...JANE VOSPER'

Freeman Wills Crofts (1879–1957), the son of an army doctor who died before he was born, was raised in Northern Ireland and became a civil engineer on the railways. His first book, *The Cask*, written in 1919 during a long illness, was published in the summer of 1920, immediately establishing him as a new master of detective fiction. Regularly outselling Agatha Christie, it was with his fifth book that Crofts introduced his iconic Scotland Yard detective, Inspector Joseph French, who would feature in no less than thirty books over the next three decades. He was a founder member of the Detection Club and was elected a Fellow of the Royal Society of Arts in 1939. Continually praised for his ingenious plotting and meticulous attention to detail—including the intricacies of railway timetables—Crofts was once dubbed 'The King of Detective Story Writers' and described by Raymond Chandler as 'the soundest builder of them all'.

Also in this series

Inspector French's Greatest Case
Inspector French and the Cheyne Mystery
Inspector French and the Starvel Hollow Tragedy
Inspector French and the Sea Mystery
Inspector French and the Box Office Murders
Inspector French and Sir John Magill's Last Journey
Inspector French: Sudden Death
Inspector French: Death on the Way
*Inspector French and the Mystery on
Southampton Water*
Inspector French and the Crime at Guildford
Inspector French and the Loss of the 'Jane Vosper'
Inspector French: Man Overboard!

By the same author

The Cask
The Ponson Case
The Pit-Prop Syndicate
The Groote Park Murder
*Six Against the Yard**
*The Anatomy of Murder**

*with other Detection Club authors

FREEMAN WILLS CROFTS

Inspector French and the Loss of the 'Jane Vosper'

COLLINS
CRIME
CLUB

COLLINS CRIME CLUB
An imprint of HarperCollins*Publishers*
1 London Bridge Street
London SE1 9GF
www.harpercollins.co.uk

This paperback edition 2020

First published in Great Britain for the Crime Club
by Wm Collins Sons & Co. Ltd 1936

A catalogue record for this book is
available from the British Library

ISBN 978-0-00-839321-2

Set in Sabon Lt Std by Palimpsest Book Production Ltd, Falkirk, Stirlingshire

Printed and bound in Great Britain
by CPI Group (UK) Ltd, Croydon CR0 4YY

MIX
Paper from
responsible sources
FSC™ C007454

This book is produced from independently certified FSC™ paper
to ensure responsible forest management.

Find out more about HarperCollins and the environment at
www.harpercollins.co.uk/green

CONTENTS

Contents

For the sake of verisimilitude the scenes of this story have been laid in real places. All the characters introduced, however, are wholly imaginary, and if the name of any living person has been used, this has been done inadvertently and no reference to such person is intended.

1

Sea Hazard

Captain James Hassell, master of the S.S. *Jane Vosper*, lay wakeful in his bunk. He had turned in shortly before eleven and now it was getting on to four in the morning, and he had not yet closed an eye.

It was not the motion of the ship that had kept him awake, which, though considerable, had many times been vastly worse. He was accustomed to being pressed by her corkscrew roll first to one side of his bunk and then to the other. It was nothing strange to him to have his head and his heels alternately though irregularly elevated, and to see his oilskins and other hanging objects sweep backwards and forwards through a thirty-degree arc. Nor was his rest affected by the howl of the wind and the crash and jar of seas striking the ship's hull. Except in a full gale or worse he was scarcely conscious of such sounds, for so many years had he listened to them. And now out there it was nothing like a full gale. Dirty a bit undoubtedly, but no more.

Captain Hassell's trouble was not from without, but

1

from within. He was suffering from a sharp attack of the blues. A feeling of depression and foreboding had taken possession of him. The present seemed empty and futile, the future dark with intangible but inevitable calamity. Grimly he thought that he had not had such a premonition of evil since that night long ago when a typhoon had so nearly overwhelmed his ship in the China Sea . . .

But Hassell was a materialist and he did not allow these dark imaginings to weigh unduly on his mind. He scorned presentiments and scouted occult influences. His thoughts turned rather towards his supper, and he mentally damned the cook as the real cause of his distress.

However, whether due to indigestion or not, he had never felt less like sleep in his life. He was sick of lying rolling about in his bunk. He must get up. He would go out on the bridge for an hour or two, and turn in again later if he became drowsy.

He switched on his light, and sitting on the edge of his bunk, looked round his cabin as he felt for his clothes. Considering the age and size of the *Jane Vosper*, it was not too bad a little place. Indeed he felt for it a sort of mild affection. It was his home, the only home he had. He had lived there now for eight years, since he had been transferred from the *Mary Clayton*, and he would probably live there till the end of his sea life.

For James Hassell was getting old. He was due to retire in a couple of years' time. And it was unlikely that he would get another ship in those two years. When the *Ann Blount* was laid down a year ago he had hoped . . . But Red Mackail had got her. Nothing against Mackail; he was a good fellow and *young*. That's where he had the pull. Young! The *Jane Vosper* was old too: twenty, if she was a day, and her plates had worn thin. She wouldn't last much longer. But she would last his time. A couple of years would do them both.

He put on his sea boots and oilskins, for though the sea was rapidly going down, spray was still coming pretty solidly over the bridge. Then he passed from his cabin, which was on the starboard side, into the swaying chart-room amidships, and out through the wheel-house into the night.

It was not wholly dark. The sky was clear of clouds and the stars were bright, though there was no moon. The sea all around was black as jet, but black bearing innumerable smudges of a ghostly whiteness, moving smudges, growing, fading, changing form and position. In front and below a deeper blackness outlined the ship's forward well-deck and fo'c'sle. A faint green shimmer came from the weather sidelight casing.

In the navigation shelter near the green light was the motionless figure of the officer of the watch, motionless save for an easy sway to the lurch of the ship. Henry Arlow, first mate, was entirely competent at his job, but like his skipper, he was growing old. He had had his master's ticket for many years, but he had never had a ship. He was beginning to believe he never would have a ship, and only the thought of the numbers of men with master's certificates who were walking the streets ashore without a job of any kind prevented him from becoming bitter in his disappointment.

It chanced that both men came from the same little watering-place, Beer, in Devon. They had known each other as youngsters and they had always been friends as well as shipmates. In private they were James and Harry to one another, though before the men the first officer was Mr Arlow, and he addressed his captain as 'sir'. Hassell now moved close to the other.

'Couldn't sleep,' he explained, though explanation of his appearance on the bridge at any hour was not called for. 'Must have been that damned stuff we had at supper. Sea's falling?'

'Yes, and about time too,' Arlow agreed.

As if begging leave to doubt the men's statement, a higher line of foam at that moment shone dimly across the sky on the *Jane Vosper*'s starboard bow, borne on a black hillock of water which moved menacingly forward towards the vessel. She put her nose down and went at it like a charging bull. There was a crashing thud, and as her bows swung up into the sky, the ocean seemed to rise in foam above her. The fo'c'sle was blotted out in white, while water poured in tons down into the well-deck and spray hit the dodger canvas with cracks like the spitting of a machine gun. Gradually the black fo'c'sle emerged like a rock with water running off it in all directions, and stopping its climbing, plunged down into the following trough, as if over the edge of a precipice. The jar of the racing engines came up through the planking of the bridge as the screw lifted out of the water, followed by a sudden cessation of vibration, as the engineers throttled down. Another heavy plunge and she settled down once again to more reasonable pitching.

'There are fewer like that,' Arlow remarked when the wave had passed.

Hassell nodded. He devoutly hoped the wind would fall. Not that there was anything in the sea that was running to hurt the *Jane Vosper*, but against that head wind she could not keep her speed. At best it was only nine knots, but with the wind she was meeting she averaged but little over five. Already they were nearly thirty-six hours late.

They had left the London Docks on Saturday afternoon, the 21st of September, just six and a half days earlier, and had made good speed to Ushant. There they had run into fog, and for twelve hours had had to creep along with horns and sirens going all round them. This twelve hours of blind sailing, surrounded by great ships whose reduced speed would still have cut them in two as a knife cuts cheese, had taken it out of Hassell. Conditions had then improved. The Bay had smiled on them, and going down Northern Portugal was like a pleasure cruise. But off the Burlings they had met a heavy head wind. This had continued ever since, though now at last it was dropping.

At this hour on this Saturday morning they should have been abreast of the Madeira Islands, but instead these were still something like 300 miles ahead. Captain Hassell was worried about the delay, though it was not in any way his fault. His company's boats ran on a regular schedule, and a captain who could not keep time was unpopular at headquarters.

The *Jane Vosper* was a small freight liner of some 2500 tons register, which worked back and forward between London and Buenos Aires, calling at Pernambuco, Bahia, Rio, Santos and Montevideo. She was a sound, well-built steamer of the three-island type, that is to say, with a high fo'c'sle forward, a high boat-deck amidships, and a high poop aft. Between these three heights or 'islands' were the comparatively low well-decks with their cargo hatchways. Indeed her long, rather narrow hull was practically all cargo space except for the block amidships, which, starting with the engine-room and stokehold below, rose through the officers' quarters to the chart-house and bridge above. Her single screw was operated by triple expansion engines, and she was divided into six compartments by five watertight bulkheads. She had one tall funnel, painted with the company's red and green colours, and her hull was black, relieved only by the white of her boats and upper fittings. She was a fine sea boat, and in bad weather rode easily, recovering quickly when she rolled, and rising nimbly enough to a head sea.

Though Captain Hassell would dearly have liked, before his time was up, to have skippered a passenger liner, or at least a larger cargo ship, he could not but recognize the good qualities of the *Jane Vosper*. Though she was small for regular ocean work, many a larger and more important vessel was a lot worse found. Nor could he complain of his crew. Without exception they were good men. There was no one he would have preferred to Arlow for first mate, and the second officer, Blair, a Scot from Dundee, was also an efficient seaman. The engineer, Mactavish, hailed from Clydeside. He was a genius in the engine-room, though inclined to take a sombre view of life. Both he and Hassell treated their respective staffs well, and both got loyal service in return. In short, the *Jane Vosper* was what is usually called a happy ship.

Hassell, pacing the bridge, paused at the wheel-house to look at the clock. Ten minutes to four. Eight bells and the change of the watch would be immediately. He would stay and have a word with Blair, and then after a few minutes he would lie down again and try to sleep.

He had just come to this conclusion and was turning back to rejoin Arlow at the end of the bridge, when there came a sudden vibration beneath his feet, followed by a dull roar from somewhere in the interior of the ship. Both officers leaped forward and their hands met on the engine-room telegraph. But for a moment neither moved the handle. Both instinctively waited for some indication of what had happened.

Thoughts raced through Hassell's brain. The engine-room! A boiler burst? The crank-shaft broken? Or the tail-shaft, or a connecting rod? Or had the screw gone altogether?

No. A moment sufficed to tell him that it was none of these things. The beat of the engines continued normal and tranquil. Nothing vital in the engine-room.

Had they fouled some floating debris? It hadn't felt like it. Still less had it sounded like it. It was an explosion of some kind, somewhere. But what, and where?

Though these considerations were passing through Hassell's mind, he had not remained inactive. He had quickly rung for Slow Ahead—just enough speed to keep steerage-way on the ship—and had called to the helmsman to starboard thirty degrees, to bring the ship's head to the sea. 'Keep her to it,' he had ordered as he whistled down the engine-room tube.

'That you, Mac? What is it?'

The chief had evidently already reached the engine-room, for it was he who answered.

'I couldna say. It sounded in No. 2 hold. Everything's right enough here.'

7

'Then better get your people out in case they're wanted.' He swung round to Arlow. 'I'll take charge. Get below and see what it was. And send Crabbe here.'

Crabbe was the single wireless operator the *Jane Vosper* carried. As Arlow ran down the bridge ladder he met him hastening to the wireless-room.

'Old man wants you on the bridge,' he cried as he hurried on.

By this time the men of both watches were streaming from the fo'c'sle, driven out principally by the knowledge that anything wrong meant that all hands would be required, but also, in the threat of an unknown danger, because of that haunting fear of being drowned in a confined space which lies dormant in the mind of most seamen. Brought up into the wind, the *Jane Vosper* had steadied somewhat. She was still pitching a good deal, but her rolling was easier.

Crabbe appeared beside the captain.

'Get in touch with anything that's near us,' Hassell directed. 'But no message as yet.'

As Crabbe hurried away, the second officer appeared, hurriedly buttoning his coat. Hassell immediately ordered him to check up their exact position and then to go down and help Arlow to find out what had happened.

Captain Hassell stood gripping the bridge rail with both hands, his mind tense and senses keenly alert. Gradually he grew more reassured. Nothing seemed to be wrong. The engines were carrying on steadily and rhythmically, the ship was steering correctly and riding easily, all apparently was as usual. The deck lights had been put on and he could see the hurrying figures of the men passing here and there. They were, he knew, sounding the wells, and if the ship proved to be dry they would follow that by a search in the various holds. Till he received Arlow's report, there was nothing to be done.

Suddenly, without the slightest warning, the shock was repeated. There was the same jar and quiver of the deck planking and rail, followed immediately by the same dull, muffled detonation from below. Certainly an explosion! An explosion in the engine-room or hold!

Hassell felt as if a huge hand had suddenly gripped his heart. Its beating seemed to fill the world and to be about to choke him. Then with a resolute effort he overcame his momentary paralysis and was once again his own alert and efficient self.

Tensely he watched and listened and felt the planks beneath his feet and the rail he still gripped. In all his experience he had never known anything like this.

But once again he couldn't discover anything wrong. Still the gentle rhythm of the engines continued unbroken. Still the ship steered and rose and fell easily to the swells. To all outward appearance, everything remained as before.

Quickly he moved to the engine-room tube and spoke down. There also everything appeared to be right. Mactavish was in the stokehold investigating, but so far as the speaker—the second engineer, Peebles—was aware, all in his department was in order. 'Here's the chief, sir,' he went on, and in a moment Mactavish's voice sounded.

'It's in No. 2 hold, whatever it is,' the engineer declared. 'An explosion of some kind. But we're right enough still.'

As Hassell took his mouth from the tube, his eye caught the flying figure of Second Officer Blair approaching the bridge. He flung himself up the ladder and reported: 'Fire in No. 2 hold, sir.'

Hassell nodded. Now that he knew what to do he was his own man. Coolly but decisively he gave his orders. The men to fire stations; pumps to be rigged, all to stand by to flood No. 2 hold. 'And, Mr Blair,' he went on, 'I want you to get those boats swung out and make sure everything's ready if we have to leave in a hurry. Then come back here and relieve me.'

It has been said that the *Jane Vosper* was a ship of the three-island type, with five watertight bulkheads. These bulkheads were arranged as follows:

The first was close to the bows, separating the fore peak, which contained stores, certain tanks, etc., from No. 1 cargo hold. The second was placed between Nos. 1 and 2 cargo holds, just under the stumpy foremast with its group of derricks and attendant winches. The third bulkhead was between No. 2 cargo hold and the stoke-hold. Then came the bulk of what might be called the operative part of the ship; boilers, engines, bunkers, galley, officers' living and sleeping quarters; the whole centre of the vessel. Behind this and separating it from No. 3 cargo hold was the fourth bulkhead, the last bulkhead being placed near the stern, between this No. 3 hold and the aft peak.

The part where the fire had broken out and where the explosions had evidently taken place was, therefore, just forward of the bridge, the hold beneath the after-half of the forward well-deck, between the bridge and the foremast. It was divided off from No. 1 hold and the stokehold respectively by solid steel partitions, so that with any reasonable luck it should be easy to prevent the fire from spreading.

As the ordered disorder proceeded of getting the

fire-fighting appliances in operation, Chief Officer Arlow found time to run up on the bridge and make his report. The ship was dry. Whatever had gone wrong in No. 2 hold, her plates seemed to be undamaged.

'Then have a look at this fire, and if it seems to have got a hold you may start to flood No. 2,' Hassell decided, and he was about to add an order to keep a man testing the wells of adjoining holds when the words were struck from his lips.

There was a third explosion!

It felt and sounded just like the others, or perhaps even more muffled, as if deeper down in the ship's bowels. Hassell and Arlow exchanged glances of horrified amazement. What could have happened? Something in the cargo, it seemed; but if so, what? And how many detonations might they expect? No ship's hull would stand many repeated shocks such as these. What did it all mean? And would the trouble be confined to No. 2 hold?

Once again Hassell felt himself paralysed by the unexpectedness of the situation, but once again it was only for a moment.

'Carry on,' he said, 'but before you begin to flood, sound those wells again and report what you find.'

Arlow hurried off and Hassell turned once again to the engine-room tube.

'What about that one, Mac?' he asked. 'Still all right down there?'

'Aye, so far as I can see,' was the reply. 'But yon was a bad one. I misdoubt me some of her plates are away. And now it sounds mighty like water running into her.'

'Then get your pumps going and let me know if you see any water yourself,' Hassell directed. He returned slowly to the rail of the bridge to await the result of the fresh sounding of the wells.

What under heaven could have taken place? Explosions in a ship's cargo were by no means uncommon, but, and this was what was puzzling the captain so much, they only occurred with certain kinds of cargo. None of the dangerous substances in question were aboard the *Jane Vosper*. he was positive there was nothing explosive or inflammable in any of the holds. No: once again he felt confronted with a situation entirely outside his previous experience.

One thing that seemed faintly reassuring was that the fire must be slight. So far Hassell had himself seen no indications of it whatever. Of course, with the head wind they were still meeting, smoke and smell would be blown aft before reaching bridge level. At the same time, if there were a serious conflagration, smoke would be pouring out in such volumes that he couldn't fail to see it, if only by the light of the deck lamps. He decided he had been right to hold back the flooding of the hold till he was absolutely sure that no more serious damage had been done.

Then suddenly his grip of the rail tightened and he stared forward with tense expectancy. In the dark and with all that swell running it was hard to be sure, but—yes, he was sure. Only too unhappily sure. Her bow was lower in the water.

He felt the motion now. It was heavier; more sluggish. She was not rising so lightly to the seas. Rather was she inclined to bury her nose in them. Yes, though the sea was falling, there was more water coming on deck. There could be no doubt. She had been holed by that last explosion, and she was settling down.

If it were only No. 2 hold that was leaking, she should pull through. Not in a gale, of course, but in this sea that was already dying down into a heavy swell, she should float all right. Provided always that the bulkheads held, and that neither of the adjoining holds were flooded. But if No. 2 filled up, would the bulkheads hold?

Normally, no doubt, yes. But Hassell reminded himself unhappily that the circumstances were not normal. Three heavy explosions had taken place in that hold. Could this have happened without damaging the bulkheads?

If they, or any part of them, had been started by the shocks, they would never bear the weight of water. And if they gave way, the ship would sink like a stone. Nothing could save her.

A man suddenly appeared running up the bridge ladder. Hassell recognized one of the deckhands.

'Chief officer reports five feet of water in No. 2 hold, sir.'

'What about No. 1?'

'No. 1's dry, sir.'

'Very good. Tell Mr Arlow to keep me advised how he gets on.'

This at least settled the question of the fire. Grimly Hassell realized that the hold was being flooded, and much more quickly than Arlow could have done it. But to the captain the fire was now an inconsequent trifle. He almost forgot its existence. The question had become one of their lives and the safety of the ship.

As he realized the position, the second officer ran up on to the bridge. 'Boats out and ready, sir.'

'Right. Take charge till I come back. I want all pumps got on to No. 2 hold, and have men placed at the wells in No. 1 and the fore peak. Speak down to Mr Mactavish. I'll be with Crabbe.'

'Very good, sir.'

Hassell passed round the port side of the wheel-house to the cabin corresponding to his own. His was at the starboard side and between the two was the chart-room. In this port cabin Crabbe sat bending over his desk and wearing his earphones. He pushed them up as the captain entered.

'The nearest ship is the *Barmore* of the British Latin States Line. She's 90 miles south of us and coming to meet us—bound for London. The next is the South African liner *Scipio*, 150 miles nor'-east, and northward bound. There's nothing else very close, but the *Para* of the Portuguese American Line is in Funchal Harbour with steam up.'

Hassell nodded. The *Scipio* was out of the question, but the *Barmore* would appear to suit very well. Hassell knew her as the crack vessel of his owner's rivals. She was a 7000-ton boat, and he believed could do 12 knots at a pinch. With the knot or two the *Jane Vosper* was making, the *Barmore* should be with them in about six and a half hours, say shortly before midday.

It shouldn't cost his firm much, Hassell thought, to get the *Barmore* to hurry up a bit. Then if the bulkheads gave and they were able to get clear of the ship, they should be picked up all right.

On the other hand, Hassell wanted to bring his ship to port, and it might be better to try to get the *Para* to come out and stand by while they worked the 300 miles to Funchal.

14

Without speaking, Hassell turned on his heel and went into the chart-room. There with the help of his charts he faced the position. It was a hell of a long way to Funchal, but it was a deal farther to any other port. Lisbon, Cadiz, Gibraltar, Casablanca; he considered them all. Funchal was by far the nearest. Moreover, it was on the line of his company's boats. His cargo could be transhipped there with less disorganization of the service than elsewhere. Further, to go towards Funchal would be to meet the *Barmore*. In any other direction they mightn't get help.

For two whole minutes Hassell weighed the matter. Then, his mind made up, he returned to the wireless-room.

'Tell the *Barmore* we've had an explosion and got No. 2 hold flooded, and ask her to come along as quickly as she can. Say we're not in immediate danger, but that we should be if anything gave way.'

Crabbe said, 'Right, sir,' and began to call, while Hassell bent over the desk. He took a message form and wrote, slowly and with thought. Heading it with the code name and address of his firm, he went on:

'S.S. *Jane Vosper* L. 36° ·19′ N. 14° ·44′ W. Stop. Regret to state have had series of unexplained explosions in No. 2 hold, which has been pierced and is flooded. Stop. Expect to be able to reach Funchal but have asked *Barmore* to look out for us. Stop. No immediate danger. Stop. Hassell.'

'Send that to Funchal to be cabled home when you've finished with the *Barmore*,' he ordered, and turned to go back to the bridge.

As he looked out of the door of the wireless-room, which, being on the port side of the ship, faced east, he saw that dawn was already breaking. The sky and horizon were lightening and he could dimly see the swells moving past, now almost smooth and free from white. Soon it would be daylight, and there would be one handicapping difficulty the less to meet.

But it was not on the sea and the horizon that his attention lingered. Turning from the consideration of their plans to the immediate present, he gave a gasp. The ship was tilted forward; unmistakably. God, but she was down by the head! A glance from the bridge horrified him. The forward end of the well-deck was down nearly level with the water, and the fo'c'sle was but little above it.

Hassell stared in dismay. Then he congratulated himself that the *Jane Vosper* was not fully loaded. She was not down to her Plimsoll marks. This had been regrettable from the point of view of the profits of the voyage, though it made her steadier and easier to manage than if deeper in the water. But now this matter had become of importance. This very buoyancy might prove her salvation. Every extra inch of freeboard she had would stand to her in her present state.

As Hassell watched, a huge swell came rolling forward. With the wind so much down, there was but little broken water on its crest. But still it was a pretty big sea. Fascinated, he watched it sweep down on them.

Normally the *Jane Vosper* would have swung up her bows and crested it with ease. But now she hung in its path, as if uncertain, as if waiting for some order to make the required move.

It came on relentless, without haste, without delay. It struck the bows a crash that jarred the planks of the bridge like another explosion. It came on over the fo'c'sle as if the latter had not been there, and fell, hundreds of tons of it, on to the well-deck. It surged against the amidships fittings, sending a burst of green water up over the bridge.

Captain Hassell, clinging to the rail for dear life, could see nothing of his ship forward. There was in front of him only a white seethe of foaming water. The *Jane Vosper* staggered as if she had received a mortal blow.

'God!' thought Hassell, 'she's gone! She'll never come up again!'

For breathless seconds her fate seemed to hang in the balance. Then slowly her bow began to rise. The water forward began to pour away, and the fo'c'sle appeared, black and rugged against the creaming foam.

Hassell moved beside his second mate. 'Go down and see what Arlow is doing,' he said quietly. 'If we can spare the men I should like to rig a sea anchor. Come up again and report.'

Blair hurried off, and Hassell went again to the engine-room tube. 'Could you spare the time to come up and speak to me?' he asked the chief.

'We have oor hands full wi' the stern being up in the air and her racing every ither minute,' answered Mactavish, 'but I'll be able to run up for a moment.'

Hassell moved back to the rail. Thank heaven it was getting light at last. And the sea was falling quickly. Perhaps he was wrong about that sea anchor. Probably by the time they got it out it wouldn't be needed. Probably the hands could be more usefully employed below. Well, he would hear what Mactavish and Arlow advised, and then he would have a look at the damage himself, and then he would decide.

'She's weel enough doon by the head,' said a voice at his shoulder in broad Scotch.

'She's down as far as she'll go,' Hassell returned firmly. 'I want a word with you, Mac. You still all right below?'

'Aye, I canna complain so far as the engine-room's concerned.'

'We'll have to shore those bulkheads. The Lord knows how they've been weakened by the explosions. If they hold, we're all right. If they go——' He shrugged. 'What about it?'

'I was thinking it would come to that and I've been getting forward stuff. I canna promise much with the stuff we've got—only a few old beams. But we'll do the best we can.'

Hassell knew the chief would never admit that any materials he had were suitable for the job he was given, nor that the work could be satisfactorily carried out. But he knew also that if Mactavish failed in it, no other man afloat would succeed.

'Right,' he said. 'Carry on, will you.' Then he caught sight of the first officer coming along the deck. 'Wait,' he went on. 'Let's hear what Arlow has to say before you go. Well, Mr Mate?'

'No. 2 hold's full, sir. Right full up to sea level. And it came in so quickly that there's no earthly use in pumping. She must have a hole as big as a ventilator in her bottom.'

'No. 1 hold still dry?'

'Still dry, sir.'

'Well, Mr Arlow, I want that bulkhead shored. The glass is rising and we'll have good weather presently, and I'm going to work her under her own steam into Funchal. All the same, the *Barmore*'s bearing down on us, though I'd rather not stop her if I can help. Go ahead with that shoring, and I'll come down to see you presently. Where's Mr Blair?'

18

'Carrying on in my place, sir.'

'Right: send him up when you can.'

Neither of the two men he was speaking to required encouragement to do their best for the ship. And yet Hassell saw that his confident manner had reassured both of them. He had given them this reassurance because that was his job as their superior officer, but it was an assurance that he was far from feeling himself. That Mactavish should be able to make a job of the shoring, he had little doubt. But it was far otherwise in the case of No. 1 hold. There the mate would be hampered by the cargo. He couldn't get it out to make room to work, because it would be impossible to lift most of it without a winch. And a winch could not be used, because, unless the sea fell very much farther, they dare not uncover the hatch. However, Arlow must just do his best. Here again it was fortunate the hold was not full. They would at least have a certain headroom.

As the mate and Mactavish went down the ladder, Crabbe appeared.

'The *Barmore*'s coming full speed, sir,' he reported. 'She expects to be here by midday or earlier.'

Hassell nodded. Midday! Would they do it! He knew the enormous stresses the bulkheads were bearing, stresses increased far beyond the normal by the pitching of the ship. He could picture only too well those stresses becoming strains, deformation taking place, an extra pull coming on some rivet, it sheering, and then—It wouldn't then be long till a whole row of them went. And if a row went . . . Well, one of those plunges she was taking would simply be her last. She would plough into a wave as she was even then doing, but after it had passed, her bow

19

wouldn't come up. And the next wave would find it lower still. The stern would rise. The water would creep up the deck. And then . . .

Hassell sighed, then glanced around him. What a blessing the sea was falling! Though every wave was still sweeping over the fo'c'sle, they were doing so with less and less violence. The wind had practically died down and the hillocks of water were almost smooth and unbroken. Given good weather, she should be able to bear another knot or two, and make Funchal under her own steam without calling on anyone for help. At half-speed, which was the utmost he dare push her to, she should do it in less than three days.

It was now six o'clock and the sun was up. It made a difference, though Hassell didn't realize it. Unconsciously as he looked at it, the outlook seemed to improve. Things grew more rosy, figuratively as well as literally. This was a nasty experience, but they were going to pull through it. His mind strayed towards the question of dry dock accommodation at Funchal . . .

Then he returned again to the question of that bulkhead in No. 1 hold. He didn't think, no matter how much the sea fell, that with the bow as deep in the water as it was, it would be safe to open the hatch. If they did so and they got a wave over, it would probably send her straight to the bottom. They would have to work the cargo back from the face of the plates, get a beam across, put back the cargo, and then make a longitudinal channel or two for the struts. Difficult, but not impossible.

Blair interrupted his thoughts. 'You want me, sir?'

'Yes. Take over, will you. I'm going below.'

He turned away, but before he reached the ladder he

was struck motionless by another terrible explosion. It came like the others, but worse—much worse. Not only was the sound louder, but the shock, coming up through the planking of the deck, was far more severe. The whole fabric of the ship seemed to stagger. She seemed to stop, as if dumbly protesting at this new calamity. Hassell gasped. For two seconds he stood motionless. Then he turned back to the engine-room tube. He whistled: without reply. At last he heard Mactavish's voice.

'Yon's about done it, I'm thinking,' the chief declared. 'The bulkhead's buckling. Some of the rivets are started, and she's beginning to weep down the joints.'

'You're getting your pumps going, I take it? Better start them for No. 1 hold too. I'll come down to see you when I hear what's happened there.' He turned to Blair. 'See Arlow and find out how things are with him.'

While waiting for Blair to return, Hassell kept his eyes glued to the ship forward. No, she did not seem to be getting lower in the water. A little more flooding aboard would show; a very little. A very little would put her down altogether. As he had only too vividly pictured, one of those dips that she took would be the last; she just wouldn't rise again. And all his crew were below. Not one of them would have a dog's chance . . .

For a moment temptation assailed him. Was it not his duty to make sure of their lives while he could? After all, the ship and the cargo were insured. His owners wouldn't be hard hit. The men trusted him. Was he justified in taking a risk with their lives?

Then Blair appeared, and Hassell became once again the master of his steamer and his soul.

'Water's leaking into No. 1 hold, sir, but only leaking. Mr Arlow thinks the pumps may keep it under.'

'Good. Then you take over here. Watch her motion, and if you think she's settling send for me. If you're sure she's going, don't hesitate to sound Abandon Ship. But don't do that,' he smiled crookedly, 'unless you are sure.'

Hassell passed down the bridge ladder, and entering the deck-house below, made his way through the officers' quarters and into the upper portion of the engine-room. The air was heavy with pulsations, not of the engines, which were little more than moving, but with the clangs and suckings and thrusts of the pumps. As quickly as he could, without appearing to hurry, he climbed down the steel ladders, past the big low-pressure cylinder with its teak covering, secured by brass bands, past the great blocks of the cross-heads, moving slowly up and down in their slide bars, and so down to the cranks, burying themselves in pits in the floor and unearthing themselves again with a slow and dignified regularity. All around was the subsidiary machinery; the pumps clacking hard, the dynamo with its low hum, the reversing engine, the rows of dials and gauges. The engine-room was deserted save for Peebles, the second engineer, who stood with his hand on the main throttle, ready to cut off steam should the screw lift out of the water and the engines race. He looked up and saw Hassell.

'Chief's in the stokehold, sir,' he shouted, indicating the low door with a backward gesture of his head.

Hassell passed through. It had been hot in the engine-room, and in here it was stifling. But the captain didn't notice it. He pushed his way along the confined space between the two single-ended Scotch boilers which supplied the ship's motive power, forward to the doubtful bulkhead. There he found Mactavish and as many of his staff as there was room for.

The chief had managed to bring forward a number of planks and baulks of wood and a couple of rolled steel joists, but he had not yet succeeded in getting these into place. Happening at that moment to swing round, he saw Hassell. He beckoned him over to the end of the bulkhead, against the ship's side.

'See yon?' he pointed.

The captain gazed with sinking heart. Down the joint in the angle a little stream of water was trickling, very quietly, very silently. It was not large, not more than the size of a stout walking stick. It was impossible to say where it was coming from, but it began some three or four feet above Hassell's head. By the time it had reached the floor, there was twice the volume.

'You see?' Mactavish repeated. 'Yon joint's weeping all the way down. And it's the same at the ither side and along the bottom. And see.' He pointed to the centre, above their heads. 'See, the whole darned affair is bulged. It was the last shot did it.'

Hassell nodded. He forced himself to speak calmly. 'I see that, Mac. But you've got to hold it. You can shore it to stand for seventy hours. Seventy hours with a falling sea. Then we'll be in Funchal, and if we can't get a dry dock we can beach her.'

'It's a' very weel. The whole—business is started, and those rivets may sheer. At any minute one of those joints may rip, and then we'd have the whole—Atlantic in here.' He spoke in a low tone, then swung away. 'Come on, you —s,' he cried, 'get that joist round with the end butted on here!'

23

That was Mac all over. Many a time Hassell had smiled at his little idiosyncrasies, though now they only irritated. He would grumble about everything and call his men by the foulest epithets, and he would carry his job to a triumphant conclusion and his men would love him and give him of their best.

But bad as the situation was here, Captain Hassell felt that it would be worse in No. 1 hold. Here, confined as was the space, you could at least get at the plates you wanted to shore. You could see where you stood and know whether what you were doing was meeting the situation. But where Arlow was working none of these things would be possible. The bulkhead would be covered with cargo. And it would be difficult to remove that cargo, for the simple reason that, unless the hatch was opened, you couldn't get power on it to lift it. He must go down into the hold and see how Arlow was faring.

'Well, I'll leave you to it, Mac,' he said. 'You'll do it all right.' He paused and was about to add that if the chief thought they ought to leave, he had only to say so. Then he thought better of it. That was well understood between them. If the chief had said, 'This is dangerous: we're going to throw away our lives: we'd better quit,' Hassell would have said, 'Right, come along,' and well both men knew it.

The captain passed back between the boilers and into the engine-room. There, save for the ominous downward tilt towards the bows, and the unusual noise of the pumps, everything seemed so normal and commonplace as to be definitely reassuring. Strange to think that their ship, and perhaps their lives, should be dependent on the staying power of a few over-stressed rivets!

He climbed up the shining ladders out of the engine-room, and watching his opportunity, crossed the well-deck, and entering the fo'c'sle, went down into No. 1 hold. There Arlow had rigged lights, and Hassell climbed across stacks of cargo to where he could see the moving forms of men. One of these with blackened face, and blood running from a cut on the cheek, revealed itself as the first officer.

''Fraid we're not going to do it, sir,' Arlow said when he saw the captain. 'The water's gaining on the pumps and we can't get at the leak. It was that last explosion. The whole bulkhead's shaken.'

'How much is there in her now?'

'Getting on to two feet. I have the hand pumps going as well as the steam, and I've been trying to clear a way to drop some more emergency suction pipes, but we can't get the darned stuff moved.'

'What is it down there that you're up against?'

'Crates. Big crates weighing the Lord knows what, and all jammed together. We could scarcely get them out if they were empty. We'd want the hatch open and the derrick on to them.'

'You can't get that.'

'Have a look, sir, for yourself.'

Hassell climbed down the sort of shaft which Arlow had succeeded in sinking against the face of the bulkhead. He had cleared about seven feet deep, and had come down to the crates he had spoken of. A glance showed Hassell that the mate had not exaggerated. Power would be required to shift those tightly-packed crates.

'We'll try if the chief can't get some more pumps on it,' he said. 'In the meantime can't you get a beam across some of that cargo with a set of blocks that would lift the crates?'

'I'm trying to do that, sir. Scholes and some men are getting a beam forward. But I doubt—' He glanced quickly round. They were out of hearing of the men. 'She's pretty near her limit, James,' he went on. 'Another foot of water here, and I believe she'll go.'

'You've a man at the well?'

'Arkwright. He keeps on sounding and reporting.'

'How quick is she making?'

'Not very quickly. Couldn't say exactly.'

'Well, we've some time yet. Get your blocks on and try to get a sump down to the water and we'll have some more hand pumps on. Don't bother about the shoring in the meantime. I'll go down again to Mac and see if he can help you.'

Hassell was almost in despair as he retraced his way from the hold and climbed once more down the engine-room ladders. It was beginning to look as if he were going to lose his ship. Momentarily he glanced back over his life. He had been in command for eighteen years. Eighteen years without a serious mishap, and now at the end of his career—to lose his ship! That it wouldn't be his fault scarcely mattered. It would be ruin in his old age just the same as if he had deliberately sunk her. For a moment his thoughts grew bitter and he felt that he had spent his years for nought. Then he saw that at the present time he must not harbour such ideas. Resolutely he pulled himself together. He forced thoughts of himself from his mind and became once more the captain, whose job it was to encourage and protect his men.

Mactavish saw him as he emerged from between the

boilers, and beckoned him once again into the corner between the bulkhead and the ship's side.

'See yon?' he said again.

Hassell looked in the angle. The water was flowing down—much more strongly. The stream which had been as thick as a walking stick was now as thick as a man's arm. Instead of flowing silently, it was now making a gurgling, loud enough to be heard against the murmur of the boilers, the scrape of a coal shovel, the noise of the pumps and engines, and all the creaks and groans of the hull, still pitching sluggishly in the swell.

'You may give it up, Captain Hassell,' Mactavish said shortly. 'The bulkhead's giving. We can't do anything.'

'The water's gaining in No. 1 hold. I came to see whether you could get more pumps on it.'

'I'll soon not be able to keep the water under here.'

Hassell now wanted to abandon ship—desperately. He did not show it, but in his own private mind and heart he was afraid. Afraid not so much for his own skin, though even that was still precious to him. But afraid for his men. He couldn't risk their lives too far.

But he had to be sure—*sure*—that nothing could really be done. A master must not give up his ship while there is a chance of saving it. But here there was no chance. Neither Arlow nor Mactavish would give up while there was hope. And both, independently, had done so. And he, Hassell, himself was no fool about ships. He knew their ways as well as anyone—none better. And he knew that it was a hopeless task. Both bulkheads were going. They might go at any minute.

For thirty seconds the captain stood in silence. Then with a quick sigh he turned again to the chief.

'Very well,' he said. 'We'll abandon. Get your fellows up.'

He turned, and not allowing himself to hurry, left the stokehold, and went forward once more to No. 1 hold. There he called Arlow.

'I'm going to abandon,' he repeated quietly. 'Get the men up.' Then again without haste he went up to the wireless-room.

'Get the *Barmore* again,' he directed. 'Send S O S and say that I am forced to abandon ship. Repeat the position and ask them to look out for us. Don't be in a hurry. There's time enough and we won't go without you.'

As Hassell reached the bridge the men were already streaming up from below. He told Blair what was being done, and passed into the chart-room and his cabin for the ship's papers and the log and one or two private and cherished possessions. When he came out he moved to the rail of the bridge.

The fore part of the ship was markedly lower in the water, in fact the front portion of the well-deck was now continuously awash. He had been considering putting out some oil to ease the embarkation, but he saw that would be unnecessary. The wind had dropped completely, and the swells—also greatly down—were smooth and glassy. They should have no trouble.

He could see what was taking place on the deck behind him. Both lifeboats were being lowered. The men had donned lifebelts and were being counted. Everything was ready. He stepped over to the wireless-room.

'I've given the message and got it repeated, sir,' Crabbe declared. 'The *Barmore* expects to be here in between three and four hours.'

'Good. Then get your belt and go.'

He turned back to the wheel-house. 'Lash that wheel, Simmonds,' he said to the helmsman, 'and get away to the boats. Blair, get away.'

'Aren't you coming, sir?' Blair asked.

'Yes, I'm coming. Get a move on with those boats. She won't last much longer.'

Blair and the helmsman ran down the ladder. The boats were lowered. First the port and then the starboard reached the water, the falls were unhooked, quickly, skilfully. The men began to climb down. In a couple of minutes the port boat had her complement and had pushed off from the swaying side. Then Hassell saw the starboard boat was also filled. With a last glance forward over the bows he had looked out over for so many years, Hassell walked, still slowly and with dignity, down the bridge ladder and climbed into the boat.

The *Jane Vosper* was still forging slowly ahead, and the men, as soon as they had pulled far enough away from her to be safe from her suckage, turned with one consent and began rowing with her, determined to see the end. In silence they watched her, plunging a little deeper into each swell, recovering a little more slowly, the stern rising a little higher . . . Not a man but was heartily thankful to be out of her, and yet she was their home. All but a few of their possessions, such as they were, were aboard. In the case of the captain his hopes were aboard too.

For ten minutes they watched, then a cry broke out. She was going! At a distance of perhaps quarter of a mile they saw her stern slowly rise. It went up and up and up, with the screw racing, while her bow up to her bridge disappeared beneath the water. The stern hung poised—for hours, it seemed. Then very slowly it began to go down, more and more quickly, till at last it disappeared behind a smooth rolling swell.

Alone on the sea, the boats instinctively drew together.

2

Sea Risk

In a private room in a suite of offices on the fourth floor of a large building in Mincing Lane three men sat talking.

The building was new. It was the last word in office design, with roomy landings and corridors, decorated with simple though slightly startling designs and lighted from unexpected places by glowing tubes. The floors were of rubber, coloured in the shapes conventionally assigned to lightning, though admittedly lightning in rather solid flashes. The four lifts had grilles of bronze, and fascinating little lights popped in and out as the cages rose and fell.

The fourth floor housed a firm whose plate read 'The Land & Sea Insurance Co., Ltd.' with below it the word 'Enquiries' and the representation of a hand pointing towards three o'clock.

The office in which the three men sat talking was at the end of the main corridor. It was the private room of the manager, Arnold Jeffrey, and he was discussing business with Wallace Crewe, his accountant, and Wilfred Leatherhead, his chief clerk.

For a private office, the room was large and ornate, providing ocular demonstration to the caller of the stability and prosperity of the company. It contained a large flat-topped desk, at which Mr Jeffrey was now seated, and two leather-covered arm-chairs, containing respectively his two assistants. All this furniture rested on a very thick, brightly-coloured carpet, which also bore a table with glass top and curved steel legs, a file case, a waste paper basket, and a nest of sectional bookcases, mostly containing books on law and insurance.

Jeffrey was a big man of about fifty, with a heavy jaw, thin, closely compressed lips, wide awake eyes, and a slightly unpleasant expression. He was an able manager, and if he was not greatly liked in a personal capacity he was respected as a sound business man and an efficient chief.

Crewe and Leatherhead, except that one was tall and thin and the other small and stout, were alike in that they were typical heads of departments in a business of the kind. Both were good men—if they weren't they wouldn't have remained long under Jeffrey's management, but neither was outstanding, and for the same reason.

They were discussing a message which had been received a short time previously from the Weaver Bannister Engineering Company Limited, of Watford, a firm with whom they had recently done business. That their information was serious was evident from the expression of all three. Indeed they looked as if they had just received the news of a disaster.

'A hundred and five thousand, wasn't it?' Jeffrey was saying, and there was something approaching horror in his tones.

'Yes,' answered the chief clerk with equal emotion, glancing at a paper he held. 'There were 350 sets and they were covered at £300 apiece: makes £105,000.'

For a moment there was silence, a brooding silence, and then Jeffrey spoke again with vicious emphasis. '*Damned* ill luck its coming just now,' he declared. 'We were badly enough hit by that Chelsea fire, and to have to pay out another hundred thousand on the top of that, as well as having had a bad year generally, is something that won't bear thinking about.'

'It's very unfortunate,' Crewe answered somewhat inadequately, while Leatherhead murmured agreement.

'I've rung up the chairman,' went on Jeffrey. 'I did it first thing when I got the message. He said he'd come across at once.'

'He'll be pretty badly hit,' the accountant considered. 'Last time he was speaking to me he wasn't too happy about our position. This'll about put the lid on it.'

'Yes, he was talking to me, too,' Leatherhead added. 'He was worried about the dividend. Said there never had been such a year of losses since the company was formed.'

'I don't know how we're going to meet another hundred thousand without something unpleasant happening, and that's a fact,' Jeffrey declared unhappily, and was going on to develop his theme when there was a knock at one of the two doors and a pretty girl looked in. 'Mr Brangstrode's here, Mr Jeffrey,' she said.

'Show him in,' Jeffrey answered, while the other two got up from their chairs.

The young woman stood back and a tall man with aquiline features and greying hair entered the room. There was a suggestion of power in his strong chin and quiet though forceful movements. He was just sixty and looked ten years younger.

Rupert Brangstrode had been chairman of the Land and Sea for the past six years, though it was small beer to him, most of his energies having been put into larger corporations with which he was also connected. However, under the combined management of himself and Jeffrey, the Land and Sea had considerably increased its business. A prosperous business, too, it had been, at least up to the present year. Within recent months bad luck had seemed to dog it. There had been burglaries and accidents which had proved heavy losses, culminating in a fire in Chelsea in which valuable old pictures, insured with the company for the sum of £250,000, had been totally destroyed. The dividend prospects for the current period were therefore distinctly unpromising.

Brangstrode having nodded to the three men, laid his hat on the glass table and sat down in one of the armchairs.

'What's all this, Jeffrey?' he asked in the words of a policeman investigating a street row.

'More trouble, I'm afraid,' the manager answered with a worried air. 'About an hour ago I had a telephone from Bannister's people of Watford, saying that they had heard that the steamer carrying their consignment of petrol sets to South America had been totally lost.'

The chairman moved impatiently. 'So you said. I remember we accepted the policy, but except that they were large, I've forgotten the figures.'

'Yes, sir, they were large,' Jeffrey agreed gravely. 'There were 350 sets and each was covered at £300. The total cover was £105,000.'

Brangstrode's face fell. '£105,000! Good God!' For a

34

moment there was silence and then he went on: 'Well, is it true, this report?'

'Directly I received it I rang up the shipping company, the Southern Ocean Steam Navigation Company of Fenchurch Street, and asked them. They said it appeared to be true. They had had a cable via Madeira from the skipper of their steamer *Jane Vosper*, the ship in question, saying that there had been some unexplained explosions aboard, and that part of the ship was flooded. The message said that there was no immediate danger and that they hoped to make Funchal under their own steam. That, the Southern Ocean people said, was the only information they had received direct from the ship.

'But later they had had a message from the British Latin States people in Gracechurch Street to say that the master of their ship, the *Barmore*, homeward bound from Buenos Aires, reported that he had just received an S O S from the *Jane Vosper*, which said that she was sinking rapidly and that they were abandoning ship. The master of the *Barmore* said the weather was good and that he expected to pick up the crew about midday, that is,' Jeffrey glanced at the electric clock on the opposite wall, 'just about an hour ago.'

'Then it looks a true bill,' Brangstrode considered.

Jeffrey shrugged. 'I'm afraid so. The British Latin States people said they expected to hear from their captain if and when he picked up the men, and I asked Clayton to let me know immediately they rang him. We might hear any time.'

Brangstrode nodded, but for some moments remained silent. Then presently he went on: 'If this turns out as you say, what becomes of our dividend?'

'I was considering that when you came in,' Jeffrey returned. 'I think,' and he drifted off into technicalities.

'I suppose,' said Brangstrode, when this point had been discussed, 'there's no chance of our not being liable? Explosions? That sounds like the engine-room? Steam pipes, or boilers, or perhaps a mechanical breakdown? If the accident were due to carelessness or improper management or inferior materials, could we make anything of that?'

Jeffrey shook his head. 'I doubt it. I should think all those things would be included in the risks we insured against.'

'What sort are these Southern Ocean people? Know anything about them?'

'Oh, yes, I think they're all right. They've got a good reputation in the City. A small firm, but quite sound and all that.'

'Have they only tramps?'

'As a matter of fact, their boats are liners, not tramps. I used to think all cargo boats were tramps, but they're not.'

'I always thought so myself.'

'We were both wrong. It appears a liner is a ship which travels backwards and forwards on a regular schedule, as these boats do—between London and Buenos Aires. A tramp is a ship that makes no regular journeys: it will take cargo for anywhere hoping to pick up cargo at that port for somewhere else, and so on. Of course, a liner and a tramp may be structionally similar, and a ship may be a liner at one part of its career and a tramp at another.'

'I didn't know that. Well, tramps or liners, are they sound ships?'

'I think so. The Southern Ocean has had very few accidents. Stewart Clayton's their manager.'

Brangstrode made a gesture. 'Clayton? I know him. A good man, I agree.'

'The ships are reputed to be well built and well found. We made, of course, the usual enquiries about them when we learned they were taking the Bannister stuff. But we've come across them several times before. They've often carried stuff covered by us.'

'A small firm, you say?'

'Yes, as shipping companies go. They've got small boats, from two to four thousand tons register. I don't know how many—not very many, I think. They run three services. London to Buenos Aires, calling at various South American ports; London to the West Indies, calling at several islands, and London to the Central American states, including Mexico.'

'Freight only?'

'Yes, they don't take passengers.'

'I happen to have met Captain Hassell of the *Jane Vosper*,' observed Leatherhead suddenly. 'I was at their offices on another job. You remember, sir, that railway stuff that we covered for Trinidad? While I was there Captain Hassell came in. Mr Clayton introduced us.'

'And what did you think of him?' Brangstrode asked.

'He seemed to me a thorough good man, sir,' the chief clerk answered with decision. 'Of course you can't be sure in one short interview. But I was very favourably impressed. Quiet and businesslike, he seemed, like a man who wouldn't lose his head in an emergency.'

'I wonder who insured the ship?'

Jeffrey shook his head. 'I've no idea. They may be their own insurers for all I know to the contrary.'

'Not very likely if they're a small concern.'

'That's true. Lloyd's, then, I expect. We can find out easily enough.'

'It would be interesting to know.'

Once again the rather desultory conversation turned to their own possible loss. Then after some time Brangstrode raised another point.

'We surely can't be the only insurance firm interested? What space would these blessed sets take up?'

Jeffrey turned to the chief clerk. 'You have the description of them somewhere?'

'I have it here.'

Jeffrey glanced down the paper Leatherhead handed him, then read:

'"Each set consists of one of our *Exo* petrol motors, connected direct with an *Alilo* dynamo, together with a separate switchboard. The sets are packed in strong wooden cases, measuring 2′ 0″ by 2′ 0″ by 4′ 0″." That would be,' Jeffrey calculated quickly, '16 cubic feet per set, and 350 times 16—5600 cubic feet for the lot, or say, a block 20 feet wide, 28 feet long and 10 feet deep. It probably wouldn't fill one of her holds.'

'Then she must have been carrying a lot more stuff?'

'Sure to have been,' said Jeffrey.

'That means that other insurance firms are also interested in the loss?'

Jeffrey agreed again.

'Interesting to find out what other cargo there was and who had covered it,' Brangstrode said thoughtfully.

Jeffrey's reply was interrupted by his telephone bell. With a gesture of apology he picked up the receiver. 'Yes,' he said, 'Jeffrey speaking . . . Oh, they have? I'm glad to hear that . . . Yes . . . Yes . . . No further statement? . . . What

do you think yourself? . . . On Thursday morning? . . .
Shortly after that, I should think . . . Then you'll let me
know? Thank you, Clayton, very much.'

Jeffrey put down the receiver. 'That was Clayton,'
he explained. 'He says they've just had a phone from the
Latin States people. A message has just come in from
the captain of the *Barmore*, saying that he's picked up the
crew of the *Jane Vosper*. At half-past eleven he came in
sight of them, and by twelve they were all on board. They
reported that the *Jane Vosper* had gone down a few minutes
after they abandoned her, about half-past eight this
morning. They say that explosions in the hold damaged
the hull, and that one watertight compartment was
completely flooded and the two adjoining compartments
were leaking more quickly than they could pump them
out. They're making no further statement till they reach
home, which, it is expected, will be on Thursday morning.
Clayton says the Board of Trade enquiry is certain to be
held almost at once, and he'll keep me advised of all that
becomes known.'

'Then she's gone,' Brangstrode concluded, 'and it looks
as if our £105,000 is gone with her.'

'Clayton had no theory as to what might have happened?'
Crewe asked.

'None whatever; or if he had, he didn't mention it. No;
he seemed as puzzled as I am.'

'It definitely wasn't a steam burst, or a mechanical
breakdown?' Crewe went on.

'Clayton said "Explosions in the hold." I should have
thought if it had been a steam pipe or something like that,
he'd have said so.'

'He might not,' put in Brangstrode. 'He mightn't want

to make any admissions. Or rather, the captain mightn't report it at this stage.'

'If it had been a boiler,' Crewe pointed out, 'some of the stokers would almost certainly have been killed. If it had been a steam pipe, it is unlikely it would have done all that damage to the hull. A broken connecting rod might have swung round and plunged through her bottom, and so might a broken tail-shaft. But if any of these things had happened it's hard to see why the captain would want to keep it a secret.'

'I've heard of the loss of a propeller damaging the stern of a vessel so much that she sank,' Leatherhead put in.

'Yes,' Crewe answered. 'If damage occurs about the after bulkhead, that's between the aft hold and the aft peak, so that both those are flooded, the average cargo boat will go down. A passenger boat should float with two adjoining compartments flooded, but not a boat of the type of the *Jane Vosper*.'

'You're quite a sailor,' Brangstrode intervened.

Crewe laughed. 'I'm interested, sir,' he explained. 'I've read a bit about ships.'

'Passengers are more valuable than freight?' Leatherhead suggested.

'I think it's not that altogether,' Crewe returned. 'There are two reasons: first, bulkheads are a nuisance in cargo boats, as they get in the way of stowing the cargo, so they have as few as possible; and second, there are comparatively so few people on a cargo boat, that they have a much better chance of getting away if there's trouble.'

'I don't profess to know anything about the sea,' said Brangstrode, 'but I always thought that spontaneous combustion occurred under certain conditions, with probable explosions. Do you know anything about that, Crewe? What about explosions of coal dust in the bunkers?'

Crewe shook his head. 'I don't know anything about it, sir. I understand there's a risk of spontaneous combustion from greasy cotton and other substances. But I don't know how far there's danger from coal dust.'

'That'll all be cleared up at the enquiry,' Jeffrey said with some impatience. 'I don't see that we'll gain much by discussing it now.'

'You're right, Jeffrey,' admitted Brangstrode. 'All the same, I confess to a good deal of interest in the cause of those explosions.' He paused a moment, then added: 'So much so that I think we should be represented at the enquiry.'

The others stared. 'Represented?' Jeffrey repeated.

'Represented. Suppose those explosions were not due to what I might call any normal cause: any explainable cause, if you like. Well,' he shrugged, 'explosions have been known to occur which damaged insured goods.'

'You mean,' Jeffrey said quickly, 'deliberate? But that wouldn't affect us. Suppose, if you like, the ship was scuttled. We'd still be liable for our hundred and five thousand.'

'Possibly,' Brangstrode admitted, then after a pause added, 'and possibly not.'

'Possibly not? I don't follow you there, sir. What do you mean?'

'Well,' Brangstrode shrugged slightly. 'Suppose a ship is insured and she's blown up by the owners for the insurance money. If this can be proved, the insurance company doesn't pay, does it?'

'Of course not. But the companies that insured the cargo would pay.'

'Admittedly. But now consider the converse case. Suppose certain cargo was destroyed for the insurance, and suppose as an accidental correlative the ship sank. Who would pay?'

'I see what you're suggesting. That if—'

'I'm suggesting nothing. I'm only pointing out that cases are conceivable in which cargo insured for safe transport by sea, and destroyed *en route*, need not be paid for.'

Jeffrey shook his head. 'We're dealing with Weaver Bannister's in this matter. They're a good firm. There's never been a whisper of anything crooked about them. I see what you mean, but I don't honestly believe there's anything in it.'

'I don't say there's anything in it myself. I say we should be represented at the enquiry and be sure.'

'I wish there was a chance of what you're hinting at,' Jeffrey went on with a crooked smile; 'but really, sir, I'm not with you there. Have you thought what a ghastly crime it would be? Not only the fraud against us, but also against the firms which covered the rest of the cargo and the ship herself. And all that fraud would be the smallest part of it. Why, it might have meant the loss of the whole crew; the *murder* of the whole crew. No, I don't see Weaver Bannister or anyone else standing for that.'

Brangstrode shrugged. 'I agree with all that,' he admitted. 'All the same, I don't see that it is any reason against our being represented.'

'Oh no, I admit that. I expect it would be a wise enough precaution. I suppose Alexander?'

'I think so. Let's consult him at all events. What about ringing him up now?'

Herbert Alexander, senior partner of Alexander, Alexander & Phillimore, Solicitors, occupied offices on the eighth floor of the same building as the Land & Sea Insurance Company. Though their practice was nominally general, the partners had specialized largely on insurance law. Nor had they neglected the criminal side of the subject, and they were recognized authorities on insurance frauds, arson, and even murder.

Alexander replied that he was disengaged, and five minutes later he entered the room. He was not unlike the chairman in appearance, tall, aquiline, and with the same suggestion of latent force.

'You just rang up in time,' he declared, as he took the armchair Crewe vacated. 'Another twenty seconds and I should have gone out to lunch.'

'Sorry for keeping you then,' Brangstrode returned. 'Perhaps as I've spoiled your plans, you'll lunch with me afterwards?'

'I never,' said Alexander gravely, 'refuse a good offer. I shall be delighted.'

'Very good.' The chairman turned to Jeffrey. 'Tell him, Jeffrey, will you?'

'It's about a consignment of petrol sets Messrs Weaver Bannister of Watford were sending to South America,' the manager began, and he recounted what had taken place. 'I think the immediate question is whether you advise our being represented at the Board of Trade enquiry? That's right, sir?'

'That's the point,' agreed the chairman. 'It was I who raised it, but I don't wish to push it against all of you.'

'There's been no explanation of these explosions?' asked Alexander.

'None,' Jeffrey answered, 'but it's only fair to add that there has been no opportunity to get one.'

The solicitor asked a number of other questions. 'Quite,' he concluded, 'I'll consider the matter and let you have an opinion. In the meantime and speaking without proper thought, it seems to me that if between this and the enquiry no explanation of the affair is put up which satisfies you people, an attendance at the enquiry would do no harm. In fact it might be better for me to apply to be made a party to it. Under the circumstances this would certainly be granted.'

'Just what exactly does that mean?' Brangstrode asked.

'Well, if for instance an underwriter suspects an insured vessel has been cast away, or a certificated officer wishes to have his character cleared of damaging imputations, he may apply to be made a party to the enquiry. It gives him a *locus standi* and enables him to see that any evidence he wants is called, and so on. In our case it would strengthen our position if we afterwards wished to. dispute the claim.'

'That seems a good idea,' the chairman approved. 'I should make the application.' He looked at Jeffrey, who nodded.

'I shall do so,' Alexander promised. 'Now there is one other point. If I'm really to go into this matter seriously, I'd like to have Sutton with me.'

John Sutton was a private detective employed by the Land and Sea, as well as by certain other insurance firms. He investigated doubtful cases, both beforehand, when the question of granting the cover was being considered, and afterwards, if what seemed a fraudulent claim had been made. Sutton was a first-rate man, extremely reliable, and as pertinacious and thorough as they were made.

Jeffrey raised his eyes at the solicitor's proposal, but the chairman declared it was only common sense. 'There's no earthly use in half doing anything; though I don't suggest,' he smiled crookedly at the lawyer, 'that without Sutton that's what you'd do. But undoubtedly if we do suspect anything, Sutton should know all there's to be known about it from the beginning.'

This was agreed to, and then Brangstrode summarized the position. 'The matter stands then in this way. Unless everything is cleared up beforehand to our satisfaction, Alexander will represent us at the enquiry, taking Sutton with him. In the meantime we do nothing about any claim that may be made.' He looked round on his little audience, and seeing approval on each face, turned to the solicitor. 'And now, Alexander, what about that lunch I defrauded you of?'

With a little further talk the conference came to an end.

3

Sea Law

In due course the *Barmore* reached London and the shipwrecked crew came ashore. But whatever statement they may or may not have made to their owners, no further information was vouchsafed to Jeffrey. Instead he was simply informed that the Board of Trade enquiry into the disaster would be held on the following Wednesday in a court in Hopeney Street off Kingsway, under the presidency of Mr Courtney Trafford, a stipendiary magistrate with considerable experience of that class of work.

The newspapers, it was true, were full of the story. But their accounts were not very illuminating. As was to be expected, they wrote up the dramatic side of the tale for all they were worth, painting vivid pen pictures of an epic struggle to save a stricken ship amid a waste of tumbling waters in the darkness of the night. But over such dull matters as practical cause and effect they slid gently. Naturally perhaps, as the very mysteriousness of the happening was but so much more grist to their mill.

Jeffrey read these accounts with exasperated scepticism.

46

He had not been content entirely to rest on his oars during that ten days before the enquiry. With some difficulty he had found out four insurance firms beside his own, which had covered portions of the cargo carried by the ill-fated ship. He had called in each instance on the manager and tactfully questioned him as to his views on the affair. In the case of three out of the four his efforts had met with a ready response.

These three managers admitted without hesitation that they viewed the circumstances with grave dissatisfaction. Mr Edwardes of the Derby & Yorkshire Company was the most outspoken.

'Explosions?' he had said. 'What sort of explosions? They won't say. They must surely know, that captain and crew. Then why all the mystery? I admit I don't at all like the thing. I may say we're not going to pay a penny till the whole matter is cleared up.'

'So far as I can gather,' Jeffrey answered, 'Doulton of the Antwerp Company and Austin of the Narrow Seas take up the same position. And so do we.'

'Of course you do. You're attending the enquiry?'

'Alexander, our solicitor, is watching it on our behalf, but I didn't think of going myself.'

'I shall,' Edwardes returned. 'If there's going to be trouble, I want to know about it from the beginning.'

Jeffrey, remembering that this was the argument Alexander had used for taking Sutton, decided that after all he might as well attend himself. If the proceedings didn't seem to be useful he could leave at any time. Besides, even if he were to wait till the end, it would not take up a serious amount of his time.

Jeffrey was more upset about the position of the Land

and Sea than he would have cared to admit. Owing to various family troubles, he had never been able to save, and now at the age of fifty-two he was still entirely dependent on what he earned. He did not exactly fear that the payment of this £105,000 on the top of the £250,000 would cripple his company, but its prosperity was too intimately bound up with his own for him not to be profoundly anxious as to the outlook.

It was therefore with a direct personal interest in the proceedings that he presented himself with Alexander and Sutton at the Hopeney Street court at some twenty minutes past ten on the Wednesday morning following.

The room into which they presently pushed their way was of good size and was fitted with the usual court furniture. Bench, dock, jury box, witness box, well containing the solicitors' table, and public galleries; all were arranged as in a criminal court—as indeed Jeffrey reminded himself this usually was. Unlike so many courtrooms, this was modern, airy and well lighted. In one other particular it looked different from the courts which Jeffrey had previously attended, and that was in the absence of policemen, of whom several had always been well in evidence.

But what most surprised Jeffrey was the number of people who were present. He had not expected the proceedings to be popular, but already there was a crowd of from eighty to a hundred standing chatting in little knots or seated as close as they could get to the central table. And nearly all of them looked as if they were there on business. There were a number of men whose black clothes, clean-shaven faces and thin compressed lips unmistakably suggested the law. Many more were obviously business men, and among them Jeffrey recognized several whom he knew. They were the managers of all four insurance companies on whom he had called, one or two other men interested in shipping, and Stewart Clayton, the manager of the Southern Ocean Company. There were men in blue suits and carrying bowler hats whom Jeffrey put down, correctly, as he afterwards discovered, as trades union secretaries. There was a rather woebegone cluster of men in poor clothes, obviously the shipwrecked crew, with, standing a little apart from them, but with a subtle suggestion of belonging to them, some half-dozen older and better dressed individuals, clearly the officers. Only a few persons who had taken seats in the public galleries appeared to be unconnected with the proceedings. These looked like unemployed, who had drifted in as a relief from the dreadful tedium of their lives. Not a single woman or girl was present: all were men.

'This is going to be a bigger thing than I had any idea of,' Jeffrey remarked to Alexander, as they squeezed their way into a seat near the solicitors' table.

'There are a good many interests affected,' Alexander replied, 'and probably most, if not all, are represented. There's first of all the Board of Trade, then the owners, then the underwriters, then at least five insurance firms who covered the cargo. You discovered four besides your own firm, didn't you?'

'Yes.'

'Well, they're probably all here. Then the British Latin States people will be called in connection with the rescue of the crew. And that's only one side of the affair. The captain, officers and crew of the lost vessel are in a way of speaking upon trial. They will be here both as witnesses and to see that they get a fair hearing.'

49

'That lot over there, I should say.'

'I imagine so. It's rather a serious business for the senior officers. The court can reprimand them, or suspend or remove their certificates, in the event of negligence or other fault being proved. They can't be sent to prison, but even a reprimand is a terribly serious thing for an officer, specially a master.'

'You mean he'd lose his job?'

'Almost certainly. And that wouldn't be the worst of it. He'd probably never get another. Particularly now, when so many qualified men are unemployed.'

'Means ruin for life?'

'It does, and so I expect the chief officers are all legally represented. And that adds to the crowd.'

As he spoke, Clayton saw Jeffrey and pushed across. 'Extraordinary affair this,' he remarked. 'Quite outside my previous experience.'

'I've only heard what you told me yourself,' Jeffrey answered, when he had introduced Alexander. 'Has your captain not been able to clear it up?'

'No, that's just it,' Clayton returned. 'He doesn't know a thing about it. His statement is simply that explosions occurred, but what caused them he can't say. Extraordinarily unsatisfactory.'

'Probably the enquiry will bring out the truth.'

'I'm sure I hope so. Not to know is bad for us from every point of view. But you're almost as much interested in it as we are?'

'A good deal more deeply than we care to be,' Jeffrey admitted.

Clayton shook his head. 'Well, let's hope for the best,' he murmured, as he moved to a seat beside his solicitor.

It was now half-past ten, the hour at which the proceedings were to open. People had continued to pour in, till the room was practically full. Almost all had found seats. The shipwrecked crew, of whom there seemed between thirty and forty, had pushed into the jury box and the witnesses' seats behind. Counsel with their formidable briefs, and their attendant solicitors with their reference books and stacks of papers, had taken their places at the table. There was still, however, movement all over the room and a loud buzz of conversation.

Presently there came a cry of 'Silence!' Everyone stood up and the stipendiary magistrate, Mr Courtney Trafford, entered, followed by two other men. He took his place in the centre of the dais, bowed to those present, and sat down, his companions sitting on his right and left hands respectively.

'The assessors,' Alexander whispered. 'Technical men appointed to advise Trafford.'

Jeffrey nodded, settling himself more comfortably in his seat. They were punctual about beginning at all events. He hoped this was an augury for the speedy conduct of the case.

There ensued a number of rather uninteresting formalities, and then all sorts of people from all over the room, Alexander among them, got up and said they were appearing for this or that interest. Their names were duly noted, and a short discussion then took place between the magistrate and his assessors. When this was over, Mr Trafford made a brief opening statement.

'As you are aware, gentlemen, this enquiry is into the circumstances of the sinking of the steamer *Jane Vosper*, while on a voyage from London to Pernambuco and other ports in South America. The court will be concerned in the first place with the fact and the cause of the sinking, but it will also take cognizance of the conduct of all those concerned, inasmuch as this may have contributed or otherwise to the sinking. This will include not only the actions of those on board the ship, both before and at the time of the disaster, but also those whose duty it was to see that she went to sea in a reasonably fit and perfect condition, both as regards the ship herself, the appliances and stores which she carried, and the nature and disposal of the cargo.

'The loss of a ship at sea is always a distressing event to all concerned, and this case is no exception to the rule. At the same time it is a matter of congratulation that in this instance the worst feature of such disasters is missing—there was happily no loss of life. That fortunate circumstance will not, however, make any difference to the course of this enquiry, particularly as we have only to remember that had the weather been different, it is possible that not a single member of the crew would have escaped.

'I shall now ask you, Mr Armitage, to open the proceedings on behalf of the Board of Trade.'

Mr Reginald Armitage, one of the barristers present, was a tall man with an impressive carriage and a dominating manner. His hawk-like face and heavy jaw bespoke a tenacity of purpose which would not easily be turned aside from the path he wished to follow. His very look of conscious power and grip was a reassurance to those for whom he appeared, and induced doubts of their case into the minds of his opponents. And when he spoke, these feelings became strengthened. He had a full rich voice with which he could make great play, modifying it, as it were between the aggressive roaring of the lion and the seductive softness of the sucking dove. It was rumoured by those who did not like him, that in civil cases he made huge sums merely by not being on the other side.

'Your Worship,' he began quietly, standing up and turning towards the magistrate, 'after what you have just said there is no need for me to waste the time of the court with prolonged remarks, and I will be very brief.'

He paused and hitched his gown up on his shoulder, a characteristic action. Then in a louder and more assured tone he went on:

'As Your Worship has pointed out, this enquiry is into the sinking of the steamer *Jane Vosper* on the morning of Saturday, 28th of last month, while she was on a voyage from London to Pernambuco in Brazil.

'The *Jane Vosper*, as you will hear in evidence, was a cargo liner of some 2500 tons register, owned by the Southern Ocean Steam Navigation Company of Fenchurch Street, and registered in London. Her length was 270 feet, beam 36 feet, and draught 16 feet. She was built in 1913 for the general carrying trade, and carried a complement of 35 officers and men.'

Mr Armitage then went on to describe the vessel, with its high fo'c'sle, bridge-deck and poop and the comparatively low stretches of well-deck between. He told of the location of the stores and of the berthing of the officers and crew. He referred briefly to the engines and boilers and went into detail about the size and position of the three holds and the number and position of the watertight bulkheads dividing them. When he had finished there was not much about the vessel that he had not covered.

'As to the actual voyage and to the extraordinary series of explosions as a result of which the ship sank,' Mr Armitage went on, 'I propose to say very little, as I think you will get a better idea of these direct from Captain Hassell, her master, who is with us today. But very broadly speaking,' and Mr Armitage went on to describe both, not indeed broadly, but in the utmost detail. He told the story vividly and well, from the loading of the cargo in the London Docks right up to the point at which the *Barmore* picked the crew up from the boats. Nothing was omitted from the tale, except the explanation of what had really occurred. Mr Armitage didn't say in so many words that this was a mystery, but indicated that all the available evidence on the point would be put before the court. Then after a short peroration on the importance of the case and the number of interests involved, he sat down.

But immediately he was on his feet again. 'James Hassell,' he called, glancing over the assembly.

Captain Hassell, looking anxious and thoroughly woebegone, rose from his seat with the other officers and moved round the room to the witness box. There he was sworn and invited to sit down.

'You are James Hassell, master of the *Jane Vosper*, the ship which is the subject of this enquiry?'

'I am.'

Then ensued a long questionnaire on Hassell's age, qualifications and career. He had been twenty-five years with the Southern Ocean Company, eighteen as a skipper, and eight in command of the *Jane Vosper*. He was adequately qualified for his job and had never before been involved in any serious mishap.

A similar but more detailed questionnaire on the ship

herself followed. Her size, age, design, workmanship and equipment were taken in turn and legally established. The captain said she was a good sea boat, steady, easy to steer, and very dry, as well as being well built and well found in every way. There was nothing about her, he declared, to account for the explosions or to warrant any suggestion that she had been sunk more easily than a ship should.

Mr Armitage then turned to the voyage and took Hassell through each step from the London Docks until the first explosion.

'Now,' he went on, 'during those six days of the passage, up till the time of the first explosion, did you notice anything abnormal or unusual about the ship or crew?'

'Nothing whatever. Except for the delays from fog and wind, the voyage was entirely normal and satisfactory.'

'You were satisfied with your crew?'

'Absolutely.'

'There was nothing to suggest that disaster might be approaching?'

'No, sir. Nothing.'

'Except that you had lost some thirty-three hours, you were entirely satisfied with your progress?'

'Entirely.'

'And before you started? Was everything perfectly normal and satisfactory?'

'Perfectly so.'

'Were you satisfied with the nature and stowing of the cargo?'

'Quite satisfied.'

'Very well. Now we come to the explosions. Will you tell us in your own words what occurred?'

Hassell told of his being unable to sleep and his decision to go on deck, of his doing so, of the sea that was running, and of the first explosion. Then he described the steps he had taken to ascertain the damage. How he had rung down the engines to SLOW AHEAD, reducing the speed as much as possible consistent with keeping the ship's head to the seas. How he had called for information to the engine-room and taken over the ship himself, so that his deck officers might go and find out what had happened.

Slowly Mr Armitage took him through the events of that dreadful night. The second explosion, the third, the fourth. The orders he had given, the wireless messages he had sent, his inspection of the damage in the stokehold and No. 1 hold, and his consultations with the chief engineer and first officer. Finally, his conclusion that the ship could not be saved, the last message to the approaching *Barmore*, and taking to the boats, the sinking of the *Jane Vosper*, and the final rescue by the *Barmore*.

The K.C. then turned once again to the explosions.

'Now at first you tell me you weren't certain of exactly where the explosions had occurred. But later you came to a conclusion on this point?'

'In the light of what happened afterwards, it was clear that they were in No. 2 hold.'

'Quite. What size was this hold?'

'About 40 feet long by the full breadth of the ship, say 34 feet, and about 17 feet deep.'

'That's a large space, very much the size of this room, I should say.' Mr Armitage looked round. 'Now can you form any opinion as to whereabouts in the hold the explosions occurred?'

For the first time Captain Hassell looked doubtful. 'I've been thinking about that, sir,' he answered. 'While I can't swear to it, I am of the opinion that they were low down.'

'Yes? Why do you think so?'

Again Hassell hesitated. 'I'm afraid it's more what the chief engineer reported than what I saw for myself,' he admitted. 'He said—'

'Well, we'll get that from him. What did you see for yourself?'

'When I went down to the stokehold after the last explosion I saw that the principal buckling in the bulkhead, what I might call the centre of the buckling, was low down: about five feet from the floor plates. That's what I saw, but there was another reason. It didn't occur to me at the time, but I've thought of it since. It seemed to me the shots were individually small. If they hadn't been, they would have blown the hatches off. But if they were small, they must have been low against the ship's bottom to puncture her plates.'

'Yes?'

'I think, sir, that without considering the puncturing of the ship's bottom at all, one could say they were low down because they didn't raise the hatches.'

'I should have thought that even a small explosion and low down would have blown off the hatches. Would a large volume of gas not have been generated, which must have gone somewhere?'

'That is so, but in the case of the *Jane Vosper* the holds were well ventilated and in my opinion the ventilators afforded the necessary relief.'

'Ah, quite so. That all sounds very clear and very

ingenious, if I may say so, captain. An interesting and important point, that the charges were probably small.' He paused for a moment, then resumed. 'Now another point. Was any adjustment made with the disposition or otherwise of the cargo since the stevedores finished with it?'

'No, sir, the hatches weren't opened.'

'But you have told us that the holds could be entered without opening the hatches?'

'That is so. But the cargo would not normally be moved without opening the hatches.'

'I see. Do you mean then that at the time of the explosion the hold contained everything loaded by the stevedores and nothing else?'

'I believe that to be correct.'

'What's your own view, captain, as to the cause of the explosions?'

'I can't explain them at all. I know of nothing that could have caused them and am entirely puzzled by the whole thing.'

'Now, here's a more difficult question. During the loading of that hold, up till the time the hatches were battened down, could anyone have placed explosives in the hold?'

A slight movement passed through the assembly. This was the first time the suggestion of foul play had crept into question or answer, and it evoked a corresponding reaction. Persons who were already looking bored sat up sharply. The atmosphere grew more tense.

But the suggestion did not seem strange to Captain Hassell. He agreed that this was a more difficult question. He didn't think anything of the kind could have been done, though he wasn't prepared to state it as a fact. In the daytime he believed it would be impossible. He pointed to the fact that during loading hours no one could have approached unseen. At night there was a watchman aboard, apart from those on the wharves, and he thought it very unlikely that anyone could have passed these men.

'Then with regard to the period between the battening down of the hatches and the disaster. During that period could anyone have smuggled in explosives?'

As to the possibility of this the witness was not so sure. Granted that someone with explosives was on board who wished to sink the ship and endanger his own life, Hassell supposed an opportunity could have been found. But he was dogmatic about its probability. He didn't believe that any of the men who were on board were capable of doing such a thing, or had done it.

Mr Armitage did not press the point, but turned instead to the question of the wireless signals. These he went over in detail, obtaining Hassell's reason for every message he had sent. He was particularly searching in his questions with reference to the final S O S, and the reason which induced the captain to abandon ship. At the end he said, 'Thank you, captain,' and sat down.

As he did so another little wave of movement passed over the room. People who had been listening intently suddenly found they had become cramped, and took advantage of the break to change their positions. A buzz of conversation arose, as whispered remarks were exchanged. Then Mr Trafford's voice was heard inviting anyone who was appearing for a client, and who wished to ask questions, to do so.

Three or four of the legal-looking men stood up, and Trafford took them in turn. But to Jeffrey their questions seemed to have very little point. In no case did they succeed in bringing out anything new. All that they got was confirmation of statements already made.

When the last had finished Trafford said he would himself like to ask one question: 'When your second officer reported that there was fire in No. 2 hold, what exactly did you do? I ask because no action seems to have been taken to deal with it.'

'I realized the danger of fire at once, sir,' Hassell replied, 'and I was quite clear as to what I should do about it. But I was more afraid that the ship might be taking water, and until the wells were sounded, I refrained from any decision as to the best thing to be done. In the end the fire was put out automatically by the flooding of the hold.'

Trafford nodded. 'I follow,' he admitted, then went on: 'That will do for the present, Captain Hassell. Please don't go away, as some further question may arise. Now, Mr Armitage?'

Hassell left the box and Armitage stood up and called, 'Henry Arlow.'

Arlow was sworn, and then in due form asked his name, position, qualifications and history. Though he was only first officer of the *Jane Vosper* and had never had a ship, he had held for eight years his master's certificate. His qualifications were therefore satisfactory and his record was good.

Then to Jeffrey and others of those present the enquiry began to drag. For all the preliminary questions asked Arlow were those which the captain had already answered.

It was not until Armitage reached the actual explosions, that Arlow had anything new to tell.

He described, as Captain Hassell had done, the feeling and sound of the first explosion, his first thought that it was an engine-room accident, and then his reassurance on this point. He felt sure from the first that it was not due to the ship striking an obstruction. When, therefore, the captain had said he was taking over the ship and had instructed him to go below and find out what had happened, his first thought had been the holds. He decided that before anything else he must find out if the ship were taking water. The men were aroused by the shock and he called the carpenter and bosun, and sounded the well first in the fore peak and then in Nos. 1 and 2 holds. All these were dry. Then he started to inspect the holds. The second explosion occurred when he was in No. 1 hold, and it sounded in No. 2 hold, beyond the bulkhead. He then went into No. 2 hold, and there he smelled smoke and burnt explosive. The smoke was hanging about rather than pouring up, and he did not think there was serious fire. He was sure the explosions had come from low down in the hold. He was satisfied from the sounds that no explosions had occurred abaft the engines, so he did not sound the well in No. 3 hold.

His researches so far had not shown that there was anything wrong with the ship, so he had gone up again on the bridge to report to Captain Hassell. While doing so the third explosion had occurred. It seemed to come from the same place as the others, and he at once ran down to sound the well in No. 2 hold again. This time he found water was coming into the ship. Moreover, it was gaining so quickly that he didn't believe anything could be done to stop it. He was satisfied that all the pumps they had on board wouldn't equal the flow.

But though he realized that they couldn't keep the water down in No. 2 hold, he believed that the ship would float all right even with this hold flooded, provided the rest of her was tight. He at once sounded No. 1 hold again. He found it dry. He then sounded the fore peak again. It was also dry.

Then he went back to No. 2 hold. There was by this time five feet of water in it, and the level was rising quickly. Arlow sent a man with the news to the captain while his thoughts turned towards the bulkheads. He knew the safety of the ship depended on their holding, and he wondered whether they had been damaged by the explosions and whether any attempt should be made to shore them.

To get a ruling on this point he went again up on the bridge to see the captain. There he found the chief engineer. It appeared that the captain was already discussing strutting the bulkheads with him, and he, Arlow, was now instructed to get the forward bulkhead shored up from No. 1 hold. He went down at once and saw to getting out beams and wedges.

Arlow then described his once again sounding the well in No. 1 hold after the fourth explosion, and his horror at finding that this hold also was taking water. It was coming in slowly, and he thought the pumps should hold it. He was about to report in person to the captain, when he heard the pumps starting. He sent a man to the captain and then carried on with his work.

He told in detail, made more convincing by its moderate language and freedom from word painting, of the terrible job he had there in the hold. Everything was jammed up with cargo. It was piled against the face of the bulkhead, and he couldn't get it clear. He began to despair of his job, thinking that they would have to wait till the hatch could be opened and the winches got to work.

They had, however, after great efforts, succeeded in getting the cargo moved back in the centre of the bulkhead for a width of some four feet, and they were gradually working down the face to make a sort of well or sump down which they could get to the water and perhaps put down suction pipes for additional hand pumps, as well as getting in some timbers against the bulkhead, which could afterwards be strutted back from the beams or the after end of the hatch. While they were working the water was gaining on them; admittedly quite slowly, but definitely. With the pumps they had they couldn't keep it down. However, they had stuck to the work until they were recalled by the captain, who said that he had decided to abandon the ship. With regard to the actual taking to the boats, seeing the *Jane Vosper* sink, and being picked up by the *Barmore*, he simply repeated what the captain had already said.

'You are the officer responsible for the stowage of the cargo, are you not?' Armitage asked, when all this evidence had been taken.

'Yes, sir, it was done under my supervision and I have a note of it all.'

At this the interest of Jeffrey and several more quickened. But their curiosity was not about to be satisfied. Armitage turned to Trafford and said that with his permission he would not take this part of the witness's evidence at the moment, but would recall him later, finishing first with what took place on the voyage.

The magistrate agreed that this would be a desirable proceeding, and said that in that case he would adjourn for lunch, ending up with the exhortation, 'Two o'clock, please, gentlemen.'

Everyone filed out as quickly as they could, Jeffrey, Alexander and Sutton among the others.

4

Sea Justice

'Well,' said Jeffrey as they turned towards the Holborn Restaurant, 'what do you think of all that?'

'I don't like it,' Alexander answered; 'I don't like it at all. A very mysterious affair.'

'And the further the enquiry goes, the more mysterious it gets.'

'Quite. Explosions in ship's holds are not uncommon. But it's extremely uncommon not to be able to explain them.'

'If the captain's telling the truth, and it certainly seemed to me that he was, it was something in the cargo.'

'It was something in No. 2 hold,' Alexander replied. 'I don't think we've had evidence that it was in the cargo.'

'But there was nothing in the hold but cargo.'

'So far as we know.'

'Perhaps so.' Jeffrey turned to Sutton. 'What's your view?'

'It doesn't look any too good to me either, sir,' the detective answered. 'There's been some hanky-panky going on, and we haven't got to the bottom of it.'

Jeffrey looked from one to the other. 'It seems to me

that both of you think the ship was deliberately sunk. Am I right?'

Alexander shook his head. 'We've no evidence for that. We've no evidence for any conclusion. And more than likely there won't be any.'

Jeffrey made a gesture of disagreement. 'If there was no natural or ordinary cause for the explosions, it could surely only mean they were deliberately brought about?'

'Quite. The difficulty is that not being able to find a natural or ordinary cause, is no proof that there wasn't one.'

'The lawyer's mind, Alexander. I agree in theory, of course, but in actual life things are different. The obvious explanation is the true one ninety-nine times in a hundred.'

Alexander smiled. 'There are two things we'll be interested to hear at all events,' he declared. 'The first is, What was the nature of the cargo in that No. 2 hold? and the second, What was the relation of the insurance cover of the ship and cargo to their value?'

'Ah yes, I agree with you there.' Jeffrey paused, then went on. 'Look here, they haven't given us any too much time to get this blessed lunch. Let's get on with it.'

'I want something light,' Alexander declared. 'These afternoon sessions are sleepy affairs at the best.'

They compromised on omelettes followed by coffee, to the secret regret of Sutton, whose ideas of lunch ran more towards Porterhouse steak and onions, washed down by draught stout. By five minutes before two they were again in their places.

The proceedings reopened by the calling of Second Officer Blair. Here again there ensued a good deal of rather wearisome repetition of questions which had already been answered by the previous witnesses. Blair indeed had very little to say which added to the general knowledge. His opinion as to the position of the explosions agreed with Hassell's and Arlow's, but he had no suggestions to make as to their cause.

The only fresh information he gave was about the fire. When sent to investigate the first detonation he had at once made for No. 2 hold, believing that Arlow was already searching the fore peak and No. 1. There he had found that the door by which the hold was reached from amidships had been blown open and that smoke was pouring out. This smoke smelt of explosives and of burning wood. He had at once closed the door to cut off the supply of air, immediately informing the captain that there was fire in the hold. Steps were taken to deal with the outbreak, but before anything could be put into operation there were further explosions and No. 2 hold was pierced and became flooded. The fire had not penetrated above the level of this flooding and was therefore automatically extinguished.

Angus Mactavish, the chief engineer, was the next witness. After the usual questions as to qualifications and experience, he was asked to tell in his own words what he knew of the affair.

He said that on the evening before the explosions they had had a little trouble with one of the main bearings of the auxiliary engine which worked the dynamo, which had been inclined to heat. He had decided to light by oil and stop the engine to remetal the bearing. This had been done in the small hours of the morning, and the engine was then tested. He had lain down earlier, but had got up to inspect the work and to be present at the test. It thus happened that he was in the engine-room at the time of the first explosion.

He did not know where the sound came from. It was not very loud, being muffled by the sound of the engines. He had wondered whether the trouble was in the stokehold, and had looked in. Everything however, seemed to be right. As he had turned back to the engine-room to make a closer inspection, the telegraph had rung for SLOW AHEAD. Directly he had slowed the engines and seen that the fire draught was reduced, the bridge speaking tube whistled. The captain had asked if anything were wrong, and he had reported all well in the engine-room.

He had left the second engineer in charge of the engines and had gone back to the stokehold to make further enquiries about the noise. The firemen and trimmers on duty agreed that it was an explosion of some sort, apparently in the adjoining hold. While he was speaking to them the second explosion had come, and it sounded close as well as very heavy. He agreed it was in the hold at the other side of the stokehold bulkhead. So far as he could ascertain, however, no damage seemed to have been done to the ship.

On his own initiative he immediately got steam to all the pumps, so that if they should be wanted they could be brought into use with the minimum of delay. He was back in the engine-room engaged in this work when the third explosion came. He ran into the stokehold but again he could not find anything wrong. However, he heard the ominous sound of water pouring into the ship, and ran back and started the pumps. The bridge whistled again on the speaking tube, and he reported accordingly.

Asked if he could estimate from what he had heard

either the size or position of the hole, Mactavish said
that he could not do so with any certainty. It sounded to
him, however, as if it were in the bottom somewhere
amidships. At all events the sound of flowing water was
loudest in the centre of the ship, and grew more muffled
as he moved towards the sides. As to the size, he had
since worked out a rough calculation from the approxi-
mate time the hold had taken to fill, and it would seem
to him that the hole must have been somewhere about
two feet in diameter.

The captain had then called him up on the bridge for a
consultation. No. 2 hold was by this time about full and
the ship was badly down by the head. The captain had
discussed the situation and it had been agreed that as the
bulkheads might have been damaged by the explosions,
they should be shored. He had then returned to the
stokehold to get the shoring under way.

He was actually in the stokehold when the fourth explosion came. This was quite different from the preceding
three. It was very much sharper and more severe, and the
entire ship vibrated as if she had got a blow from some
sort of giant hammer. The bulkhead had buckled; he had
actually seen it coming forward. For a moment he thought
it was going to give way entirely, which would, of course,
have ended all their lives. It hadn't done so, fortunately. It
had remained curving inwards and for a moment it didn't
seem as if a great deal of harm had been done.

'Can you estimate how far the bulkhead curved in from
its former plane?' Mr Armitage asked.

Mactavish thought about a foot. It was happily not
enough to tear the bulkhead away from the sides of the
ship, though it was enough to start the joints. Immediately

the rivets down each side and along the bottom began to weep. The whole bulkhead had been shaken, and in his opinion it was only a question of time till it gave way altogether. He reported to this effect to the captain, who said he would come down to see the damage and discuss what was to be done.

He, Mactavish, continued getting his beams and struts into place, but as they worked the flow from the bulkhead grew steadily stronger. At that time the pumps were easily able to cope with it, but he was aware that if it continued to gain on them, the ship was doomed. She was low enough in the water as it was, and she could not carry much more weight.

The captain went away but returned after some time. The flow was then much stronger. He, Mactavish, was by now convinced that they could do nothing to stop it, and that they would be unable to save the ship. His pumps were still keeping the water down, but the increase in the flow was so rapid that they would not be able to do so long. He had tried to ease up the pressure with shores, but it took time to get the beams into position in the confined space of the stokehold, and he could not get a great deal of force to play. He admitted advising the captain to abandon ship. Under similar circumstances he would do it again. It had proved to be sound advice, for if they had delayed another half-hour they would all have gone to the bottom. The captain agreed after a short time, and he mustered his men and sent them on deck. He made them fire up the boilers before leaving, so that there would be steam for the pumps till the boats got away. He remained below himself till a call from the bridge told him that the boats were out. He and the captain were the last to leave the ship.

'Now about the explosions,' Armitage went on when the chief's story had come to an end. 'You say that the fourth shock was very much more severe than the other three. You mean that a bigger charge of whatever the substance was went off?'

'No,' Mactavish returned, 'I didna say that. They might ha' been the same as far as that was concerned.'

'I don't think I follow that. Would you please explain.'

'Weel, the condeetions were no' the same. In the case o' the first three you had airr cushioning, the fourth occurrred in water.'

'You mean the water would carry the shock?'

'Aye, but I mean more than that. If you explode against water, it's nearly like a solid. The water would get driven outwards all round, but it wouldna compress like air would do. It couldna get out of the hole in the ship's bottom, so it could only go outwards and upwards. And it couldna go very much upwards with the carrgo.'

'So it went outwards against the bulkheads?'

'That's so. And if the bulkheads hadna given in the centre by bulging, they would ha' torn away, and she would ha' gone strraight down.'

'How do you account for the first two explosions doing no apparent damage?'

'I canna be sure, but I thought they had likely blown through the upper plating of her double bottom. If so, that would explain the thirrd holing the lower plating.'

'You mean that its protection would have been removed?'

'That's so.'

'What space was there between the upper and lower plating?'

71

'About three feet.'

'Now, Mr Mactavish, from all you know of the affair, can you form any opinion as to the cause of the explosions?'

This was one of the questions that had been asked of each of the witnesses. And now the chief gave the same answer as his predecessors. He had no idea. There was nothing that he knew of about the ship or cargo which could possibly account for them.

'Does that mean that in your opinion some explosive must have been deliberately smuggled aboard the ship?'

Mactavish was not going to be pinned to anything so definite. As the explosive went off aboard, he supposed it must have been brought aboard in some way, but he had no idea how.

Some further questions followed, and then the chief left the witness box. For a time the proceedings lost a good deal of their interest. The next dozen witnesses, though their examination was no doubt necessary, added nothing of value to the evidence. After the chief came his two assistants, a greaser, two firemen, a trimmer, the bosun, the carpenter, and certain members of the crew. All these gave their evidence clearly enough, but it simply confirmed what the principal officers had already said. All this weight of testimony did, however, tend to increase the belief of those listening, that the truth, the whole truth, and nothing but the truth, was being told.

By the time all these members of the crew had been examined, it was after five o'clock, and the proceedings were adjourned till the following morning. It was generally believed that the next day would complete the enquiry.

When the court reopened at ten o'clock the first witness called was the third officer of the *Barmore*. He described the receipt of the wireless messages from the *Jane Vosper*, the race to the scene of the disaster, and the picking up of the crew from the boats. This confirmed the statements already made, but there was one line which Mr Armitage opened up with him, saying he had omitted to obtain Captain Hassell's views upon it.

This was the question of the amount of shipping which was in the neighbourhood at the time of the S O S. The witness was unable to state exactly what ships were close by, but he pointed out that both his own ship and the *Jane Vosper* were on a frequented traffic path. Practically all ships from Europe to South America—certainly all coming from north of the Mediterranean—and *vice versa*—passed through the waters in question, and this represented a very considerable fleet. He was of opinion that a crew in distress in such locality would have a very good chance of being picked up by a passing ship.

Mr Armitage asked leave to recall Captain Hassell to put this point to him. Hassell thereupon returned to the box and when the question was asked, said he fully agreed with the opinion of the last witness. When he put out his call, he had no doubt that there were steamers not far off. But he pointed out that the call at Pernambuco took him slightly westward of the most frequented path—that to Rio and beyond.

'I want to ask you another question, captain,' Armitage went on. 'You said you were thirty-three hours late, and that if you had been running to time you would have been abreast of Madeira. How far from the islands do you pass?'

'On this trip I was aiming to pass within about twenty miles.'

'There is more than one island?'

'Yes. They stretch in a curved line from Porto Santo in the north to the three Desertas Islands in the south, a distance of over thirty miles. Madeira itself is south of halfway between them, to the west.'

'Then supposing you were running to time and the explosions occurred at the same hour that they did, you would have been comparatively close to land?'

'That is so.'

'Given reasonably good weather, could you have made land in your boats?'

The captain thought that there was every probability that they could, though he did not seem cheered by the suggestion.

'Then,' went on Armitage slowly, 'would it, in your opinion, be true to say that assuming these explosions were to take place, the position which you normally should have reached when they occurred would have been as good, from the point of view of the safety of your crew, as any along the whole course of your voyage?'

Captain Hassell paused for a moment to take in this question, then answered that unless it had been round the coast of Kent, he supposed it would.

'Armitage believes it was malicious,' Jeffrey whispered.

'Looks like it,' Alexander agreed. 'Looks as if he held a brief for the criminal too.'

'One other question, Captain Hassell,' went on the deep voice. 'The date of the disaster was the 30th September, wasn't it?'

'That's correct.'

'Now what kind of weather might you reasonably expect

74

about the end of September in the neighbourhood of Madeira?'

'Pretty good; better a good deal than we did get.'

This line of enquiry, unexpected and suggestive, reawakened the somewhat flagging interest, and when Captain Hassell left the box there was a small orgy of movement and whispering. It certainly seemed as if Armitage believed there had been foul play, but if so, his object in attempting to whitewash the evil doers was not so clear.

However, the matter was not followed up, and the next witness, Mr Peter Davis, was immediately called.

Davis described himself as a technical representative of Messrs Ferris & Bloom, of Newcastle, the builders of the *Jane Vosper*. He produced plans showing not only the general arrangement and dimensions of the ship, but also details of the construction, particularly the steelwork of the bulkheads, and the method of securing the latter to the sides and bottom of the vessel. He said that the ship had been built to these plans, and that all steel was of the full dimensions shown and all workmanship of the best standard and thoroughly well carried out. The hull indeed was of extra strong construction, as he thought was proved by the fact that she stood three of these explosions and remained afloat.

In reply to a question from Armitage, he said the ship was designed to float with one compartment flooded, but not with two.

Charles Cruthers, the next witness, said that he was a naval architect employed by the Admiralty. He had some experience of the design and construction of ships of war, but most of his life had been spent on auxiliary ships approximating to the ordinary commercial freight carrier.

He had examined the plans of the *Jane Vosper*, and he agreed with the last witness that she was a thoroughly well and substantially designed ship. He was of opinion that she was well up to the average of her class, if not above it. He had heard the evidence given as to the explosions which had taken place aboard and he thought these had revealed no sign of weakness in either design or construction; rather the contrary.

'Witness probably brought by the owners,' Alexander whispered, and Jeffrey nodded in reply.

Stewart Clayton, the managing director of the Southern Ocean Steam Navigation Company of Fenchurch Street, the owners of the *Jane Vosper*, was then called. He said the ship had been built for his company in 1913 and had remained in their service ever since. Thanks to their former chairman she had been in advance of her time when built, and though she was no doubt getting old, twenty-two years, she was still in excellent condition and quite serviceable. No money had been spared in her construction and no money had been spared on keeping her in repair since then. She had proved a satisfactory ship, never having been in serious accident, and bringing in a reasonable return on her capital cost.

Her last big overhaul was carried out before her previous trip to South America, some four months before the disaster. Certain small renewals were then made, and she was left in thoroughly good condition.

His firm and he himself were entirely satisfied with the officers and crew of the *Jane Vosper*, In Captain Hassell they had every confidence. He had served them conscientiously and well for many years, and they were satisfied that in this case he had done everything possible to save the ship. These remarks also applied to the chief engineer, and indeed to all the remaining officers and men.

Mr Armitage then turned to a point which at once raised the public interest to greater heat, particularly to those who were connected with the insurance of her freight. 'Can you tell the court,' he asked, 'just in what her cargo consisted?'

Mr Clayton took some papers from a folder. 'I have that information here,' he answered. 'The cargo on this trip was rather unusual, in that it was limited to the products of five firms. With general carriers, such as we are, it is usual to have on board a single ship freight from dozens of firms. This time, as I say, there were five rather large consignments from only five firms. They were as follows: There were 200 large cases of cloths and serges for dresses and suitings, from Messrs Holroyd & Cartwright of Hackney. That was valuable stuff, and the consignment was divided almost equally between Rio and Buenos Aires. There were 350 large-sized cases containing petrol-electric lighting sets from the Weaver Bannister Engineering Company of Watford. These were separated into four lots, for Pernambuco, Rio, Montevideo and Buenos Aires. Then there were 178 cases containing ornaments and metal fancy goods of various kinds from Messrs Walker Higgins and Son of Croydon. There was a lot of radio material, also in cases, from the Nightingale Company of Bermondsey. And lastly, the principal item and by far the greatest bulk was agricultural machinery from Messrs Dennison & Meakers of Reading. Some of this latter was crated, but most of it was loose. I have all details of sizes of cases and crates here and so on, and I can read it out if you desire.'

'You distinguish between cases and crates?'

'Yes. Technically a case is a box, completely closed in. A crate is an open structure: I might describe it as a box with alternate side boards missing.'

'Quite. I think if you will hand in your memorandum of the cargo it will be sufficient without reading it.'

To this the magistrate agreed and Armitage went on: 'Was there then nothing in the cargo to account for the explosions? No chemicals, which by accidentally coming in contact or being wet, might have formed a dangerous compound?'

'Nothing of the kind.'

'What about petrol having been left accidentally in the sets?'

'They were guaranteed to be empty and I've no reason to suppose they weren't. Besides, I doubt that petrol would have produced such explosions. On the other hand, it would probably have started a fire.'

'Then can you make any suggestion as to what might have caused the explosions?'

'Absolutely none whatever.'

Armitage then turned to the question of insurance.

The *Jane Vosper* was insured for £20,000 and the witness estimated that before the accident she was worth just about that sum.

Mr Clayton was subjected to a good deal more cross-examination by the various solicitors present than had fallen to the lot of the previous witnesses, but here again Jeffrey did not see that anything material was gained. He simply repeated his former statements in different words.

Edgar Trevenna, inspector of the Marine Department of the Board of Trade, then testified that in the normal course of his duties he had inspected the *Jane Vosper* after her last overhaul, some four months previously, and he had found her in good order and properly equipped.

Arthur Jefferson, inspector for Lloyd's, followed, and gave similar evidence.

Both the technician's evidence and that of Mr Clayton had taken a considerable time, and the president now pointed out that it was past one o'clock and time for lunch. With his 'Two o'clock, please, gentlemen', he vanished with his assessors, and once again the hall quickly emptied.

'It doesn't seem to be getting any simpler,' Jeffrey declared, as he and his companions headed for their restaurant.

'It looks at all events as if Armitage thought it malicious,' returned Alexander. 'And Armitage means the Board of Trade.'

'Surely nothing else could be possible?' As he spoke Jeffrey glanced at Sutton as if asking his opinion.

'That's my view,' the detective put in. 'There's nothing in the ship and there's nothing in the cargo to blow her up. She was blown up. Therefore some explosive was deliberately put aboard with the object of sinking her. I don't see how you can escape from that.'

'And the motive?' put in Alexander.

'Why not insurance?'

Alexander shook his head. 'We've had no evidence to suggest it so far, but probably the point will be dealt with after lunch. You don't suppose the owners sank the ship for the £20,000, I presume?'

'I suppose not,' Jeffrey admitted. 'But they're not the only firm concerned. I shall be interested to hear the value of the cargo and what was its cover.'

This point was, as a matter of fact, the first taken on the resumption of the proceedings. Representatives from the five firms who had dispatched cargo by the *Jane Vosper* were called and gave estimates of the cost of their various consignments and the amounts for which they were insured. If these figures were correct, and there seemed no reason to doubt them, the amount of cover in each case was reasonable, if not moderate. Certainly there was nothing to account for so desperate a step as the blowing up of a ship for the insurance money. Indeed Jeffrey had to admit that no adequate motive had yet been suggested.

During this somewhat tedious portion of the enquiry attention flagged, but it revived when Chief Officer Arlow was recalled, particularly among the representatives of those insurance companies which had covered the cargo.

Arlow said that in the ordinary discharge of his duty he had been present during the whole of the loading, and had seen that the cargo was stowed in a thoroughly workman-like and proper manner. He had there the bills of lading and other records of the work, and from these he was in a position to say in what part of the ship each item of cargo had been stowed.

'Then,' said Armitage, 'you might tell us in as complete detail as you can, just how No. 2 hold was loaded.'

Arlow replied that in the bottom were stowed the 350 cases from the Weaver Bannister Engineering Company of Watford. These were heavy and he had had them put on the floor of the hold, arranged in order of unloading. These cases covered the entire floor of that hold to a depth of some four feet. On them he had had built to the height required agricultural machinery invoiced to Pernambuco and Rio. None of the holds was quite full.

In No. 1 hold, about which Armitage next enquired, the cargo placed against the after bulkhead was at the bottom crates of agricultural machinery for Buenos Aires, and above it cases of radio material for Montevideo. They were tightly wedged, and in his opinion it would have been impossible to get them out without opening the hatch.

'Was the agricultural machinery covering the Weaver Bannister cases in No. 2 hold, in crates, or if not, how was it packed?'

'It was not in crates, sir. Parts of it were lapped with straw ropes and stiffened by being attached to pieces of wood, but for the most part it wasn't packed at all. We roped and wedged the various implements together to prevent them shifting with the movement of the ship.'

'Then would you say that between the crates and the top of the hold there was a good deal of open space, through which the gases of an explosion might become diffused?'

'Yes, sir, that is so. There were ploughs, for instance, and while a man couldn't have crawled between them, there was a lot of hollow space surrounding the metal.'

'Now I want you to think carefully before you answer this question. Explosives undoubtedly got into that No. 2 hold. How, in your opinion, could that have happened?'

Arlow shook his head over this. He knew nothing of any explosives. He couldn't see how explosives could have got into the hold. He admitted they must have done so, but how was entirely beyond his knowledge.

When the usual non-productive questions had been asked by various solicitors, the next witness was called.

Abel Garstone said he was employed as a foreman

stevedore at the London Docks. He had been in charge of the squad which had loaded the *Jane Vosper* and had worked under the supervision of First Officer Arlow. He had heard the first officer's evidence and he corroborated it on every point. He was positive that no explosives could have got into No. 2 hold while he was working there, unless these were hidden in the Weaver Bannister crates. Nothing of the kind could possibly have been secreted in the agricultural machinery, as this was much too open.

A Mr George Hislop then gave evidence. He said he was second in command in the export department of the Weaver Bannister Engineering Company of Watford. He had been directly concerned with the packing and dispatch of the cases which he had just heard had been loaded into No. 2 hold on the *Jane Vosper*. With obvious indignation in his voice he declared that the suggestion that explosives could have got into the cases was entirely false and absurd. The whole operation of assembly, packing and dispatch was carried out by experienced and trustworthy workmen under a very complete system of supervision, and no explosives or other unauthorized objects or materials could under any conceivable circumstances have been included. He wished to take strong exception to the suggestion that such might have occurred.

Mr Trafford here intervened to point out smoothly that according to his notes no such suggestion had been made. He thanked Hislop for his evidence and asked Armitage if he had many more witnesses.

It appeared there was just one, a Mr Hulbert Morris. He stated that he was a representative from Messrs Dennison & Meakers of Reading, and with reference to his own firm he repeated Hislop's assurance that no explosives could have been included in the stuff sent for shipment.

When this witness stepped down Trafford said that if any of those gentlemen who were appearing for interests involved had any further material facts to put forward, he would be glad to hear them.

No one produced further witnesses, but a number of the legal-looking men and some of the trade union officials availed themselves of the invitation to address the court. Once again it did not seem to Jeffrey that their contributions very much advanced the common stock of knowledge. Most of what they had to say was devoted to showing that the person or interest for whom they appeared had acted throughout in an exemplary manner, and that if blame were to be allocated, it must be apportioned elsewhere.

Then Armitage replied for the Board of Trade. His speech was not biased towards or against any interest, but took the form of a summing up of the evidence which had been given. It ended by reciting a number of questions which he said the Board of Trade would like the court to answer. These were rather obvious and included such demands as, What was the cause of the sinking of the *Jane Vosper*? Was any person to blame for the sinking, and if so, who? Had the officers and crew done all that could be reasonably expected of them to save the ship? and several more of a similar kind.

Trafford listened carefully and then had a long conversation with his assessors. Finally he said that that concluded the immediate proceedings. He thanked everyone very much for his attendance and help, and explained that the findings of the court would be delivered in due course. With a bow he and the assessors withdrew, and with the same lack of drama that had marked its opening, the enquiry came to an end.

5

A Further Puzzle

On the afternoon of the following day Jeffrey, Alexander and Sutton met in the former's office to discuss the situation which had arisen as a result of the enquiry. Jeffrey was anxious to reach a conclusion as to the course he would recommend his directors to follow when the claim for the £105,000 came in from the Weaver Bannister Company.

He was far from clear in his own mind as to what that course should be. Naturally he wished to avoid payment if this were possible, but he did not desire, and was not going to suggest, anything which was not strictly honourable. To evade its liabilities on some legal quibble was to him the worst possible policy for an insurance company.

But in this case there really was a genuine doubt as to where they stood. They still didn't know what had happened aboard the *Jane Vosper*. The enquiry had not cleared up the one point in the whole affair that really mattered—the origin of the explosions. Until they knew that, how could they decide their own position?

He had put these points to Alexander. 'My strong feeling,' he continued when they had talked them over, 'is that we shouldn't pay. The thing is too suspicious. It seems incredible to me that it could have been anything but foul play.'

'It looks like foul play, I admit,' Alexander returned, 'but you can't prove it. What's more to the point, you can't prove that the Weaver Bannister people were mixed up in it. If their deal with you was carried out legally, you remain liable, even though some other person may have committed a fraud which incidentally damaged their property.'

Jeffrey leant forward. 'I know all that,' he said. 'But look at it this way. The four explosions came from the same part of the ship, and the evidence was conclusive that that was near the bottom of No. 2 hold. Now the entire bottom of No. 2 hold was filled with these Weaver Bannister crates. Therefore does it not follow that the explosions came from the crates?'

'It certainly looks like it,' Alexander admitted cautiously.

'And that view is further supported by the bulging of the bulkheads. The chief engineer said the fourth explosion must have come from low down, owing to the place in which the bulge occurred. It seems to me that the presumption that the explosive was in the crates is overwhelming.'

Alexander shrugged. 'Suppose it was,' he parried. 'I don't just see what you're getting at.'

'Well, I think that should be clear enough. If it came from the crates, there's fraud against us, and we don't pay.'

'Not exactly,' the solicitor pointed out. 'If you can prove that the Weaver Bannister people put the explosives

86

into their crates with the object of sending them to the bottom of the sea and so obtaining the insurance money, then there would be fraud which would relieve you and see some of the Weaver Bannister people in prison. But you're very far from being able to prove anything of the kind.'

'But if the Weaver Bannister people didn't put the stuff into the crates, how could it have got in? No one else had anything to do with them.'

'You don't know that.'

'The stevedore said they were stowed exactly as they came into the docks.'

Alexander shook his head. 'Scarcely convincing, I'm afraid. Besides, you'd have to prove that no one else dropped explosives between them after they were loaded.'

'I admit all that. All the same I'm hanged if I think we ought to pay as things are now.' Jeffrey paused, shrugged, and then went on: 'By the way, talking of another matter, I had four visitors this morning.'

Alexander looked his question.

'One after the other, as if it had been arranged between them, and each with the same air of secrecy and mystery. I couldn't help smiling.'

'Representatives of the other insurance firms?'

'Yes. Each came in, hemmed and hawed, and then pointed out that the trouble was obviously connected with our consignment, and what were we going to do about it? They all sincerely hoped we weren't going to pay.'

'You bet they did. And what did you tell them?'

'I said we hadn't made up our minds, and asked them would they care to help us in whatever action we decided on.'

Alexander laughed outright. 'Trust you, Jeffrey,' he said. 'And what did they answer to that?'

'Very non-committal. Glad to do anything vague and unspecified, but cautious about definite action.'

'They wanted to shove the dirty work on to you?'

'Of course.'

Alexander took a case from his pocket and carefully selected a cigarette, then as an afterthought held the case out to the others.

'They'll succeed there, I should think,' he declared. 'You've just been at pains to explain why only your firm could be interested.'

'Well, what do you advise?'

'I'm coming to that. You have, as I say, shown an *a priori* reason for suspecting that the Weaver Bannister people may be at the bottom of the thing. Now if so, the first question that arises is: What was their motive? That would have to be established before any proceedings would have a ghost of a chance of success. I'm not trying to crab your idea—far from it. But as you know, the strength of a chain, and so forth. Therefore these difficulties must be faced.'

'I understand that, of course, old man. Go ahead.'

'Well, I think we have to admit that no suggestion of motive came out in the evidence. The firm insured 350 sets, and there was evidence that 350 sets went aboard. They stated that they sold those sets at £350 and they insured them at £300. That means that if they destroyed them they would get £300 each for them, but if they didn't destroy them they'd get £350. Not exactly what you'd call a motive there.'

'I see that,' Jeffrey agreed slowly. 'But that mightn't have been the particular line they would take.'

'How do you mean?'

'How do we know those crates containe c sets at all?'

'Oh, I see. You mean they might have filled them with stones?'

'Something of the kind. By that means they would have made £100,000.'

Alexander shook his head. 'Impossible, I should say. How many of their men would know of a thing like that? Why, it would be common property. No, they simply wouldn't dare to put themselves in the power of so many of their workers.'

'H'm,' said Jeffrey. 'I agree there's a difficulty there.' He paused and for a moment there was silence in the room. Then he turned to Sutton. 'You haven't expressed any opinion, Sutton. What's your view of the whole business?'

Sutton moved uneasily. 'It's not so easy to answer you, sir,' he answered. 'I'm blessed if I know what to think.' He paused in his turn, then went on. 'So far as the question of the ship being sunk deliberately is concerned, I think that's proved. I can't see any way in which it could have been accidental. And the fact that the four explosions came so close together seems to me to show that they were worked by carefully set timing mechanism. Clockwork bombs, probably.'

'I think we both agree with Sutton so far?' Jeffrey said, glancing at the solicitor.

Alexander nodded. 'Yes,' he said rather surprisingly, 'I think we may assume that. That question of the time seemed to me almost conclusive. And Armitage appreciated it too.'

'You think so?'

'I'm sure of it,' the solicitor returned. 'You see, there was not only the point that the four shots went off practically simultaneously—though not simultaneously enough for one to have caused the others—but also the even more important point of the time at which they did go off. Anyone wanting to sink the ship—I mean anyone except an absolute devil—would want to give the crew as good a chance for their lives as possible. Now that was done. Armitage brought it out very well. Had the ship not been unexpectedly delayed, the explosions would have taken place when it was close to land. The captain admitted that excepting round the coast of Kent, it was about as safe a place as could be found on the whole voyage.'

'I follow you. I admit I didn't see what Armitage was up to in those questions.'

'That was it, I imagine: to show that deliberate sinking was not unlikely. Plenty of people would sink a ship for the insurance money, who would hesitate about drowning thirty-five men.'

'I agree. You agree, Sutton?'

'Yes, I do, sir. I'm satisfied the thing was deliberate. But when it comes to saying who did it, it's not so easy.'

'Well,' Jeffrey suggested, 'it seems to me that only six lots of people were interested, the owners of the ship and the five lots of cargo. Of those I think we can eliminate four; the owners of cargo which was not stowed at the bottom of No. 2 hold. That leaves two possibles, Weaver Bannister's people and the owners of the ship.'

Sutton nodded. 'Yes, sir, that's my view also.'

'I don't think that's quite proved,' Alexander put in, 'though I admit it as a provisional working hypothesis.'

'Very well,' said Jeffrey, 'let's assume it in the meantime. That is that either Weaver Bannister or the Southern Ocean people have been going in for fraud. Though hang it all,' Jeffrey made a worried gesture, 'I can't see either doing anything of the kind. They're decent firms with good reputations. You both know Stewart Clayton. Can either of you see him a party to such a thing?'

Alexander shrugged. 'I know. I've been pointing out the difficulties myself. Too much so, I imagined you thought.'

'If you hadn't known, sir, you would have said that it was incredible that any one of the five would have sunk the ship, wouldn't you?' put in Sutton. 'And yet it was done.'

'Yes, that's true,' agreed Jeffrey. 'Very well, provisionally we suggest that it must have been one of those two firms. Now the question is, What are we going to do about it? There'll be a demand for £105,000, probably in the morning. What do you say, Alexander?'

The solicitor did not reply for some moments. 'I'll give you my opinion,' he said then, 'first as a lawyer, and secondly as a friend.' Again he paused and the others bent forward, obviously hanging on his words. 'As a lawyer I am of opinion that with the knowledge you possess, you must pay. I can see nothing else for it, and I certainly should not refuse or put it in Weaver Bannister's power to take you into court to recover the money. Now for unofficial advice as a friend. I should temporize about the payment, and I should put Sutton here on the job of trying to find out something more about what really happened. He might learn something that would put a completely different complexion on the whole affair.'

'It's good advice,' Jeffrey declared. 'As a matter of fact I thought we'd have Sutton investigate it in any case. Well, Sutton, what do you think about that?'

'There are certain things that I think I could find out, sir, and there are others that I'm doubtful about. I think I should be able to find out if the 350 sets were of normal good quality, same as Weaver Bannister's actually sell for the £350. And I should certainly be able to find out if they were really packed up and put on board. I'd have less chance of finding out whether the Southern Ocean people dropped in bombs after the cargo was stowed, though I'd do my best on that too.'

'If Sutton can find out if Weaver Bannister's 350 sets were of normal quality, and whether they actually sailed, I think that's all you want,' Alexander commented. 'If that is proved you couldn't refuse payment. Whether the Southern Ocean people sank their ship or whether they didn't would be nothing to you.'

Jeffrey was obviously unwilling to come to any conclusion which might involve payment by his firm. But he had to admit that Alexander's view was sound. They thereupon went on to discuss with Sutton the details of his investigation. Finally it was arranged that the detective was to concentrate on the two questions already referred to: first, the quality of the Weaver Bannister sets sent, and second, whether 350 of these actually left in the *Jane Vosper*. If he could get any further information, so much the better, but he was not to go out of his way to seek it.

By the very next post Jeffrey received the claim from the Weaver Bannister firm, a claim for the whole sum in question, £105,000. For some time he sat thinking over the situation, then he decided that he would go out to Watford and have a talk with the partners. This would have the additional advantage that while it showed a desire to settle the business amicably, it put nothing in writing.

Accordingly he rang up the firm and went out early next morning. He had already decided to put all his cards on the table. These Weaver Bannister people were reasonable and would appreciate the position in which the Land and Sea Company found itself. They would not, he felt sure, object to Sutton's enquiry. Under the circumstances indeed they should welcome it. If they were innocent they should be glad of anything which would help to remove the unpleasant suspicion of their firm which necessarily existed. On the other hand, if they were guilty they would almost certainly have prepared a demonstration for insurance detectives, and would be glad of the opportunity of making it.

Jeffrey was courteously received by the senior partner, Mr Bannister, a man of about sixty with a pleasant manner and a look of quiet efficiency. It was evident that he was gravely troubled by what had taken place. He spoke with transparent sincerity and a very short conversation was sufficient to convince Jeffrey that he at least had had no part in anything underhand. He expressed his complete bewilderment as to what had really taken place, and admitted without hesitation the equivocal and unpleasant position in which his firm had been placed.

This gave Jeffrey his opportunity. He admitted that he also was utterly puzzled by the whole affair, going on to point out what a very serious matter it would probably prove for his company. 'Now, Mr Bannister,' he went on, 'I'm going to be quite straight with you. I want you to understand at the outset that we intend to meet our full liabilities. That, I think, should be made clear before I go any further.'

He paused, while Bannister, evidently relieved, murmured

politely that with a firm like the Land and Sea, no doubt of this could possibly arise.

'Presumably,' went on Jeffrey, 'no action should be taken on either side until after publication of the Board of Trade findings on the enquiry. I don't want to go into that, it can be settled later.' Mr Bannister did not look quite so pleased. 'What I should like to say now is this. Owing to the very exceptional nature of the circumstances, my directors will naturally require me to take certain obvious steps before any payment can be made. You know as well as I do what those steps are.' Jeffrey smiled. 'We are now talking formal business, not touching on our individual relations nor upon our private beliefs, which I imagine are identical.'

Bannister nodded with a certain air of anxiety. 'Go on, Mr Jeffrey,' he invited.

'I think you will agree that as a matter of formal business we should have a report from one of our representatives that he had satisfied himself that all the terms of the contract had been strictly carried out. You will agree also that our requiring this is not intended to, and in point of fact does not, throw any slur whatever on your firm.'

Bannister made a deprecating motion. 'I hope I am not so foolish as to object to that. What exactly do you want me to do?'

'I should like you, if you will, to grant our representative, Mr Sutton, facilities to enquire into and report on the sending out of the crates, right from the loading here in your works up till the departure of the *Jane Vosper*.'

Once again Bannister seemed relieved. 'I shall not only agree to that,' he said with some warmth, 'but I shall welcome his enquiry. I shall give him my authority to go anywhere he likes about the works, to interrogate any of our staff, including myself, and to inspect any documents for which he may ask. I am only anxious that the truth should be demonstrated and am delighted at the prospect of its being done. But,' he added with a searching look at Jeffrey, 'you on your part will send a discreet man who will not give unnecessary trouble, and who will keep to himself anything he may see which is irrelevant to the enquiry.'

Jeffrey leaned back in his chair, also with an expression of relief. 'That's very satisfactory,' he declared. 'I should like to express my appreciation of the way you have met me. As to Sutton, I don't think you will have any fault to find. He's a good man, tactful and discreet. He'll carry out his job with the minimum of annoyance.'

'I should be glad to have the affair cleared up,' Bannister said, passing his hand wearily across his forehead. 'Very glad indeed. Though we are not in any way responsible for what has happened, all this has been a great worry to me. Until the truth is known there is bound to be— well, I needn't go into that; but it's unpleasant for all concerned. I confess I was disappointed with the enquiry.'

'It wasn't very illuminating, was it?'

Bannister, it appeared, had been present and they began to compare impressions. Jeffrey had taken an instinctive liking to the man, and before he left they had grown almost cordial.

Jeffrey returned to his own office in a rather despondent mood. His interview had made him more certain than ever that the Weaver Bannister people were innocent of the fraud, and he could see no possibility of his company escaping payment. And this would be nothing short of a disaster. It would mean a serious reduction in the dividend, which would have a far-reaching effect on their general prosperity. It would mean a backset in his own personal finances, a backset which he could ill afford. Altogether the outlook was far from rosy.

For the next two days Jeffrey was engaged with other work and had not time to give much attention to the Weaver Bannister claim. But at intervals his thoughts slipped back to the subject. Particularly he wondered what Sutton was doing. The one unsatisfactory point about Sutton was that he was extraordinarily secretive. It was hard to get him to make regular reports of his proceedings. He seemed to have a rooted objection to describing his activities—until he had attained a result. Then admittedly he reported it promptly enough. But even then he only gave the result itself, omitting all reference to the steps by which he had reached it. 'From information received' was his favourite phrase, though he had never been in the official force. With the object of keeping in touch with what was going on, Jeffrey had instituted a daily report. But Sutton, while religiously sending it in, had filled it with such remarks as, 'Working on the—case,' or 'Visiting Scotland Yard relative to Mr—,' or 'Investigating at—' So Jeffrey found himself but little further on.

On the Tuesday morning, however, he came face to face with Sutton in the office corridor. 'Come and let's hear what you're doing,' he buttonholed him. 'Got anything interesting yet?'

With apparent unwillingness Sutton followed him into the office. 'I'm not quite ready to report yet, sir,' he answered when he was seated before the great table desk.

'I hope to be able to do so in a day or two. But I can tell what I've done up to the present.'

This was an unexpected concession. Jeffrey glanced keenly at the man. He had a slight air of eagerness, sufficiently foreign to his usual undemonstrative manner to make Jeffrey wonder if he really had discovered more than he had admitted. But his statement was commonplace enough.

He said that the Weaver Bannister people had been sympathetic to his enquiry. They had given him all the facilities for obtaining information that he required, and he had made an exhaustive investigation in their works. He was entirely satisfied that the 350 sets sent were of the standard quality, and also that they really did sell for £350 apiece. Moreover, they were correctly packed in their crates and were dispatched by rail from the works. There was no doubt whatever that the full value of the claim had been sent out.

He had then gone to the London Docks, and he was equally certain that the crates had been correctly received and stowed on the *Jane Vosper* and that the vessel had sailed with them on board.

When at the works he had seen Mr Dornford, the head of the export department, and Mr Hislop, his chief assistant, who had given evidence at the enquiry. They had supplied him with details of how the stuff had been transported from the works to the ship. He had not yet had time to trace the journey and he would of course do so, but in his opinion it would be a mere matter of form, as during the journey nothing could have been done in the way of tampering with the crates.

Here Jeffrey interrupted him to ask what kind of man

Dornford was. It seemed he was old and shortly due, so Sutton had heard, to retire. Hislop seemed to have the real power and it was said he would succeed his chief. Both were exceedingly civil, and Sutton repeated that they had given him every facility he could possibly have wanted.

Then came the explanation of the detective's eager look. 'I don't know if I should mention it, sir,' he said with some hesitation, 'but I heard a chance rumour that interested me quite a bit. I heard that the Southern Ocean people were going to break up the *Jane Vosper* after she had completed this voyage. Of course, I don't know if it's true; but, if it is, £20,000 would seem a tidy sum to get for her. I don't want to say too much about this at present, but I hope to get in touch with a man who may be able to confirm.'

This was worse and worse. If the rumour were well founded, here was undoubtedly a motive. Not perhaps a very adequate motive, but still the first glimmering of a motive that they had come on.

'What would she be worth for breaking up?' Jeffrey asked.

'I don't know, sir. I should guess about £5000.'

This was the figure Jeffrey had in his own mind, and if it were correct the fraud should bring the Southern Ocean people in about £15,000. Would a shipping company of their standing, particularly with a manager of the calibre of Stewart Clayton, commit so serious and dangerous a fraud for so paltry a sum? Jeffrey couldn't believe it. No, it was out of the question.

'Did you get the yarn on good authority?' he asked presently.

'No, sir, I didn't. It was only a couple of stevedores I

heard talking. And I couldn't get from them where they had heard it. It may be only nonsense. But, of course, those sort of fellows do pick up things pretty quickly.'

Jeffrey shrugged. The idle talk of stevedores was not a very convincing source of information. At the same time the idea was supported by more than their talk. It certainly looked as if the Weaver Bannister people were innocent. And, if so, no other alternative than the guilt of the steamer firm seemed possible.

For some time the two men discussed the matter, and it was finally arranged that Sutton should continue his investigations to cover the journey of the crates from Watford to the London Docks. He was not to make a formal investigation into the rumour about the breaking up of the *Jane Vosper*, but he was to keep his ears open, and if he could pick up any relevant information, so much the better.

That afternoon Jeffrey rang up the four other insurance firms interested to ask if any of them had learnt anything which might help in the general dilemma. None of them, however, had done so, and in the tones of each he recognized the growing belief that they should have to pay.

That night Jeffrey found it hard to sleep. His business had taken a grip of his mind, and, as usually happens at night, it was not its optimistic side that was uppermost. For some reason also Sutton dominated his thoughts. It occurred to him that he had omitted to speak to the man on another claim which, though small, had been giving him a lot of worry. It was the case of a shop fire, and there were reasons to suspect arson. Sutton had been going into the affair, but had been taken off it to attend the *Jane Vosper* enquiry. Now the negotiations had come to a head, and Sutton's evidence was required. Jeffrey noted mentally that he would have to get the man back to the office on the following day, so that the claim might be dealt with.

It was with this object that, when Jeffrey had completed his letters and routine business next day, he telephoned to the detective's home to tell him to drop what he was doing and call for further instructions. But this, as it turned out, was only to learn of a fresh worry.

Mrs Sutton replied. She said that she had just been about to ring up the Land and Sea. He husband had not returned home on the previous night, and she was rather anxious about him. She wondered if Jeffrey knew where he was.

Jeffrey felt slightly exasperated. However, he was outwardly sympathetic and reassuring. He did not know Sutton's whereabouts, but he had seen him on the previous day, and everything about him was then normal. He had said that he was going out in the afternoon to the Weaver Bannister works at Watford. If Mrs Sutton liked, he, Jeffrey, would ring up the works and find out if he had done so.

Mrs Sutton said that she would be greatly obliged. It was quite unlike her husband to remain away at night without letting her know.

Jeffrey accordingly got through to Mr Bannister. Bannister knew nothing about Sutton, but he said he would make enquiries as to whether he had been seen on the previous afternoon, and reply as soon as possible.

A few minutes later he did so. Yes, Sutton had called at the works on the previous afternoon. He had seen their Mr Hislop of the export department. It was with this department Sutton had dealt in his enquiries about the sets for South America, and it was on this same business he had called. Hislop stated that Sutton had asked about the transport of the sets from the works to the docks, and he, Hislop, had given him all the information in his power. It happened that Hislop had to go down to the City that afternoon, and the two men left in company. They had gone as far as Baker Street together, and then their ways diverged.

Jeffrey at once repeated this information to Mrs Sutton. But instead of reassuring her, it seemed to make her more apprehensive. She repeated that it was very unlike John and that she didn't like it at all. Jeffrey didn't altogether like it, either, though he didn't say so. Instead he told Mrs Sutton he was sure she would soon have some news and asked her to ring him up again later and let him know if she had heard anything.

Though Jeffrey thought the affair surprising, he did not really believe there could be anything wrong, and in the pressure of other business it slipped from his mind. But after lunch he was reminded of it when Mrs Sutton was shown into his room.

She was a small, dark, vivacious woman with a capable face and a pleasant manner. Jeffrey had seen her on one or two previous occasions and had been attracted by her lively conversation and bright smile.

But this afternoon she wasn't smiling. Her features, instead, were pale and drawn with anxiety. Eagerly she asked if Jeffrey had heard anything more.

'John's always so careful,' she went on, 'to let me know if he's making any change in his plans. He seldom stays away at night unexpectedly, but if he does he always rings me up. It's not even as if we weren't on the telephone: we must be for his job. I can't understand it. I'm perfectly certain he would have let me know if he could.'

Jeffrey murmured sympathetically.

'And last night in particular, he had an engagement. He was going to a debating society that he's fond of. He was going to take part in the debate. It's not that he was so very specially keen on it, but all the same he wouldn't have missed it if he could have helped. I've been to see the secretary. They were expecting him last night, and he didn't turn up or send any message.'

For the first time the possibility of something serious having happened entered Jeffrey's mind. If all this were true, as of course it must be, the circumstances were more disquieting than he had realized. It was easy to suggest reasons why the detective should have been prevented from returning home, but it was scarcely possible to explain why, if nothing were wrong, he had not sent his wife a message.

Jeffrey moved uneasily. 'He might have met with some slight accident,' he suggested slowly. 'He might have been taken to a hospital and they mightn't have yet got in touch with you.'

Mrs Sutton shook her head. 'No,' she answered, 'I thought of that. But I don't believe it's possible. I happen to know that his name and address and telephone number were in his pocket-book. If he had been taken to hospital I'd have heard of it.'

Her earnestness impressed Jeffrey. He had to admit to himself that things were not looking at all well. He wondered where Sutton could have gone after parting with Hislop at Baker Street. Then he remembered what at first had slipped his memory—the rumour about the breaking up of the *Jane Vosper*. Had the man gone down to the shipping office in the hope of learning something about that?

In Mrs Sutton's presence he rang up the Southern Ocean manager. He was trying to get in touch with his inspector, Mr Sutton. Could Mr Clayton kindly inform him if he was there?

Clayton replied himself. He would have enquiries made, and answer in a few minutes.

While waiting, Jeffrey tried the London Docks. Here there was a similar delay, but presently there were replies from both places. Sutton had not been seen at either of them for a couple of days.

All this did not tend to reassure Mrs Sutton, who, Jeffrey could see, was on the verge of tears. She was obviously acutely uneasy, and at last Jeffrey began to think that murmured reassurances were only exasperating her. He turned to her and gravely asked her if she was afraid of anything?

In her turn she hesitated, as if she didn't like to put her thoughts into words. 'It's his job,' she said at last. 'God knows he's been fair and straight with people—I mean people suspected of crime. But in his job you can't escape making enemies, and that's a fact. Because of what he's done—done rightly and in the course of his job, I mean— many a man's gone to prison. They won't forget that, some of them.'

'I don't know that you're right there, Mrs Sutton,' Jeffrey protested. 'It's not a subject I know much about, but I have read more than once that criminals don't resent the efforts of police and detectives. They recognize they are not following them out of malice, but only because it's their job. I see, of course, what you're hinting at, but I really don't think you need have any fears on that score.'

'Then what has happened?' she returned quickly. 'Is there any other way in which you can account for it?'

This proved a very searching question. Jeffrey found it extremely hard to tackle. For some minutes they discussed it, and then he asked her plump and plain if she would like him to report the matter to the police?

It was obvious at once that this was what she wanted. While she had hesitated about making her fears public, she was now so frightened that she would only be satisfied if some drastic action were taken. Jeffrey stretched out his hand to the telephone, then withdrew it and turned to her.

'His job must have brought him into contact with the police,' he said. 'Is there anyone, say at Scotland Yard, who knows him, or with whom he was friendly?'

'There were a number,' she answered. 'There was one officer at the Yard he knew well; but, of course, since his promotion he hasn't seen so much of him. That's Inspector French—now Chief Inspector.'

Jeffrey nodded as he again picked up his receiver. He asked for Whitehall 1212, and then after a short delay went on: 'Is Chief Inspector French in the building . . .? Yes, please put me through. Mr Jeffrey, manager of the Land and Sea Insurance Company.'

There was a short further delay, then a strange voice said, 'Chief Inspector French speaking.'

Jeffrey told his story and the strange voice said, 'Very good, sir, I'll look into it. Perhaps you would ask

Mrs Sutton to wait at your office till someone arrives. It would be quicker to see her there than elsewhere, and I presume you could grant the use of a room?'

Jeffrey said he would be pleased to do so, and French replied that someone would be sent at once.

6

French Takes Charge

Though Chief Detective Inspector French had replied in a
formal way to Jeffrey's call, he was distressed enough by
the message.

He had not been exactly intimate with Sutton, but he
had met him in connection with various cases and had
developed a genuine liking and respect for him. Though
Sutton had never been in the police force, he was a fellow
detective, working through different machinery it was true,
but still working towards the same great end as was French
himself. If anything had happened to him, French would
treat it almost as a personal matter.

And it might well be that something had happened to
him. Those guilty of insurance frauds were as dangerous
a type of criminal as any other, and men in Sutton's position were much more vulnerable to attack than were the
official police. They worked alone. They had behind them
no great organization such as that which sustained French
and his colleagues. Their discoveries were much more likely
to be known only to themselves than in the case of a Yard

officer, who worked as a member of a team rather than as an individual. Correspondingly their 'removal' was much more likely to safeguard a dangerous secret than would the murder of a policeman.

Another reason why French took a personal interest in the matter was that on one occasion when they were both engaged on the same case, Sutton had taken him home to supper. There French had met Mrs Sutton and her two daughters. He had liked all three, and now that they were in trouble he felt it was up to him to see that everything possible was done to help them.

French was feeling very keen and fit. It was not long since he had returned from his annual holiday—long enough to have got rid of the holiday slackness, but not long enough to have lost the benefit of the change.

He had had a splendid holiday, one of the best he had ever taken. He had not gone to Amsterdam, as he had intended at the conclusion of the case of the jewellery stolen from Nornes, Limited. A friend had recommended south-western France, and he and Mrs French had gone on a General Steam Navigation boat to Bordeaux, and from there had worked south to Biarritz and along the Pyrenees as far as Bagnères-de-Bigorre. They had spent a few days at Cauteret and had loved exploring the beautiful valley and its surrounding hills, and they had been thrilled by the drive up into the mountains to the Cirque de Gavarnie. But it had been hot in the plain: too hot for pleasure.

French's first consideration on receiving notification of a possible crime was to decide whom he should send to make the preliminary enquiries. But in this case with its personal reflex he quickly determined to go himself. If necessary as the matter developed he could put someone else in charge. But he felt he would like to hear the circumstances at first hand.

He went along the corridor to Sir Mortimer Ellison's room, reported the call, and obtained the Assistant Commissioner's approval of his plan. Then calling Sergeant Carter, he set off. They took the District Railway to Mark Lane and walked to the Land and Sea Company's offices in Mincing Lane. There French asked for Jeffrey, and was immediately shown into his office. Jeffrey was alone.

'I asked Mrs Sutton to wait for you,' Jeffrey said when greetings had passed. 'Perhaps you would like to see her first?'

'Yes,' French answered. 'I won't be very long with her, and then she can go home. Then, sir, I should like a word with you, if convenient.'

'I shall be here,' Jeffrey agreed, ringing for his pretty secretary to take the visitors to the waiting room.

Mrs Sutton jumped up as they entered and came forward with hands outstretched. 'Oh, Mr French,' she exclaimed, 'I'm so glad to see you. I'm in such trouble. Have they told you?'

'They've told me that Sutton didn't turn up last night and that you're anxious about him. But, my dear lady, you mustn't be upset. A thousand things may have prevented him getting home.'

'Oh, no, it's something serious,' she declared. 'I know it! I feel it! He was so good that way. He never stayed away without letting me know. Something dreadful has happened.'

'Now, now,' said French cheerily, 'that won't do at all. You mustn't meet trouble halfway. Tell me all about it and we'll see what can be done.'

'There's nothing to tell: that's just the difficulty. Nothing except the one thing—that he didn't come home last night, and that there's been no news from him.'

'Don't you worry, we'll soon find him for you. But I shall have to ask you a lot of questions, just as I would do in any other case.'

'Anything! Anything I can do! And I'm so grateful to you for coming so quickly and undertaking the search.'

'We'll do our best for you. You may be sure of that. Well, now, let's begin at the beginning. When did you see Sutton last?'

'At breakfast yesterday morning. He left at his usual time: everything just as usual. He never comes in for lunch, and he was due for supper at seven. But he never came.'

Soon French had the whole story; and he had then to admit that Mrs Sutton was right: it contained only the one outstanding fact—that the man was missing. French took notes of what he was told—the normality of everything in the immediate past, the fact that Sutton had intended to be in punctually to supper on account of his debating society's meeting, his unfailing habit of ringing up when detained, his practice of keeping his name, address and telephone number in his pocket book, the serge suit he was wearing of grey with a tiny check pattern. Then French began to ask more general questions.

'What cases has he on hand at present, Mrs Sutton?'

'He was acting for this company on that steamer case, the *Jane Vosper*. You may have seen about it in the papers?'

French had read of it, but had not followed it closely.

'It was sunk, the steamer,' Mrs Sutton went on. 'Explosions took place on board, and they thought they were done on purpose. The Land and Sea had insured part of the cargo, and John was trying to find out if there was foul play, so that perhaps the Land and Sea wouldn't have to pay.'

'That all?'

'No, he was on a fire case for the Land and Sea as well. Also a case for Appleby's of Henrietta Street. You know them: another insurance company. A fire, too. He didn't think anything was wrong there. And there was a personal injury case for Johns and Wilcox. I think those were all.'

French noted the names. 'Any recent letters, or phone messages, or callers?'

'You can look through his desk. There was nothing that he made any remark about. And I don't think there were any phone messages. But Mr Murphy was in the night before last.'

'Mr Murphy?'

'Mr Peter Murphy. He's in the same line of business as John: an insurance detective. He acts for Lloyd's, I think, though I'm not very sure. He's an Irishman, and a very nice man. He and John were good friends.'

'That the only recent caller?' said French, noting Murphy's name.

'The only one.'

'Very good. I think that's all I want at present. You go home now and I'll follow you and have a look through his desk. You haven't a photograph of him, I suppose?'

'Not here, I haven't. But there are some at home.'

'Then I'll get one when I call. Well, Mrs Sutton, that's all we can do here. I hope we'll soon have some good news for you.'

'I'm so grateful,' she said as she got up. 'It is an ease to my mind, your knowing about it.'

'Doesn't look well to me,' French said to Carter when

110

the woman had left. 'I read about that *Jane Vosper* case, and it's a big case. If a bunch of crooks are willing to sink a ship in mid-Atlantic and run the risk of drowning thirty or forty men, they wouldn't hesitate long to put an insurance detective out of the way if he got to know too much.'

''Fraid I didn't read about it, sir. It was when I was on my holidays.'

'Better employed, I suppose. Well, we'll go and hear what this Jeffrey has to say while we're here.'

Jeffrey was very willing to tell them all he could, and not only because Sutton was his employee, though he was sincerely concerned about him. But he felt that any information Scotland Yard could obtain about the missing man might also be information about the loss of the *Jane Vosper*. By all means this chief inspector must be helped in every possible way.

Accordingly he gave French all particulars about the case so far as he knew them. He described the negotiations which had led to his company's insuring the sets. The Weaver Bannister people had first written, mentioning the consignment they were sending to South America, and asking for a quotation for its cover *en route*. The Land and Sea Company had replied, asking for a description of the goods and a declaration of their value. This had been given, and a rate had been quoted, accepted and paid. His company was now facing the question of liability.

In a reply to a question from French, Jeffrey explained the position regarding liability. As French would understand, if the ship had been lost through the action of Messrs Weaver Bannister, they would not have to pay. Under all other circumstances they would. It was on this point Sutton had been particularly engaged at the time of his disappearance.

'Had he come to any conclusion upon it?' French asked.

'He thought everything connected with Weaver Bannister's was straight.' Jeffrey hesitated, then went on. 'But he mentioned a rumour he had heard.' And he went on to repeat Sutton's story about the breaking up of the *Jane Vosper*. 'Of course,' he added, 'this was the merest hearsay.'

'I haven't gone into it, of course,' French answered, 'but I've always heard the Southern Ocean was a sound concern. Does it seem likely, on the face of it, that they'd put through a fraud like this? What's your own view, Mr Jeffrey?'

Jeffrey shrugged. 'I agree with you. I should say it was most unlikely. But precisely the same applies to all the companies concerned. So far as I can see, one of them must be guilty, for the ship didn't sink by accident. The question is simply: Which one?'

'Did you get the insurance figures of the other companies?'

'Yes, they were all given in evidence at the enquiry.' Jeffrey took a folder from a drawer and passed it across. 'I had them noted and copied out.'

'These certainly look all right—if they're correct,' French agreed when he had read the statement.

'All except possibly that for the ship herself. If they intended to work the *Jane Vosper* for a few years still, £20,000 would be reasonable enough. If, on the other hand, they were going to break her up after this voyage, it would be high.'

French nodded. 'Sutton acted for other firms besides yours?'

'Yes, with our approval. He was employed by us irregularly—when required.'

French's further questions produced but little fresh information. As soon as he had satisfied himself that he had learnt everything possible, he rang up the Yard, detailed Sutton's description, and asked that an advice be sent round that he was missing.

'I shall probably be back to trouble you again shortly,' he said to Jeffrey before leaving, 'but I have enough information now to start looking for the man, and I should like to get that under way as soon as possible.'

The next item on his programme was to get Sutton's photograph and to look through his papers. This meant a journey to the man's home at East Croydon, and he and Carter took the first train from Victoria.

They arrived after Mrs Sutton, but in time to witness her bitter disappointment on finding that no message from her husband had been received during her absence. She handed French the photographs, and showed him Sutton's desk. It was characteristic of her that while he was going through the papers it contained she insisted in making him and Carter a cup of tea.

The contents of the desk showed that Sutton was a tidy man with an orderly mind. The papers, carefully placed in folders, were neatly filed and cross-indexed. In spite of it they took some time to read through. French, however, read them all, on the principle that any one of them might contain a clue which would put him on the right track. Unhappily none of them did. While he learned a good deal about Sutton's recent activities, he obtained no hint of his fate.

By the time he had finished at East Croydon it was too late to carry out further enquiries that night. Offices would be closed and staffs have gone home. French therefore returned to the Yard, and, having corrected and enlarged his description of the missing man, he arranged for this and a photograph to appear in the next day's issue of the *Police Gazette*.

Though he arrived home late for supper, French spent an hour before going to bed in thinking over what he had learnt and planning his work for the following day. He was despondent about the case. The whole circumstances looked badly. The evidence was convincing that if Sutton had been able to inform his wife of his whereabouts, he would have done so. As he had not done so, it followed that he had not been able. But, so far as French could see, if he were not able, it could only be because of one of two things: Either he had met with an accident or he had been murdered. But if he had met with an accident someone would surely have found him and his name and address would have been discovered. As this would certainly have meant a communication with his home, it looked as if the other alternative must be the truth.

But if Sutton had been murdered, it must surely have been due to something connected with his work. In this case it might be necessary for French to go himself into the cases which the detective had been investigating.

Of course it was not certain that the man had been murdered, and therefore the need for tracing his steps in these cases had not yet arisen. All the same, French told himself that if by the morning there was no news, he might assume the worst.

Next morning there was no news. Nothing had come in to the Yard, and when he rang up Mrs Sutton she said she had heard nothing, either.

French thereupon got busy. First he sent a man to Lloyd's

to find out just who Peter Murphy was, and then to arrange for an interview with him that evening. A second officer he sent to the Marine Department of the Board of Trade, to ask for any information which might be available about the sinking of the *Jane Vosper*, including, if possible, any conclusions which might have been come to as a result of the enquiry. If these were not yet available, the officer was to try to make an appointment for French with someone in authority who had studied the case.

French had decided that he himself would visit the Weaver Bannister works, where Sutton was last seen. When, therefore, he had completed his routine business at the Yard, he set off with Carter for Watford.

The Weaver Bannister Engineering Company turned out to be a larger and more important concern than French had somehow anticipated. It was housed in some fine modern buildings in Foxley Road, white concrete structures whose sides seemed almost entirely glass. The surrounding space, so often in large works a dump for rubbish, was here turned into a sort of park, with well-kept grass, shrub borders, winding paths and a neat railing.

At the entrance to the office block was a porter in a blue uniform. To him French gave his official card and asked if he might see Mr Bannister.

The senior partner was engaged, but after a short wait the two officers were shown into his room. French at once felt the man's personal charm just as had Jeffrey. He listened courteously while French briefly apologized for his intrusion and explained his business. Sutton had disappeared, and as his last known call had been at the works, he, French, must necessarily make the works the starting point of his enquiries.

Bannister said he had been sorry to hear of the disappearance, though he had only met Sutton a couple of times. He had, however, told Mr Jeffrey of the Land and Sea Company all that he knew about him. Had the chief inspector not seen Mr Jeffrey?

French admitted that he had heard Jeffrey's report, but explained that he wanted to get his facts at first hand. He would probably have to go into the business on which the missing man was engaged, so if Mr Bannister would tell him anything he could about that, as well as about Sutton himself, he would be grateful. 'If you could see your way to do this now, sir,' he added, 'it might save my troubling you again.'

'Oh, yes, I'll tell you,' Bannister answered; 'not that there's a great deal to tell. It happens that we make a rather large type of petrol-electric set for the lighting of isolated buildings. It is similar to the Petter and other sets on the British market, but larger than most of these, and designed to light a larger area. It was developed to meet certain special requirements in foreign countries, notably the Argentine. There one of our sets will light the whole group of buildings of the ordinary hacienda or ranch.

'We have for some time been trying to push our South American trade in these sets, and recently we sent a special representative from home to meet the foreign dealers. As a result we got a fairly good order. 50 sets for Pernambuco, 100 for Rio, 50 for Montevideo, and 150 for Buenos Aires; 350 sets altogether, with the prospect of a large demand if these gave satisfaction. The sets were completed and forwarded by the steamer *Jane Vosper*, which, as I suppose you know, was lost near Madeira. You probably know all about our insuring with the Land and Sea people, and our present claim. That, of course, was what Sutton was enquiring into.'

'Yes, I've heard about that part of it. I'm obliged to you, sir. I think that's all I want from you at the moment. But I should like, if I may, to see the gentleman who interviewed Sutton when he called on Wednesday.'

'Mr Hislop. He's the second in command in our export department.' As Bannister spoke he touched a bell, and when a clerk answered he told him to conduct the callers to Mr Dornford. 'Mr Dornford is the head of the department,' he explained. 'He will put you in touch with Mr Hislop.'

Dornford was a frail-looking old man with a rather weak face, though his eyes were sharp and intelligent. He greeted French civilly, heard his business and said he had not personally seen Sutton on the Wednesday, but that his assistant had done so, and he would send for him. Presently a good-looking man in the late thirties entered and was introduced as Mr Hislop.

A glance at the newcomer's face showed that here was the real head of the department. Energy, decision, competence and aggression were printed there. And the suggestion was confirmed by the deference with which the older man spoke to him.

'Better take the chief inspector to your office, Hislop,' he ended up. 'Then he can ask you what he wants to know.'

French repeated the little introduction he had made to Bannister, and then asked Hislop if he would tell him what passed at his interview with Sutton on the Wednesday.

Though French had not taken either to the assistant's

appearance or manner, he had to admit that no fault could be found with his response to the request. Hislop gave a full account of what had happened, adding that if there was anything else the chief inspector wanted he had only to ask for it.

It appeared that after lunch on that Wednesday Sutton had rung him up, saying he wanted a little further information about the South American sets, and would Hislop be there if he came out immediately. Hislop had replied that he was going down into the City, but that if Sutton came at once he would wait for him. Sutton had agreed to this, and had duly arrived.

He had previously been given very full details of the sets and of their dispatch, and Hislop had been somewhat at a loss to know what more he could require. However, it appeared that what he wanted was the numbers of the railway wagons in which the sets had been loaded.

'I didn't know they had gone by rail,' French said. 'That seems strange to me, because, if my recollection is correct, there's no siding into the London Docks.'

'You are correct in that,' Hislop replied. 'However, it was a matter of £s. d. We found that it would cost us less to send the stuff by rail than by road. You may imagine we went into it carefully enough.'

'I'm sure you did,' French admitted. 'What was the route used?'

'That I can't tell you. We have a siding into the works, an L.M.S. siding. The sets were loaded in the works and were run—I don't know how—to the L.M.S. Haydon Square Goods Station. If you don't know it, it's close behind the Minories, just beside the docks. From there they were, of course, carted down. It's quite convenient.'

'I know the place,' French agreed. 'And Sutton came to get the wagon numbers that were used?'

'Yes. He said that as a matter of form he was going to trace their journey to make sure that the cases were not tampered with *en route*. I got him the numbers from our loading department.'

'And was that all he wanted?'

'Yes, that and the time the wagons had left our yard.'

'I understand. Then I think you told Mr Jeffrey that you and Sutton left the works together?'

'Yes. I had, as I had told him when he rang up, an appointment down at St Katherine's Docks. We went together as far as Baker Street. There our ways divided.'

'You travelled Metropolitan?'

'Yes, the Metropolitan station's the nearest to the works.'

'Quite. Did Sutton mention where he was going?'

'To Waterloo Station. He changed to the Bakerloo Tube, while I carried on Metropolitan to Mark Lane.'

'Quite. Did he say what he was going to Waterloo for?'

'No, gave me no idea.'

'What sort of mood did he seem in, Mr Hislop?'

'A perfectly ordinary mood. I noticed nothing in any way out of the common. But, of course, you understand that I had only seen him twice before, so I couldn't be sure of his normal manner.'

'I understand. Now, Mr Hislop, I want you please to think carefully. Did Sutton make any remark, or otherwise, which gave you any hint of what was in his mind? I mean as to his plans or what he thought about his enquiry—anything at all, no matter how vague, which might help me in tracing him?'

Hislop hadn't noticed anything. 'To tell you the truth,'

he admitted in a burst of confidence, 'I didn't worry myself overmuch about the affair. I was rather fed up with all the questions. Of course, I didn't blame either Sutton or his company; they were bound to satisfy themselves as to the *bona fides* of our claim. But I knew it was all right, and going over what could only have one result rather bored me. Besides, I had my own business. I was making arrangements about sending some refrigerating machinery to Stockholm, and my mind was partly engaged with the interview I was about to have.'

French realized that while this was probably true, it was also a hint, and as he saw that he had obtained all the information he could hope for, he tactfully brought the interview to a close by thanking Hislop for his patience and courtesy. Five minutes later he and Carter had left the works on their return to Town.

When French reached the Yard he found that two reports had come in, one each from the men he had sent to Lloyd's and the Board of Trade.

The officer who had been to Lloyd's stated that Peter Murphy was a detective employed by the underwriters of Lloyd's on the same kinds of jobs as Sutton himself undertook. He was in fact connected directly with the *Jane Vosper* case, as it was he who had been entrusted with the work of seeing that the insurance claim on the ship was straightforward.

This news interested French a good deal. On the Monday night Sutton had seen Murphy at his home. On the Tuesday morning Sutton had come to Jeffrey with the suggestion that the *Jane Vosper* was to have been broken up had she survived the trip in question. Was there here any connection? Had Sutton discussed the rumour with Murphy, and had Murphy corroborated it?

'Did you arrange for an interview with me?' French asked the constable.

'Yes, sir. Murphy was out of town, but I got him at Gravesend on the phone, and he will call here at six tonight.'

'Good,' said French, and turned to the other officer.

'I made the enquiries you told me to, sir,' this man reported, 'and I found a gentleman named Clifford who said he thought he could give you the information you required. I gathered he was a sort of superior clerk. At all events, he was present at the enquiry, taking notes of the evidence. The inspector's report has not yet been issued, but he thought that a fairly accurate forecast of it could probably be made. If you wish to see him, he said you might ring him up.'

This was satisfactory enough also, and French dismissed the man with a word of acknowledgement.

So far the trail led to Waterloo Station, and there French decided he must next concentrate. He called for a number of men, therefore, and, going with them to the station, set them to work. Armed with photographs and descriptions of the missing man, they began interviewing everyone who by any stretch of the imagination could have seen him. Two men took the clerical staff, visiting in turn the various public offices at which he might have called. Others interrogated the platform men, the ticket collectors, porters, inspectors and constables, while still others dealt with those holding special jobs, the cloakroom men, the waiters and waitresses, the bookstall attendants, the hairdressers. French realized that the chance of obtaining information was but small; however, he did not see what more he could do.

As soon as he saw his staff well under way he rang up the offices of the Southern Ocean Steam Navigation Company to know whether Mr Stewart Clayton, the manager, could see him if he were to call in half an hour. It appeared that Clayton would be disengaged, and with Carter, French presently set off to the Fenchurch Street offices.

He was, however, not quite easy in his mind as to the wisdom of making the call. He was strongly tempted to leave it till after he had seen Murphy, who was investigating the action of this very firm. But, on the other hand, it was not unlikely that Sutton had called in his efforts to test the rumour of their bad faith. If so, he, French, would not be justified in allowing so important a clue to remain unworked.

If the Land and Sea offices were spacious, airy and modern, those of the Southern Ocean Company were the very reverse. Steep, winding staircases and narrow, twisting passages with odd steps at irregular intervals led to small, dark rooms filled to overflowing with desks and furniture. Everything was dingy and wanted paint, and the layout suggested the maximum of inconvenience and the minimum of efficiency.

Stewart Clayton, however, when they were admitted to his presence, showed no signs of inefficiency. A tall, well-built man, he had clearcut features and a decided manner. Briefly but courteously he asked French's business, which French stated with equal directness.

Clayton was unable to answer French's question as to the last occasion on which Sutton had called, but he made

enquiries by means of his desk telephone. He had a telephone, and not, as French thought would be more in
keeping with the offices, a speaking tube. But the replies,
when they came, were of no use to French. Sutton had not
been at the offices for two days.

'Perhaps, sir, you wouldn't mind asking your
representatives at the London Docks? If you could do
so, it would save me the time of going there to put the
question.'

French was, of course, aware that a visit would be necessary before the point could be considered absolutely settled,
but there were so many other more urgent lines to be
developed, that he felt the information Clayton obtained
would be sufficient for the time being.

The reply was soon received. Sutton had been at the
dock, but not within the last two days.

French looked at his watch. It was just half-past three. He
had a couple of hours before he must return to the Yard to
meet Murphy. Stepping into a street telephone booth, he
rang up the Board of Trade offices, enquired for Clifford,
and asked whether if he were to call in a few minutes
Clifford could receive him.

The reply was satisfactory, and soon French and Carter
were seated in a small office with a shrewd-looking man
who expressed himself as anxious to do anything in his
power to help.

'Very good of you,' said French. 'What I want is to get
as correct an idea as I can about the sinking of the ship.
I'm given to understand it was malicious, but I want to
be sure that is so.'

Clifford shrugged. 'The report of the court of enquiry
has not been issued yet, and won't be, I expect, for some

time. Would it be indiscreet to ask how the Yard comes to be interested in the affair?'

'Not at all,' French answered, going on to tell of the disappearance of Sutton. 'I'm trying to get a motive for that, and the question of whether the sinking was malicious, and if so, the position of the explosives, might be material points.'

Clifford was considerably impressed. He at once said that he had a typed copy of the whole of the evidence, and given proper authority, he could lend this to French.

'I should be obliged for that,' French returned. 'However, as it's probably a bit too technical for me, I wonder if you'd just give me a synopsis and your view as to what lines the report is likely to take.'

Clifford nodded. 'Under the circumstances, chief-inspector, I should advise you to read the evidence for yourself. But if you like I'll tell you my conclusions, for what they're worth. Won't you smoke?' He held out a cigarette case, and the three men lit up.

'This,' Clifford went on, 'is naturally unofficial. It's only my own opinion. I can't guarantee that the report will repeat it.'

'Of course, Mr Clifford. That's understood.'

'Well, personally, I think there's no question whatever that the ship was sunk maliciously, and I feel sure—indeed I happen to know—that the president of the court takes the same view. I really think you may take that as proven. But when we go to the question of who was responsible for it there's not so much to go on.'

'So I should imagine.'

'The evidence is that the explosions came from the bottom of No. 2 hold, where were stowed cases from

Messrs Weaver Bannister, of Watford. Above them was agricultural machinery, not in cases. It was sworn that the explosives could not have been fixed to this machinery, as, if so, they would certainly have been seen.'

'Does that mean that bombs were put in the crates?'

'Not necessarily. They might have been in the crates, or they might have been dropped in between the crates after the latter were loaded.'

'Which suggests serious crime by one of two reputable firms,' commented French. 'Tell me,' he leant forward confidentially and lowered his voice, 'what about the replacement of the ship? Was she up to date? I mean, is she likely to have been running at a profit or a loss?'

'All that information is in the evidence,' Clifford returned. 'You'd better read it.'

'I shall, but what is your opinion, Mr Clifford?'

'The *Jane Vosper* was twenty-two years old. The average profitable age of a steamer is usually taken at twenty years. You can draw your own conclusions. On the other hand, the *Jane Vosper* was substantially built and had had overhauls and renewals which would undoubtedly have lengthened her life.'

More than this French could not get. He was disappointed in the interview. He had learnt practically nothing new, though, on the other hand, he had checked what he had already heard and found it true. It seemed to him beyond question that a very serious crime had been committed in connection with the loss of the ship. If so, was it not possible that Sutton had got on to it, and had been murdered because of what he had found out?

If so, again, the criminals should be the same in each case, and whichever crime he investigated should lead to the same result. From this did it not follow that he should enquire into both crimes? Two separate avenues of approach should double the chances of success.

French decided he would work on both lines. His primary enquiry would be directly into the disappearance of Sutton, but he would consider the loss of the ship as a second string to his bow.

George Hislop

The interview with Clifford had occupied longer than French had anticipated, and when he left the Board of Trade offices he found he had only just time to get back to the Yard to keep his appointment with Murphy. In fact, when he reached his office, the Irishman was already there.

Peter Murphy proved to be a large, genial man with a twinkle in a very shrewd eye. He looked the type which would make the speech of the evening at a convivial dinner. All the same, French suspected that in that admirable speech there would be precious little information, and none that the speaker didn't want to give away.

'I was going to call on Mrs Sutton tonight,' he observed with but slight traces of brogue when French had explained his business. 'Not that I had anything to tell her, worse luck, but just to enquire. I didn't know you people were handling the matter.'

'Apparently she had the wind up from the very start,' French answered. 'She went round to see Mr Jeffrey of the

Land and Sea, and said she would like us to deal with the thing. He rang us up.'

Murphy nodded. 'She did the right thing. But I'd be afraid that neither you nor anybody else would bring the man back.'

'You think he's dead, Mr Murphy?'

'Well, and what do you think yourself? He wasn't the man to go off like that without letting his wife know where he was.'

'That's what she tells me. Did you know him well?'

'Not I. I've come across him in his work now and then, and I've been home with him to supper twice, and he's lunched with me. That's about all, I think.'

'You were home with him on the evening before he disappeared?'

'I was, but not to supper. We were both at the enquiry, you understand, and we had some talk there. Then on Tuesday he rang me up and suggested another chat. We discussed a place to meet, and he proposed his house. That suited me all right, so I went.'

'I wish you'd tell me just what took place.'

'Surely. I'd do a lot to get the thing squared up, both for his own sake and his wife's, too. A nice little woman, Mrs Sutton.'

'I agree with you,' said French. 'I had met her a couple of times before this affair.'

'She was very fond of him, too. If he's dead it'll be a knock-out blow to her.'

'I'm afraid so. It was about the *Jane Vosper* case he wanted to speak to you?'

'It was. He was bothered about it. Couldn't get on with it. Well, of course I was working on it, too, on the steamer

128

side of it. He wanted to know if I had got anything useful.'

'And had you, if I may ask?'

'No, I hadn't. I was just as much in the dark as he was himself.'

'Perhaps you'd tell me what passed?'

'Well, we had a talk at the close of the enquiry. It seemed to us from the evidence that the explosives must have been put into the ship by either the Weaver Bannister people or the Southern Ocean—the very two firms that we were supposed to be considering. I mean, it looked like a personal matter for one or other of us.'

'I understand.'

'He rang up that day to say that he thought Weaver Bannister were all right, and what about the Southern Ocean? He wanted to know what I had done. Well, as you can understand, for similar reasons I wanted to know what he had done—and so the meeting.'

'Quite. And at the meeting?'

'At the meeting we swopped yarns. He said that he'd been out to Weaver Bannister's and found that standard sets had been sent out of the works and that the prices they had stated to his people were correct. He had been down to the wharf at the London Docks and seen the man who loaded the sets, and was satisfied they had been correctly loaded, and had not been tampered with beforehand. He had only to trace the journey between the works and the docks to be quite certain the whole Weaver Bannister business was OK. He intended to do that on the following day, the day he disappeared. But he was satisfied enough and said that, so far as he could see, the Land and Sea would have to pay.'

'That's pretty well what he told Mr Jeffrey.'

'Then he put it to me: If the Watford firm was all right, what about the shippers? You see, we had already agreed that one or other must be guilty.'

'Quite.'

'So he was hoping I'd have had some proof against them. But I hadn't.'

'You found no reason whatever to doubt them?'

'None.'

French moved a little uneasily. 'I wonder if you'd tell me how far you had gone in your enquiry?' he said with some hesitation. 'It's not to criticize, as you know, but just to see how far your enquiry is complete.'

'I don't mind if you do criticize it,' Murphy returned. 'In fact, if you could show me any line I haven't tried, I'd be only too glad. So far as I can see now, the underwriters will have to pay. And there's a bad swindle in it somewhere. I'll tell you.

'I began by concentrating on the loading. I've seen everybody concerned, right down from when the first cart came on the wharf until the hatches were battened down and the steamer passed out through the dock gates. Now someone may have been squared and may be lying, but all I can say is that I found no trace of it. And, what's more, I don't see how any explosive could have been smuggled aboard. Too many people were there. In the daytime there were a dozen or more about those two foreholds, and at night there were watchmen both aboard and ashore. There's no evidence against anyone. I might say there's no suspicion against anyone.'

'Sounds convincing.'

'Then I've been on to another line. Putting explosives aboard would be a risky job to take on. It would mean a pretty good stretch for anyone who was caught. And that would mean a pretty big bribe. Now, so far as I've found, none of the men who could have done anything have shown signs of having come into money. I don't say that's conclusive, but it counts.'

'It certainly does.'

'Lastly, I looked at it from the firm's point of view. I tried to get a motive.'

'Did you get it?'

'I did not.'

French turned in his chair and became more confidential. 'Sutton had heard a rumour that the Southern Ocean people were going to break up the *Jane Vosper* after this trip. Anything in that?'

'I don't know. He told me about it. I couldn't confirm it, but I'm going into it now.'

'We know the ship was old, but they said at the enquiry she was in good condition?'

'And that was true. She had a good name as a well-built and well-found ship, a fine sea boat and with comfortable quarters. And there's no doubt she'd had her overhauls and had been kept in first-rate order.'

French turned to the last item on his notes. 'Did Sutton say anything about Waterloo?'

'Waterloo?'

'Yes, the station.'

Murphy shook his head.

'Because he told Hislop, one of the men at Weaver Bannister's, he was going to Waterloo. It's the last thing that's been heard of him.'

'He must have been on to something after I saw him. He said nothing to me about Waterloo.'

131

When Murphy had left French sat on alone, thinking over what he had heard. He was a good deal disappointed by his interview. Really he had learnt little or nothing from Murphy. The affair was growing more and more mysterious. Here were two trained detectives, both convinced that they were investigating a fraud, and yet neither of them could find any evidence to support their belief. All the detailed information they had acquired tended to show that they were wrong.

But this was all in connection with the *Jane Vosper* mystery, which to French was really only a side line. About his own case, the disappearance of Sutton, he had learnt from Murphy nothing whatever. And his own investigation had been equally unproductive. Waterloo Station had been thoroughly combed, but had yielded nothing. Enquiries had been made at all hospitals within a reasonable radius, without result. No unidentified bodies had been found. Practically all the police and detectives in the country had been looking out for Sutton, but none had seen him. His wife had heard nothing. It was practically certain he had not left the country. French was beginning to feel at a complete loss.

As he walked slowly home his thoughts turned back to the last occasion on which the man had been seen. He had travelled with Hislop to Baker Street, then going on to Waterloo.

The only evidence for this, French reminded himself, was Hislop's statement. He began to think about Hislop.

Hislop's appearance and manner showed that he had force of character, determination, and ability. He was a man, French felt sure, who would not hesitate to take a risk if he thought the result worth while. And a decision to take that course once made, he almost certainly would not be put off by difficulties from carrying it out.

But there had been no corresponding suggestion of high moral traits. French believed the man would take the expedient way, without worrying much as to what codes might or might not be infringed. Was it possible that the story about the parting at Baker Street was an invention, put forward to cover up some more sinister tale?

Suppose Weaver Bannister were guilty after all? Suppose Sutton had stumbled on the truth. Suppose Hislop were one of those involved? Suppose Hislop had learnt of Sutton's discovery? Could these suppositions be true, and could Hislop have taken the only certain way of preventing Sutton speaking?

It didn't seem likely. There was the difficulty of the firm's reputation. There was the further and greater difficulty that Sutton had gone into the point and on the day before his disappearance had told Murphy—and Jeffrey—that the sets had definitely been sent out of the works, and were up to standard. No, it didn't seem likely. And yet . . .

From French's point of view the idea was certainly attractive. Suppose, instead of travelling from Watford to Baker Street, the two men had gone somewhere else? Suppose that in some way Hislop had killed his companion and succeeded in disposing of his body in some place as yet undiscovered?

Not a very hopeful assumption. There weren't so many places in which bodies could be hidden, even in London. And such a murder would require time—quite a lot of time. Hislop couldn't account for that time were he asked.

No, the more French thought over the idea the less

promising it seemed to grow. However, it was the *only* possibility he could think of which might explain the affair. He felt he must look into it. It shouldn't take long. If Hislop were innocent, he should have no difficulty in proving it.

Next morning when French reached the Yard there was still a complete absence of news. He was unable, therefore, to improve on his plans of the night before, and as soon as he had gone through his letters he and Carter started off again for Watford.

The same blue-uniformed porter was in charge of the office entrance. He saluted when French bade him good-morning. He had the cut of an old soldier, and, as he was lame, French diagnosed War service.

'I wonder,' said French in a friendly way, 'if you could help me to clear up a small point? I dare say you know I'm a police officer from Scotland Yard, trying to find out what has happened to Mr Sutton?'

The man saluted again. 'Yes, sir, so I heard.'

'I'm trying to find the hour at which he and Mr Hislop left here on Tuesday last. Mr Hislop tells me it was after lunch, but he cannot remember the exact time. You'll understand it's important to clear up the point, as Mr Hislop was the last person to see Sutton.'

'I understand, sir.' The porter hesitated. 'I'm afraid, sir, I'm not very sure of the time. I saw them go out after lunch, but it was a busy afternoon, with a lot of people in and out, and I didn't take any particular heed to the time.'

Here was practically all that French wanted—confirmation of Hislop's statement that the two men had gone off together. At the same time it would be valuable if he could find not

134

only the hour at which they started, but that at which Hislop had returned.

To obtain this information was little more than a routine job, and French settled down to it. Who else had come in and gone out during that afternoon? Of the A, B, C, etc., whom the porter remembered, who had passed before Hislop and Sutton and who after? Because, as the porter would see, enquiries from these people might fix the time they had passed, and so the limits of that required would be narrowed down till it became fixed.

As French had hoped, this detailed examination brought back small incidents to the porter's mind, which enabled him to supply the answer without recourse to anyone else. He had noticed that as Hislop and Sutton turned out of the main entrance they had all but run into a man who had swung quickly round the corner to meet them. That man proved to be a Mr Adair, who had mentioned that he had an appointment with Mr Bannister for three o'clock.

'That's very good,' French said encouragingly. 'Now, if you can fix Mr Hislop's return, it will be all I want. Of course, you understand that this has nothing to do with Mr Hislop personally? It's simply that I have an estimate of how long he was away, and the time he returned will therefore check that of his departure.'

To French's surprise, this proved an easier question. A very little help brought it to the porter's memory that the time must have been about 5.40, for he, Hislop, arrived just after Mr Bannister had left for the day, a matter of importance of which the occurrence was noted.

Only one more enquiry was needed. French saw Bannister to ask whether on the Tuesday a man named

Adair had called to see him, and, if so, at what hour? On being assured that this information was required in connection with checking up Sutton's day, Bannister said that Adair had had an appointment for three, and had been punctual.

So far nothing could be more satisfactory, and French and Carter left the works well satisfied with their progress.

The next point was to try for confirmation of the men's having travelled by rail. The enquiry was simple but tedious, and consisted in interviewing each member of the station staff in turn, asking if the man knew Hislop, and, if so, whether he had seen him on the previous Tuesday afternoon. For some time the officers worked away without result, and then Carter signed to French.

The ticket collector who had been on duty at the main entrance had seen Hislop. He knew him well as a frequent though irregular traveller. On this occasion his attention had been called to him by the fact that Hislop had arrived as the train was just about to start, and he had had a sharp run to get on board. He had been accompanied by another man, but the collector had not specially observed the latter's appearance. Nor could he say what train it was the travellers had caught, though he thought the time was not long after lunch.

Though this testimony was not as complete as French would have liked, he had to admit that it was unexpectedly good fortune to have got any information at all. So many people passed in and out of the station that the officials could not be expected to remember isolated passengers. The fact that Hislop and Sutton had run for their train was just a piece of undeserved good fortune.

But the next step in the enquiry was less simple, and French could scarcely hope for two strokes of luck in succession. Could he find out at what hour Hislop had reached St Katherine's Docks? He considered what he had to work on. Hislop had stated that he had gone down in reference to the sending of some refrigerating machinery which was being shipped to Stockholm. It didn't seem much upon which to trace the visit, yet French thought it might do.

Taking the next train, he and Carter went to Mark Lane. He had timed the walk from the works to the station, and now he timed the run from Watford to Mark Lane, and the farther walk from thence to the entrance to the docks. He made it 67 minutes altogether.

At the docks he consulted the policeman on the entrance gate as to steamers to Stockholm, and was advised to apply to Messrs Jacks & Wilkinson, who, the officer thought, were agents for the line in question. Five minutes later French and Carter were seated in the tiny wooden office of Jacks & Wilkinson's quayside manager.

'My business,' French began after showing his official card, 'is only very indirectly connected with your company. It's about a recent consignment of refrigerating machinery sent to Stockholm by Messrs Weaver Bannister of Watford.'

The manager nodded. 'I know it,' he admitted. 'You mean for the Aktiebolaget Ohlsson?'

'That's it,' French agreed, glad to have got over this fence so easily.

'I remember about it. What did you want to know?'

'Did you have any communication about it from Messrs Weaver Bannister on Tuesday afternoon last?'

'Tuesday?' The manager thought. 'Yes, I remember now.

It was on Tuesday afternoon that Mr Hislop called. He wanted to fix up details about the loading—date and time the stuff should be here, and so on—and also whether he would give us the carting or fix that up himself. What about it?'

French could scarcely hide his satisfaction. Obtaining just this information might have been overwhelmingly difficult; in fact, it might have proved impossible. And here, almost without effort, French had got what he wanted.

'I'll tell you, sir,' he went on. 'What I want is connected neither with your company nor with Weaver Bannister's, nor with Mr Hislop personally, but only with the hour he arrived with you and left on that afternoon. I needn't go into a long explanation, but I want to find the time at which he parted from a man named Sutton at Baker Street while on his journey here. That's the Sutton who's disappeared—you may have seen about it in the paper. Now Mr Hislop can't remember the time, so I'm trying to check it up from his other movements. Can you help me?'

The manager expressed keen interest. 'Is that the way you people work?' he commented. 'Making what you call a reconstruction?'

'Yes, that's one of our methods,' French agreed. 'You will understand, for example, that if we could get the time Mr Hislop left his own works and that at which he arrived here, it would give us the time he must have passed Baker Street. Then we'd be in a position to search for taxis or question the men on duty about Baker Street. You follow? One thing leads to another in our business.'

'I understand that. It's very interesting. Well, I think I

can help you there. Mr Hislop came about quarter-past four, and he didn't go away till half-past. I remember that, because I have a cup of tea about that time, and I was wishing he'd go so that I could get it.' The manager smiled and French did the same.

'I'm afraid, sir, I can only be pleased that your tea was delayed, as otherwise I mightn't have got my information. Thank you very much. You've helped me quite a lot.'

French could scarcely wait till he was out of the office to commence the reconstruction of Hislop's timetable. It was completed in a few seconds, and very convincing it proved.

Hislop had left the works about 3.0 and reached the dock office about 4.15, which gave a total time for the journey of 75 minutes. French's timing of his own journey had been 67 minutes, plus about 3 from the dock entrance to Jacks and Wilkinson's office, say 70 minutes altogether. But he, French, had taken the actual travelling time only, allowing no margin for variation in their respective speeds of walking, incidental delays, or inaccuracy of the hours given in Hislop's case. From these facts, added to that that Hislop and Sutton had been seen getting into the train at Watford, it followed beyond any possibility of doubt that Hislop's statement was true. He could not have murdered Sutton, for the simple reason that he would not have had time.

The return journey did not really affect the case, but French worked it out as a check. Hislop had started back about 4.30 and arrived about 5.40, thus taking 70 minutes. This was 5 minutes less than the outward journey, but exactly French's own time—a very complete and over-whelming check.

It was with a deepened feeling of depression that French left the docks. The momentary satisfaction he had experienced at having obtained his immediate object was quickly dispelled by the knowledge that it left him no further on with his case. In fact, he was now in a worse position than before. What had seemed a promising line of research had gone west. The one theory he had developed to account for Sutton's disappearance had been proved false, and he had no other left to take its place.

Admittedly there was still no actual proof that Sutton had parted from Hislop at Baker Street with the intention of going to Waterloo. But now that the major part of Hislop's statement had been proved true, it was very unlikely that he should have lied about a non-essential detail. French felt he must accept the story in its entirety.

What, then, must be his next step? He was by no means sure. The only thing he had thought of was to repeat the investigation Sutton had been engaged on, in the hope that he might come on whatever had led the man to his doom. It wasn't a very promising line, but he could see no other.

Finally he decided, as it was Saturday and it would be impossible to reach the people he should want to interrogate, to leave this new enquiry over till Monday, and spend the afternoon in another call on Mrs Sutton. It was conceivable that she might have heard her husband speak of a call at Waterloo, or have some idea of why he had gone there.

Accordingly he let Carter return to the Yard, while he himself went to Victoria. Getting some lunch at the station, he took an early train to East Croydon.

He was rather shocked at Mrs Sutton's appearance. Her face had gone a pasty white and her cheeks had dropped in, while her hair showed streaks of grey. Altogether she looked ten years older. She greeted French with an eager question, but she read its answer in his face, and turned away to hide her disappointment.

'I've traced him to Baker Street, as I think you've already heard,' French told her a little later on, 'and I think to Waterloo, but I can't find out where he went to at Waterloo. I was wondering if you could help me there? Did you hear him speak of Waterloo, or do you know anyone that he might have gone to see in that neighbourhood?'

Mrs Sutton had no idea. If she had, she would have mentioned it long before. Her husband must, she thought, have got on to some clue, and been led into a trap. She said directly that she had no doubt that he was dead, and that he had been murdered by someone whose guilty secret he had penetrated.

French did his best to comfort her, but as he really agreed with her, his efforts were not very successful. As soon as he could decently do so he took his leave, feeling that the interview was painful to them both.

On Sunday he spent three hours reading over his notes and considering his next move. He did not, however, gain much light from the proceeding. More and more he became convinced that his fundamental conclusions were true, but that their proof, so far, was beyond him. He felt satisfied that the *Jane Vosper* had been sunk deliberately, probably by the owners for the insurance on the ship, that Sutton had discovered this dangerous secret, and that he had been murdered because of it. But personal belief was no good to him or to anyone else. He *must* get proof.

But how to get it he didn't see.

8

The Dispatch of the Sets

A weekend of desultory thought left French with the conviction that his most hopeful line of progress lay in the repeating of Sutton's enquiry. This, with luck, might lead to results in two separate directions. First and more important to French personally, it might reveal the fate of the missing man. Second and more important, perhaps, to the community at large, it might clear up the mystery of the *Jane Vosper*.

On Monday morning, therefore, he set off with Carter to begin the work. According to Sutton's own statement, he had checked the loading of the sets at Weaver Bannister's and their stowing in the *Jane Vosper*'s hold in the London Docks, and was about to trace their journey from one place to the other. French must now do the same in his own way and as if it were his own enquiry.

Once more the chase led to Weaver Bannister's at Watford. It was a charming morning, one of those autumn days when summer seems to have come back and the sun has regained his former heat and brilliancy. French, looking

143

out of the train at the rows of houses and builders' 'estates', thought them almost cheerful in the warm light, and felt heartened by what seemed a good omen for his success.

On reaching the works he asked to see Bannister. He was sorry, he explained, to trouble him again, but the situation he had foreshadowed in his previous interview had materialized, and he was going to have to repeat Sutton's enquiries in the hope of forming the contact which had led to the man's disappearance. He had called to request Bannister's good offices in the matter.

'What do you want me to do?' Bannister asked.

'I want you, if you will, sir, to give me a note to your employees, asking them to assist me with any information in their power. Of course, you understand I can't demand this officially, but it would be a considerable help to me if you could see your way to do so.'

This was a request French frequently made under similar circumstances. Not only would such a letter be of practical value in dealing with the staff, but the principal's willingness or otherwise to give it would be to a very real extent a test of his guilt or innocence. If he were guilty he would not willingly take such a risk.

Bannister, however, agreed without hesitation. Calling in his secretary, he dictated a letter, telling the girl to have it typed at once.

While the typing was in progress, French continued talking about the case. 'Tell me, sir,' he asked, 'why you chose the Southern Ocean Company to carry your sets? I should have thought that with such a valuable cargo you would have employed one of the big liners, instead of this comparatively small *Jane Vosper*?'

'That,' Bannister answered, 'I cannot answer officially,

144

as I had nothing to do with the choice. It was Mr Dornford's business, and he settled it. But,' he went on dryly, 'I can form an opinion as to the reason. Freights are naturally less on small cargo boats than on the large passenger liners; and, as far as safety is concerned, in a way the matter doesn't greatly interest us. Our stuff, as you know, was covered by the Land and Sea Insurance people, and it was up to them to be satisfied as to the safety of the ship before issuing the policy.'

'I understand that, sir,' French agreed.

'But, as a matter of fact,' Bannister went on, 'I don't think a small cargo boat is a bit more likely to go under than a liner. Look at the great ships that have gone down, from the *Titanic* and the *Waratah* to the *Vestris* and that Ward Liner; I've forgotten her name. However, that's only an opinion, and doesn't affect your enquiry.'

'The line that was chosen doesn't really affect my enquiry, sir,' French admitted. 'I was asking only out of curiosity.'

This, however, was not strictly true. French wanted to be sure there was no guilty understanding between Weaver Bannister's and the shipping company. He therefore determined to put the question to Dornford also.

He continued chatting about sea disasters till the letter appeared. Then, thanking Bannister for his help, he asked if he could see the export manager.

To Dornford he explained his call as he had to Bannister. He produced his letter as evidence of the latter's sympathy with his efforts, and asked if he might have all the details about the shipping of the sets.

'What exactly does that mean?' Dornford asked.

'The history of the affair from beginning to end, sir, if you please. The choice of the shipping firm, the

145

negotiations which passed between you, the arrangements about getting your stuff on board: everything connected with it.'

'The man Sutton asked for and obtained something like that,' Dornford answered. 'But we'd better have Hislop in. It was really he who handled the business.'

'Thank you. I should be obliged.'

Dornford spoke through his desk telephone, then turned again to French. 'I don't know if you're aware that I'm retiring shortly and Hislop is succeeding me. He is therefore carrying on under my general supervision, so that he may be quite qualified to take charge when I leave.'

'I gathered so, sir, but I hadn't heard it officially.'

Further talk on the subject was interrupted by the entrance of Hislop. He nodded to French and asked was there something fresh on the carpet? French explained again.

'Yes,' Hislop said when he had finished, 'Sutton asked for all that information. He got it, too. I don't suppose he was actually entitled to it, but we realized his position and were anxious to help him.'

'Then I hope you will help me in the same way,' French suggested.

Both men seemed agreeable to do what they could. Hislop's statement, supplemented by the answers to a few questions, gave French all the information he wanted.

It seemed that for years the Weaver Bannister firm had been sending its products to South America, though this was the first occasion these particular sets had been dispatched. They were indeed a new line which had just been got out, and a special representative had been sent to South America to introduce them. The resulting order of 350 was in the nature of a trial, and if the sets gave satisfaction there would be large repeats.

For years the firm's stuff had been carried by the Southern Ocean Company. It had been chosen in the first place because its freights were lower than those of the passenger lines, and secondly because it had a good name for the careful handling and prompt delivery of its cargoes. This good name had been amply justified so far as the Weaver Bannister people's experience went, and the question of changing the shippers had not therefore arisen.

The correspondence which had taken place was perfectly normal and commonplace. Hislop had advised the Southern Ocean Company that they had 350 cases, of about 2 feet by 2 feet by 4 feet, and weighing about 15 cwts. apiece, for various South American ports, and asked for a quotation. This was received, it being pointed out that it included stowage, but excluded delivery on the quay of the London Docks. The price was agreed to, and then Hislop went into the question of transport between the works and the docks. He obtained quotations for road and rail transport, and found the rail was slightly the cheaper. This L.M.S. quotation he had asked for in two forms, one for delivery on the quay and the other for delivery at the nearest L.M.S. goods station, which proved to be that of Haydon Square. The reason he had done that was that he had had a canvass from a firm of carriers, Messrs Waterer & Reade, of Otwell Street, Cannon Street, soliciting a trial order. He thought the present would be a good case in which to see what they could do, so he asked them to quote for the carriage of the sets between Haydon Square and the quay. Their quotation was lower for this cartage than that of the railway, therefore the order was given to them.

'That is to say,' said French, 'the L.M.S. Company picked up the stuff here in the works on your private siding, and carried it to their Haydon Square Goods Station, then Waterer & Reade carted it from there to the London Docks and handed it over on the quay to the Southern Ocean people, who loaded it on the *Jane Vosper*?'

'That's correct,' Hislop answered. 'I made the actual arrangements, but each particular item of it was submitted to Mr Dornford and received his approval before action was taken.'

'I understand, sir. Now I'd like to get the dates of all that before we go on.'

'The dates of the correspondence we can supply without difficulty,' Hislop answered. 'Here they are.' Then when French had got what he wanted, he went on, 'The dates on which the stuff was actually moved I can't give you here. You'll have to go to the dispatch sheds. I'll take you down presently.'

'I think I may go at once,' French returned. 'You've very kindly told me all I want. Did Sutton get any more information than I have?'

'Not as much,' Hislop answered. 'He didn't ask about dates, for instance.'

'Dates are useful for pulling a story together,' French said easily. 'I'm sure I'm obliged to you for what you've told me.'

'Well, will you come along?'

French found himself conducted downstairs to a large shed containing two railway sidings with a platform beside each, roadways for lorries and vans, Decauville tracks leading back into the buildings, and over all a large travelling crane. Goods and crates were everywhere, and a

148

number of men were transhipping from the Decauville trucks to lorries and wagons. Hislop called up an elderly man in dungarees.

'This is Holmes, the foreman packer,' he explained. 'Holmes, give Chief Inspector French all the information he requires. If you want me again, chief inspector, I shall be upstairs.'

Hislop discreetly vanished, and French wished the foreman good day. 'I'm enquiring about Mr Sutton,' he went on—'you know, the man who disappeared. I understand that he made some enquiries from you?'

'Yes, sir, he was interested in a consignment of petrol sets we had sent out to South America.'

'Quite. I'm repeating his investigation in the hope of finding that he went somewhere or did something that will explain his disappearance. Now will you please tell me just what you told him?'

Holmes was willing enough. 'First, sir, he asked to see a sample set and the case it was packed in. If you'll come along I'll show you.'

The man led the way back into the depths of the building, following a Decauville track. Here, in another shed, the actual packing was going on. Machines of all kinds were being lifted into crates, or strengthened for transport with wooden frames. In one corner two men were packing sets. These consisted of an extremely compact-looking petrol motor, directly connected to a dynamo, both on the same base plate, and a separate switchboard. The cases were of $1\frac{1}{8}$-inch deal of good quality, very strongly jointed and bound with hoop-iron rings. The packing was shavings and sawdust.

French was not an expert, but to his amateur eye

everything looked of excellent quality. The machined parts of the sets, so far as these could be seen, were admirably finished, and the green-enamelled castings were smooth and even. The cases looked as if they would stand any amount of knocking about.

French's first care was to find out whether it would have been possible for inferior sets to have been loaded up. On this point he questioned indirectly the foreman, and when the latter excused himself to attend to another caller, the two packers. All three declared stoutly that all the sets they had loaded were of identical pattern, and that no cases contained anything different.

French then turned to a more ticklish point—whether anything which could have contained a bomb could have been loaded as well. Here the enquiry involved a good deal more work. Determined to be thorough, French went back to the assembly shops and saw both foreman and mechanics concerned. However, he soon satisfied himself that it would have been impossible to place a bomb inside either motor or dynamo castings, unknown to several of the men. Apart from the assurance of all concerned that nothing of the kind had happened, French was satisfied that no one would have taken the risk of such an act in circumstances of such publicity.

Similar detailed enquiries in the packing department led him to the same conclusion. Here, again, to have placed bombs in the cases would have been impossible without the connivance of at least six men. French interviewed all these, and he was convinced none of them had been party to any such action.

Nor, he believed, could the bombs have been put in at night. Cases were not left half packed in the evening, lest on taking up the work again some item which should have been included might be forgotten. They were filled and closed down, and if there would not have been time to finish one before the closing hour, it was not begun, and the man in charge occupied himself in getting forward stuff for the next day. Nor could a packed case have been opened without leaving traces. Besides all this, the sheds were locked at night and there was a watchman on duty close by.

French went into the whole question very thoroughly, and found himself forced to the conclusion that wherever the bombs had come from, it was not from the Weaver Bannister works. No doubt was left in his mind that 14 wagons of cases had left on the four days from the 13th to the 17th of September, containing 350 of the special sets and nothing else.

The papers Hislop had shown him proved conclusively that the cash value of the sets was as stated, so that French felt himself entirely satisfied that the Weaver Bannister people had acted correctly throughout, and were in no way concerned in the fraud. Also, it seemed beyond question that nothing that Sutton had learnt here could have had any connection with his fate.

Armed with the numbers of the wagons containing the cases, and the dates and hours at which they had left the works, French went to the stationmaster at Watford to pursue his enquiries. These cases had been consigned to the Haydon Square depot. How had they gone?

On this point French couldn't get a great deal of satisfaction. It seemed they were first brought into the Watford goods yard and there lay until the evening, when they were picked up by a train going south. They did not go direct to Haydon Square. They were thrown into different goods yards and remarshalled, and it was not till they had passed through a number of stages that they reached their destination. The stationmaster himself could not give the exact details.

But on the essential point he was very clear. It would, in his opinion, have been absolutely out of the question for them to have been tampered with *en route*. While in the goods yard at Watford they were under the observation of a number of men, and it would have been impossible for anyone to have got into a wagon and opened and closed a case unseen. These conditions, further, obtained at all the stopping places, and the stationmaster supposed that even French would not suggest they had been opened while the wagons were actually moving.

A consideration of the general possibilities led French to agree with him. To have attempted any interference with a case—much less four—while in the Railway Company's charge would undoubtedly have been out of the question. First it would have been necessary to ascertain in which particular yard the wagons were at the given moment. Then this private and well-fenced yard would have had to be entered unseen. Once inside, the wagons would have had to be located, involving a search along, perhaps, many miles of sidings. Then, still unseen, the wagons would have had to be entered, four cases opened, the bombs put in, and the cases closed, again without leaving any trace. Lastly the criminal would have had to leave the yard in the same secret manner as he entered it.

French saw that it simply could not have been done. As far as the rail portion of the journey was concerned, it was clear that Sutton's conclusion had again been correct.

'We're not getting any forrader,' he said to Carter as they stepped into a train for Euston.

Carter agreed that things were not looking any too good and said that it was much more likely to have been the shipping people.

'That's not what we want to know,' French reminded him. 'It's what happened to Sutton that we're up against.'

Carter agreed again and skilfully led the conversation to the question of lunch. He supposed they were going to the Haydon Square depot, and it would be a pity to have to break off in their enquiries there to have it.

French, who was himself hungry, decided to notice the hint, and said he knew a restaurant near Euston that would suit.

After lunch they went to Haydon Square. It looked a very old place with the sidings on ground level and the main line overhead. It was jammed with vehicles of all descriptions, waiting their turn at the cranes. French asked to see the agent.

He proved civil and helpful. Sutton had been to see him and had been given all the information possible. But the agent was afraid it hadn't helped him in his enquiry.

'Well,' said French, 'I'm sorry to trouble you to go over it again, but I'm afraid that's what I want.'

The agent was quite willing to repeat himself. He said the wagons containing the cases came in during the early morning and were shunted beside the cranes before the yard opened for outside traffic. The cases were booked forward to the depot only, to be handed over to Messrs Waterer & Reade, for cartage to the docks. Two of Messrs Waterer & Reade's 5-ton lorries were on the job, and the cases were loaded on these lorries and taken away by them. He admitted he had not known these details at the time, but had obtained them for Sutton.

This was convincing, but not convincing enough for French. He went down to the sheds, saw the foreman who had assisted with the unloading, and questioned him thoroughly. His replies, however, put the matter beyond doubt. Not only were all the cases removed on the lorries, but it would have been utterly impossible for anyone to have tampered with them while at Haydon Square.

Every step in this chain of investigation was making more and more perplexing the two puzzles with which French was dealing. Every step made the blowing up of the *Jane Vosper* more inexplicable, and the disappearance of John Sutton more unaccountable. It was true French had still to go into the cartage to the docks and the loading on to the ship, but it was unlikely, on the face of it, that the explanation of either mystery would be found there. It was, indeed, beginning to look as if a second investigation into the actions of the Southern Ocean people would be necessary.

But Sutton surely hadn't had time to make such an investigation? Surely it was while still engaged on the Weaver Bannister enquiry that he had met his fate? French put the point to Carter, and was surprised to find that he wholly disagreed. Sutton, in the sergeant's opinion, must have switched over to the question of Southern Ocean guilt. 'We're wasting time with these sets,' Carter continued. 'The thing was done by the steamer people—must have been. At least that's what I think, sir,' he added hastily.

'You may be right,' French admitted. 'However we've got to finish what we're at. What's the address of these blessed carriers?'

'Ten Otwell Street, off Cannon Street,' Carter answered, glancing at his notebook.

Twenty minutes later the two men reached the premises, which bore a large sign: 'Waterer & Reade. General Carriers.' The office facing the street was small, but through a covered entry they could see an enormous yard, stretching back into mysterious distances and filled with vans and lorries of all shapes and sizes. French pushed his way into the office and at a window marked 'Enquiries' asked if he might see the manager. His official card worked wonders, and without delay they were shown into that gentleman's private room.

Mr Keene was a sharp-looking man with an aggressive jaw, thin, clean-shaven lips, and very light blue eyes. He greeted his visitors briefly and asked what he could do for them.

French delivered his usual opening address and asked for all details possible about Sutton and about the transit of the cases.

Keene seemed slightly bored, but answered without objection, though sparing his words. He had heard of Sutton, but had not met him. The detective had rung him up on the Wednesday—the day he disappeared, French noted—asking could he see him that afternoon if he were to call. Keene had enquired at what hour, and Sutton answered 4.30, if that would suit. It had suited Keene, and he had noted the engagement. But Sutton had not turned up, nor had he sent any message of apology or explanation.

'At what hour did he telephone?' French enquired.

'Let's see,' the manager hesitated. 'Some time about the middle of the morning. About eleven, I think.'

French took a note to try to trace the sending of that call and asked Keene to proceed.

'That's all I know about Sutton,' he said. 'You also want to know about our handling of the Weaver Bannister cases? I can tell you that in a few words.

'For some time we have been anxious to develop our business, and I have been paying personal calls on likely firms to try to obtain their custom. Messrs Weaver Bannister was one of these firms. I called there about a month ago, and they promised us a trial order. For some time they made no move, then we received a request for a quotation for conveying these 350 cases from the L.M.S. depot at Haydon Square to the Southern Ocean boat *Jane Vosper* in the London Docks.

'We knew we should be up against the cartage departments of both the railway and the steamer companies, so we quoted a very low rate. In fact, I may say it didn't pay us. But we got the order.

'In due course we received the advice from Haydon Square that the cases were beginning to come in, and I arranged for two of our 5-ton lorries to start the job immediately. They worked—' He broke off and pressed a button on his desk. 'I'm not sure how long it took them, but I'll get the sheets.'

A clerk brought the papers and Keene passed them over.

'You see,' he explained, 'these are the timesheets of the lorrymen in question, Joseph Grey and William Henty. They began to cart on Saturday, 14th September, and continued on the following Monday, Tuesday and Wednesday. Four days they were at it. Perhaps you would like to see the correspondence and the receipts from the Southern Ocean people?'

French hesitated. He would like to see the documents,

but he could not claim that it was essential to his case. 'I should, if convenient,' he said.

'It's convenient enough, though I don't know that I understand how it's going to help you to find Sutton,' Keene responded. 'However, that is your affair.'

He rang for a file and passed it across. All the papers he had referred to were there, the original request for a quotation, the quotation itself, its acceptance, a note from Weaver Bannister saying that loading of the cases would begin on the Friday, a note from the goods depot that they were beginning to come in, the number of cases carried by each carter on each load, and the steamer people's receipts for these. It was all very complete and satisfying.

French indeed was strongly tempted to accept this mass of evidence without further enquiry as covering the carting transaction. But training, habit and experience all urged him to be thorough, not to accept *any* evidence without first obtaining all the checks upon it that were possible. Accordingly, when he had extracted what he wanted from the papers he asked if he could complete his job by a word with the two carters.

'You can with one of them,' Keene answered, 'if you like to wait till he comes in. The other I'm afraid has left, and I don't know that I can give you his address. They were temporary men, those two, taken on to cover a sudden rush of work. Grey has left, as I said, and Henty will be leaving in a day or two, as the rush is now over.'

Once more Keene rang for his long-suffering clerk. 'Take these gentlemen to the yard,' he directed, 'and find Henty. They wish to speak to him. Also look up and see if you can find Grey's address—you know, the lorryman who left recently.' He turned to French. 'If you go with Mr Paine, he'll do what he can for you.'

French expressed his thanks and he and Carter followed the clerk. The latter asked them to wait at the entrance to the yard, vanishing instantly among the mass of vehicles.

'Seems to me we've overshot the mark,' French remarked as they moved out of the way of a lorry which had just turned in from the street. 'Sutton hadn't got as far as this in his enquiry.'

'He's heard something,' Carter returned. 'Something about the Southern Ocean, I should say. He's given away what he's heard to the wrong parties, and so—' Carter made a significant gesture.

'I dare say you're right,' French admitted. 'All this part of the business looks correct to me. However, I'm going to make certain. I'm not going to leave a loophole for error.'

'It's the best way, sir; then you're sure.'

French glanced suspiciously at his sergeant, but the clerk returning at that moment, the conversation ceased.

'Henty has just come in, gentlemen,' said Paine. 'Just this moment. Lucky for you, for if he had gone out again you mightn't have seen him for hours. This is Henty. Would you like to come into the office?'

French said that, for all he wanted, where they were would do very well, and thanked the clerk with a gesture of obvious dismissal. Then, turning to the lorryman, he bade him good-afternoon.

Henty was a man of ordinary qualifications. Of medium height and middle age, he was neither thin nor stout, nor remarkable looking in any way. But his jaw was firm and he looked intelligent.

French briefly explained his business. 'It's simply about the carting of those cases from Haydon Square to the *Jane Vosper*,' he went on. 'You and another man were on the job?'

'That's right,' Henty answered. 'Grey it was. 'E's left. Tempor'ry men, we was took on as, both of us.'

'Well, tell me just what you did?'

Henty stared uncomprehendingly. 'There ain't nothing to tell,' he returned. 'We loaded up the cases at the goods depot and ran them to the quay—and that's the 'ole story.'

And so indeed it seemed to be. The loading was done by the railway staff, though he and Grey had given a hand. The unloading was carried out by the stevedores, and the cases were swung right from the lorries to the hold. The whole business was absolutely normal.

'Very good,' said French. 'That's all right.' He fumbled ostentatiously in his pocket. 'I want you to come to the goods depot and to the quay with me and point out the men who helped you to load and unload, and that'll be all.'

Henty, his eye on French's hand, agreed without demur. 'I'll go ahead,' French went on to Carter, 'and you see if they can turn up that address.'

The visits were uneventful. At each place Henty pointed out the men with whom he had dealt, and they in their turn recognized Henty as one of the lorrymen who had handled the cases. French thought he had perhaps been too meticulous in requiring the visits, but, after all, if they had done no good they had done no harm, and they had made his work all the more complete.

Left standing on the quay, French could not resist a look round before proceeding with his investigation.

159

Though—perhaps because—he knew little about it, the sea and all connected with it was to him a source of never-failing romance. This old dock in the heart of London was, he thought, one of those links connecting this stout little country of England with the great world beyond. It was a bottle-neck or clearing house, stretching out its tentacles into the factories and shops of England on the one hand, and into all the globe on the other. Or, rather, it had been, for it was now able to take few but coasting vessels. The average modern ocean-going steamer had so grown that it now berthed on the South Side in the Surrey Commercial, or farther down the river. But French stood thinking of the congested little place as it once had been. The ships which had loaded so prosaically along these quays had a few days or weeks later been sweltering in the Red Sea or the ports of India or China, the pitch bubbling from their seams and their crews languishing in the heat or, shrouded in ice, had been meeting furious seas off the Horn, that dreaded Cape Stiff where hurricane and blizzard reign supreme. How French longed for a year, for six months, to go and explore the world! Even to be scorched or frozen! How infinitely it would be worth it!

But dreams of the Far East or the Remote South would not help him to find Sutton or to earn his bread and butter. With a tiny sigh he was moving away when he heard Carter's voice behind him: 'They can't trace that man Grey's address, sir.'

'It doesn't matter. The other man was OK. Let's go round now to the Southern Ocean office. In Fenchurch Street, isn't it?'

Stewart Clayton was engaged when they reached the

head office, but, after keeping them waiting for half an hour, he saw them.

'Well, chief inspector, back again?' he greeted them, his tone dry. 'What can I do for you this time?'

French explained the point upon which he was now working, and Clayton agreed to give him all available information. But it did not amount to a great deal in the end. Clayton explained the whole affair in detail: the intimation from the Weaver Bannister people that they had a consignment of sets for South American ports with a description of sets and packing; the sending of a quotation for the freight; enquiries from the Land and Sea Insurance Company as to the steamer, etc., the stuff was going by; the arrival of the cases at the dock and their stowage; the sailing of the *Jane Vosper*, the receipt of the news of her foundering: everything, indeed, that French asked. As he spoke Clayton backed up his statements with the documents concerned, the various letters which had passed, the accounts, waybills, vouchers, copies of the ship's 'papers', in so far as they were relevant. French could not have desired more complete information.

But this very expansiveness, coupled with Clayton's straightforward manner, simply added to French's bewilderment. It was certainly very hard to believe that this man had blown up one of his firm's ships for its insurance money, or that he was party to such a crime. And French couldn't imagine it being done on behalf of the firm without Clayton's knowledge and co-operation. But if he hadn't been party to it, and if the Weaver Bannister people hadn't, as seemed even more certain, who had? Someone had! Who was it? And, more puzzling still, what had happened to Sutton?

By the time they had finished with Clayton it was too late to do any more that night, and the two men returned to the Yard, lost in sombre imaginings. French in particular was a good deal discouraged. He had covered practically all the ground, and he was no further on than when he started. The net result of his researches up to the present was to prove that no one could have blown up the ship, and that no one could have wanted Sutton's life. He shook his head. Somewhere he had gone badly wrong. But where? He could not see a single unexplored avenue remaining, or single explored one in which he could have reached any other conclusion than he had.

Nor did he find any help at the Yard. Nothing had come in. None of the enquiries which were being made all over the country had produced any result whatever. The case seemed to grow more and more hopeless.

'We'll do those docks in the morning,' French told Carter, as he turned to write up his notes.

Next morning it was again fine, and as the two men emerged from Mark Lane Station and looked down over Tower Hill their spirits rose in unconscious reaction to the bright sunshine. Yesterday might not have been a very successful day, but then they couldn't possibly expect success from their first efforts. Yesterday represented little more than the start of the enquiry. It also, French reminded himself, represented a lot of good work, conscientiously carried out. Good work, he had often told his subordinates, was never lost. Now he wondered if this were true. He hoped it was.

'Ever been through?' he asked in an effort to change the subject of his thoughts, nodding his head towards the great pile of the Tower.

Carter, it seemed, having been brought up on Harrison Ainsworth, knew the Tower well. He interested French with his talk, and French, who had not been over it since he was a boy, vaguely determined to try Ainsworth himself and pay it another visit.

They passed round the Tower and reached the entrance to the docks. A few enquiries led them to Harkness, the foreman stevedore who had loaded the *Jane Vosper*. Though busy, he made no difficulty about knocking off to answer French's questions.

He remembered Sutton. Sutton had been at the docks asking those very questions which French was now putting. And Harkness had given him all the information he could French, however, was more lucky. For there was now in the dock another Southern Ocean steamer, the *Kate Moxon*, which, though not a sister ship to the *Jane Vosper*, was of very similar size and build. He would take French aboard and he could see for himself just how and where the crates had been stowed.

They crossed a plank gangway to the forward well-deck and climbed down into the hold. French was amazed at the size of the space, because from the wharf the *Kate Moxon* looked a small ship. Four men were at work stowing the cargo, which came down in bunches at the end of a rope from the sky above, like gigantic spiders swinging on their webs. They came down on the floor of the hold, the rope slings were unhooked, the slings from the previous bundle were hung on to the hook instead, and as the hook vanished heavenwards, the goods were moved back into the hold and stowed securely.

'That's 'ow we stowed them there cases wot was mentioned at the enquiry,' Harkness explained. 'All over the floor; two layers there was.'

'Put close together?' asked French, who was watching the stowage of similar boxes.

'You couldn't 'ardly get a finger between them,' Harkness returned. 'They was tight packed. We 'as to, you know. You don't want your cargo shifting in a gale.'

This was a new and interesting point, and French seized on it. Did the foreman seriously mean that the cases had been packed so tightly that explosives could not have been dropped between them? If so, what about the edges, along the ship's side?

It seemed they were packed touching, side to side and end to end. There would have been room for nothing larger than a dagger between them. As to the sides, they were wedged up with packing, so that the cases couldn't move, no matter how bad the sea.

French interviewed the men who had done the actual stowing, and their statements confirmed that of Harkness. French could not but believe that the centre of the hold had been packed tight, though he was less convinced as to the continuity of the side packing. This side packing, however, did not matter. The evidence had been that the explosions came from the centre.

Mentally French swore. Did this mean that the explosives had been in the Weaver Bannister consignments after all? Hang it all, they couldn't have been! He didn't know what to think.

However, he completed his dock enquiry with his usual thoroughness. He saw everyone he could find who, he thought, might be able to give him any information. Then he obtained the names of the various night watchmen, went to their homes, and questioned each of them. But from no one did he learn anything further. He only became more firmly convinced than ever that no unauthorized person could have approached the hold, and that owing to the numbers present, none who had a right to be there had any opportunity of secretly planting bombs.

Filled with disappointment and exasperation, French left the docks. He had now traced the petrol sets from their manufacture up to their stowage in the *Jane Vosper*, and indeed until the steamer sailed, and he was absolutely convinced that everything connected with their packing, dispatch, carriage and stowage was entirely normal and in order. Quite definitely the explosives had not been in the cases. But now these enquiries at the docks seemed to show they could have been nowhere else. Confound it all! It was damnably puzzling. What ghastly oversight had he made, to lead him to such a conclusion?

And if his progress in connection with the blowing up of the ship had been poor, he had made none at all in his real enquiry: the fate of John Sutton. John Sutton had disappeared into the blue: vanished into thin air. He, French, had been called in, and after several days' work with the entire resources of the Yard behind him he had learnt nothing. Nothing! It wouldn't do. What was he to tell Sir Mortimer Ellison when he reached the Yard? Was he to make a complete confession of failure?

French felt badly up against it, and Carter, to whom in the depths of his extremity he turned for sympathy, had but little to offer. In a moody silence the two men reached the Yard.

9

The Shed in Redliff Lane

Scientists and philosophers alike tell us that the darkest hour is that preceding the dawn, and in a metaphorical sense French was to experience the truth of the adage on his arrival at the Yard. Again and again he had noticed that confidence and self-satisfaction were more often than not the prelude to disaster. The converse did not in his experience obtain so frequently, but occasionally a period of depression and a sense of failure did seem to end in a real step forward.

It was so on this occasion. Returning to the Yard discouraged and bankrupt of ideas, he found that the first reply to his questionnaire had come in. The officer in charge of the Leman Street Police Station had something to tell him about Sutton, and had sent a message asking him to ring up as soon as convenient.

French did not delay many seconds in doing so. His mood had suddenly changed. Instead of the hopeless baffled feeling he had been experiencing, he was now filled with optimism. Subconsciously he knew he was in for a stroke of luck. Or not luck—his reason countered—rather cause and effect. He had circulated an exhaustive question-naire, and it would be a strange thing if his efforts did not meet with some success. What he was going to hear was simply the answer to some of the questions he himself had asked. There was no luck about it: only the result of his own thought and trouble.

But when he heard the superintendent's message his bubble of self-satisfaction was suddenly deflated. Not only was the so-called information not an answer to any of his questions, but it was, so far as he could see, entirely useless and extraneous. It was simply that on the Tuesday evening, the evening before his disappearance, Sutton had rung up one of the men in the station, a constable named Osborne, to ask if he knew anything about a firm of builders in his area. The name was Rice Brothers. Osborne had known the firm only by name, and had so replied. It had happened that the next morning Osborne had gone on sick leave, and he had only just returned. As soon as he had read of Sutton's disappearance and the questionnaire sent out by the Yard, he had reported the incident to his superintendent. The superintendent passed on the report for what it was worth.

'Not very much,' French thought at first, but as he reconsidered the matter and recalled his complete bank-ruptcy of ideas in the case, he began to feel that even so unlikely a clue must not be neglected. 'I'll go down and see Osborne,' he therefore replied. 'Will you kindly keep him at the station till I arrive?'

'Come along, Carter,' he called. 'The Leman Street station.'

'What's it now, sir?' Carter asked as they set off.

167

'Wild-goose chase,' French returned bitterly. 'We have so few that I thought we'd both like one for a change.'

For the third time that day they passed through the portals of Mark Lane Station and after a short walk found themselves at the police headquarters. The superintendent, whom French knew, greeted them warmly and sent for Constable Osborne. 'Just tell the chief inspector what you told me,' he instructed him.

The constable, however, had but little to add to what French already knew. He had made Sutton's acquaintance over a case of arson, in which both men were interested. That had been in North London, from which area Osborne had been transferred some couple of years previously. The two men had become rather friends, having met in a social way on different occasions. Osborne, the superintendent had found out, was the only man in the Leman Street force known to Sutton, and this explained his request being made in a private way to him, rather than officially to the superintendent.

The address of the firm about which Sutton had enquired was 29 Redliff Lane, a street leading from Great Prescott Street, which turned out of Leman Street not a hundred yards from the station. The place was a yard, or at least it had what looked like the entrance to a yard, and it had over it a board with the name, 'Rice Bros. Building Contractors. Temporary Premises.' The constable had noticed the board, which had been up a couple of months or more, but he had been unable to give Sutton any information about the occupants. He had since walked round to Redliff Lane, and he had found that the yard was locked up and the notice gone.

'I follow,' said French. 'Sutton just asked you if you knew anything about the firm?'

'He said if I knew anything about them or could find out anything about them, he'd be glad to hear it.'

'Did he say why he wanted to know?'

'Not exactly, sir. He said he had a suspicion that they were wrong uns, but that as he wasn't sure I wasn't to report the matter officially. Just if I could get hold of anything myself I might let him know.'

'Rather a lot to ask, wasn't it?' French considered. 'What do you say, super?'

The constable spoke quickly. 'Maybe I should tell you, sir,' he said to the superintendent. 'I was anxious to help him, if I could do so in accordance with my duty. He had given me a tip about that arson case, that enabled me to make an arrest, and he let me get the credit of that and said nothing about what he had done. I said if I could ever do him a good turn I'd be glad to do it.'

The superintendent nodded. 'No harm in that,' he admitted, 'but I don't think you should have started making enquiries without reporting it.'

'No, sir, certainly not,' the man agreed hastily. 'I didn't do so, sir.'

The superintendent nodded again, and French asked, 'Can you remember the last time you saw the notice on the yard gate?'

'Yes, sir, it was there on the day that Sutton rang up—in the morning, at all events. I was on beat duty in that district, and I saw it that morning.'

French considered. 'I think, super, I'd like to look into this matter. Any objection?'

'Of course not, chief inspector. Can I help you?'

'Only by letting Osborne show me where the place is. If I want anything else I'll come back and ask you.'

'Right-o. Good luck in your hunting.'

'Now,' said French when they had left the room, 'I don't think I want to be seen with a constable in uniform. You go slowly ahead, Osborne, as if you were on beat, and when you get to this yard just try the gate, as you would the door of any unoccupied house. Then you can fade away and the sergeant and I will take over.'

Osborne saluted and set off, and when he had got a reasonable start French and Carter followed him out of the station. He turned first out of Leman Street and then out of Great Prescott Street, French and Carter stopping and arguing at the corners so as to give him time to keep ahead.

Presently they saw him cross the pavement and try the gates of a narrow entry between two tall, rather decrepit-looking houses. The lock was evidently satisfactory, for he passed on after a few seconds, disappearing round the next corner.

The gate was on the left side of the street, and on the near side was a tobacconist's and on the far a public house. French, after a look at the gate, which was of an ordinary pattern about six feet high, close sheeted and in two halves, pushed open the door of the tobacconist's. Carter, in response to a sign, strolled on.

It was a dark and dismal little shop, sadly in need of a brush and some soap. The tobacconist was old and short-sighted, and probably didn't see what an improvement a higher standard of cleanliness would have made. French greeted him pleasantly and asked for some cigarettes. A little discussion ensued as to the brand, but upon this important matter a conclusion was speedily reached. Then, while waiting for change, French turned to the question at issue.

'I see the yard next door's vacant,' he remarked.

'So I see,' the old man agreed. 'Nine shillings change.'

French thanked him. 'It's not your yard, is it?' he went on. 'I'm looking for a yard in this district for a temporary store, and that might suit.'

It wasn't the old man's. Nor could he tell who it belonged to. No, he did not know the parties who had had it recently. They never troubled him for tobacco, and he hadn't even spoken to them.

'Was the tenant,' French went on, 'a tall man with white hair and moustache? If so, I think he was a friend of mine.'

The tobacconist didn't know. His eyesight was not what it had been once. He couldn't see who went in and out. All he knew was that tradesmen worked there, and vans and lorries came and went. But he couldn't say what they were doing. In fact, the only other information that French could get out of him was that, except when in actual use, the gate was kept locked.

Seeing that as a source of information the tobacconist might be ignored, French wished him good day and moved along to the public house. Here he was in luck, for the bar was empty. He called for a pint of bitter and asked the landlord to join him.

The landlord was very willing, and soon they were chatting like old friends. Not till then did French steer the conversation to vacant yards. But even here he didn't get as much information as he had hoped. The yard adjoining did not belong to the landlord, and he had no idea whose it was. It had been taken by a firm of builders for the last eight or ten weeks, and the boss was a big, heavily-built man with a heavy face, clean shaven except for a small moustache. He drove a Ford van and was in and out with

171

it a good deal. He seemed to be making something in the yard, for workmen came to it and left it morning and evening. Lorries of materials came also at intervals. What they were doing the landlord didn't know.

The landlord spoke moderately enough, but French could sense the disgust he evidently felt when he went on to explain that he didn't know much about the men because they never used his house. 'Not good enough for them,' he said sarcastically. 'You'd have thought that here at their very door, so to speak, would have been the place they'd have had their drop of beer. But no, not one of them ever as much as crossed my doorstep.'

French did not wish to appear curious, so he finished up his beer, praised its excellence, and, having created a good impression, took his leave. But the landlord called him back. 'If you want to know the agents for next door,' he said, 'I'll see if I can find out for you. There was a sign on the gate before Rice took it.'

French thanked him and, thinking the matter worth it, invited him to share a second pint. This worked well, and when the man left to make his enquiries French felt sure he would do his best to get the information.

And so he evidently did. After a considerable time he returned to say that his daughter remembered the agents were Messrs Duckworth and Something. She could not remember the second name nor the address.

'I'm greatly obliged,' French declared. 'I'll get it easily from the directory with that help.' He and the landlord parted friends.

At the nearest post office French looked up a directory. There were a great many firms of which the first name was Duckworth, but only one of them were house agents.

'Got it first shot,' French murmured, as he read out the address for Carter to note. 'Duckworth & Crozier, 75B Fenchurch Street. Got that? Then let's go to Fenchurch Street.'

Mr Duckworth, whom after a twenty-minutes' wait they succeeded in seeing, was one of those small, stupid and intensely self-opinionated men who are such a nuisance to their fellows. French was positive that they had been kept waiting simply to pander to the man's vanity, and as a result he took a much sharper tone than he otherwise would.

He began by producing his chief inspector's card and saying that the police required some information from Mr Duckworth and that he would be obliged if he, Mr Duckworth, could let him have it without delay. Was he agent for the yard at 29 Redliff Lane, which had recently been let to Messrs Rice Brothers?

At once the little man began to make difficulties. What was the chief inspector's authority for asking about business which he, Duckworth, considered confidential? Was anything wrong about Rice Brothers or about the tenancy?

French said shortly that the police were making enquiries about the yard, and if anything illegal were found in connection with it, any refusal to answer would be noted and dealt with in due course. Whereupon Duckworth declared he had not refused to answer, but only to know where he stood in the matter.

'Where you stand, sir, is this,' French said sharply. 'You are at present delaying the police in making an enquiry into what may prove to be a serious crime. You are going to carry the responsibility for that delay. If it helps a possible criminal to escape, you will answer for it in court.

Now are you going to give me my information, or would you prefer to come with me to Scotland Yard and go into it there?'

To some extent, of course, French was bluffing. But the bluff worked. Duckworth climbed down. He said sulkily that he had nothing to hide about any of his transactions, and what did the chief inspector want to know?

'I want,' French said, 'to know the details of your transaction with Rice Brothers in connection with the letting of that yard.'

Even then the man could not bring himself to answer. He rang for his clerk and asked him did he remember how they came to let the shed in Redliff Lane to Rice Brothers? French could have sworn that he knew the particulars perfectly well, and was only showing that he was so occupied with important matters that he couldn't remember trifles. However, it was a step in the production of the information, and French waited with patience.

Finally the clerk was told to bring the correspondence, and at long last French got what he wanted.

It appeared that towards the end of July a man giving the name of James Rice called and said he was a partner in a firm of builders, and that they wanted to rent a shed somewhere near the docks for two or three months until their own new premises were ready for occupation. It was principally to deposit some plant in, but he might employ a few carpenters on forms and the like, if such proved necessary. Had they anything to suit?

Duckworth gave him three or four addresses and sent a clerk round with him. After seeing all these he said the Redliff Lane shed, though not exactly what he wanted, would do sufficiently well. He said he would take it for three months from the 1st August, and then and there signed the necessary agreement and paid the three months' rent in advance. They gave him the key and he went off.

They heard nothing more from him until the previous Friday. Then they had received a letter from Rice saying that as his own yard was ready rather earlier than he had expected, he had moved his things there and consequently was finished with the shed. He enclosed the key. The previous Friday was the 17th of October, so he had given up possession about a fortnight earlier than he need. Duckworth had sent a man to inspect the shed, and he reported that it had been left in good order. Unfortunately the Duckworth & Crozier board had been mislaid and he, Duckworth, was having another made. That was the reason there was no board on the gate.

French continued his questions methodically. He saw all of the staff who had interviewed Rice, and got from their joint efforts as good a description of the man as he could. He borrowed and gave a receipt for all documents which bore the man's writing or signature, and he asked for his address. This latter was the Kelvin Hotel in the Whitechapel Road. Finally he borrowed the keys of the shed, saying that he wished to inspect it. Duckworth had by this time come off his high horse, and was now obviously anxious to give all the help in his power.

A few minutes later French and Carter were back in Redliff Lane. Opening the gate, they passed through and locked it behind them.

They found themselves in a cartway, little wider than the gate, which, passing through a deep canyon between high buildings, led forward to a covered shed. It was not very large, about 50 feet by 35. It was well lighted by a skylight which ran down the centre for the whole length of the roof. French noted incidentally that the glass was rough rolled, so that no one from a window or elsewhere could see into the shed. Except for the door by which they had entered, there was no opening in any of the walls. The walls were whitewashed brick and the roof of the type usually known as a Belfast truss.

The paving of the floor showed that the area had formerly been a stable, coach house and open yard. The divisions of these could be traced by the areas floored respectively with stable brick, concrete and cobbles. The position of the drains bore similar testimony.

At one end was a light wooden hut with a glass front, containing a rough desk, some shelves, a sink with water laid on, a gas fire, two chairs and a telephone. It was littered with a few old newspapers. A double-sided carpenter's bench stood near the wall opposite the entrance and in one corner was a brick fireplace. The floor had obviously been swept, but still sufficient traces of shavings and sawdust remained to show that carpentering had recently been in progress. On the floor, also, were traces of sand and stone, with two or three empty cement bags, and large grey blotches showing where concrete had been mixed. In the small amount of rubbish still remaining French saw wire nails of various sizes and a small heap of cinders. There were also indications that a load of clay had recently been deposited and removed. Except for the hut and bench, the shed was empty.

Glancing up, French noticed that the tie-beams of the roof trusses had been recently notched. At these places the wood, which was dark and grimy with age, showed white and fresh. The notches individually were small, but they were distributed over the tie-beams to make a pattern. They made, in fact, a trace round the shed at a distance of about ten feet from the walls, the trace having two straight lines connected by semicircular ends. French was puzzled.

'What do you make of those marks?' he asked Carter, pointing upwards.

Carter rubbed his chin. Then after a while he shook his head.

'They're fresh marks, those,' French went on, 'and there, that looks like a new plug.' He pointed to a glossy black power plug which was attached to the middle of the centre tie-beam, just in the centre of the shed. It was connected to the electric meter by what was evidently a new cable running along the tie-beam and down the shed wall.

'Place is well lighted,' French went on, glancing again at the roof.

Six 100-watt lamps hung from the roof, and in addition there were two over the bench and one over the desk in the office.

'I wonder if that would be a runway?' Carter said suddenly, pointing up at the notches.

French stopped and looked at him. A runway! Yes, it just might be.

'If so, sir,' Carter went on, 'there might have been an electric hoist on it, fed by a flex from that plug.'

'You're scintillating this morning right enough,' French observed. 'Take particulars of it, so we can trace its purchase if we want to.'

Carter began to sketch and measure, while French continued prowling about, noticing everything that was to be seen.

The only thing which he had not examined was the fireplace. He now moved over to it and stood staring down. There appeared to have been a recent fire, as there were the remains of burnt sticks and papers. The papers were, so far as he could see, in ash, and he wondered whether anyone had stirred the fire to break the flakes. If so, it would be a little suggestive. He didn't think any scraps of paper were left, but there might be some beneath the wood. If the examination of the shed became serious, it would be worth looking.

French brought over one of the empty cement bags and very carefully plugged the chimney opening, so as to prevent a down draught damaging any paper not yet crumbled to ash. Then, having washed his hands at the sink, he rejoined Carter.

'Got those details?' he asked.

'Yes, sir. There's not much but the size of the thing and the shape of the notches.'

'Height of tie-beams from the floor?'

'I've got that, sir.'

'Well, we've done enough here in the meantime. There may be nothing in this; so far we've come on nothing suspicious. We'll go down to that Kelvin Hotel and have a word with the manager. Then if it still seems worth while we'll find Rice's new yard and see Rice.'

'There's certainly nothing here to worry about,' Carter returned. 'There's just what you'd expect in a shed hired temporarily by a builder.'

French agreed, and they let themselves out.

The Kelvin Hotel was a small, dingy establishment, of which the bar seemed to be the most important adjunct. But when the two men went inside they found that in a rough way it was not uncomfortable. French asked to see the manager, and a man with the cut of a retired butler appeared and said that his name was Smith and that he was the proprietor.

'Then I want your help, Mr Smith, if you please,' French said in a friendly way. 'You'll see who I am,' and he produced his official card.

Smith seemed impressed. 'Come into my room, gentlemen,' he invited, leading the way into the recesses of the building. 'Will you,' he hesitated slightly, 'take anything?'

'Not when we're on business, thank you,' French answered, and went on to explain that he was making private enquiries about Mr James Rice, who he understood had stayed for some time in the hotel.

'That's right,' Smith agreed. 'He was here for ten or eleven weeks, off and on.' He twisted his head on one side and screwed up his eyes knowingly. 'Anything wrong?'

'Not that I know of,' French said stolidly, 'but we want to trace him, as we think he was a friend of a man who's disappeared, and we hope to get some information from him.'

Smith nodded. 'Well,' he said, 'in that case I'm afraid I'm not going to be of much use to you. He's gone and he didn't leave any address.'

'I wish you'd describe him, Mr Smith, to be sure it's the same man.'

'He was a big, heavy man, with a heavy face. Fairish hair and blue eyes, and clean shaven, except for a small moustache.'

'That's the man. Has he left you long?'

The proprietor turned over the leaves of a book. 'On the 17th, last Thursday. He'd been here since—' Again he

179

turned over the pages. 'Monday, the 29th of July. About eleven weeks off and on.'

'Off and on? Perhaps you'd give me the dates?'

Smith did so, and French continued. 'And you say he left no address? Tell me, how did he leave?'

'How?'

'I mean, did he walk or get a taxi?'

Smith smiled. 'He took his bag in his hand and he walked on his two feet,' he said. 'We don't see many taxi folk down here.'

'A man might have luggage,' French pointed out.

'Well, he hadn't. Not more than he could carry.'

'What sort of man was he? I mean sociable or silent, or what?'

Smith smiled again. 'I'd say that sociable is about the last word you'd use to describe him. A very silent man was Mr Rice. Kept himself to himself. Never came and had his pint in the bar with the others. Not that I had any fault to find with him, you understand. He was easy to attend to and paid on the nail. But he was close. I never even got to know what his business was.'

'A builder,' French explained. 'Partner in a small firm.'

'Ay, he would just be something like that. Well, he must have had an office, for none of his letters came here.'

'I was just going to ask you that. No letters at any time?'

'None. I don't think a single letter came.'

'Telephone messages? Telegrams?'

'None at all.'

'Or callers?'

'Not a caller, either.'

'Not what you'd call expansive,' French commented. 'I wonder if you have his signature? Could I see it?'

There was, somewhat to French's surprise, a visitors' book, and Rice had signed it. French compared the signature with those given him by Duckworth. They were obviously the same.

'Well,' said French, 'I don't suppose I'll learn more than what you've told me, but when I'm here I might as well see the servants who attended him, and if his room's not occupied perhaps I might have a look at it.'

Smith had no objection, and French interviewed the waitress and chambermaid, though without gaining any additional information. Then he examined the room Rice had occupied, which was still unlet. But here again he found nothing of the slightest interest. Presently, thanking Smith, he and Carter took their leave.

'That'll do for tonight,' French said as they sat in a District train, bound for Westminster. 'I don't know that all this is getting us anywhere. So far we've come on nothing suspicious. I'll think it over tonight, and decide whether to carry on with it tomorrow.'

But all that his cogitations led to was that, though this line might not be profitable, it was the only one he had to work on. And, after all, the fact that Sutton had been suspicious was a fairly strong argument for continuing. Sutton was no fool, and though he had not had the training of the Yard, he was a skilful detective. French returned to the Yard in the morning determined to carry the matter a stage further.

The most important thing seemed to be to find and interview Rice, and he began by putting some men on the first of these two jobs. They were to begin by examining the London and Telephone Directories, though, if the new yard had just been opened, it was unlikely that it would be in either. The telephone people, however, might have had an application for a phone, and this was to be the next enquiry. Finally, if these efforts led nowhere, the police in Town were to be circularized, and the various rating and other authorities were to be approached, as plans for new buildings would probably have been submitted.

While these enquiries were in progress French went down again to Duckworth & Crozier's office to ask one or two further questions. Mr Duckworth he found in a chastened mood and ready to give him any further help he could.

But his information didn't amount to very much. There was electric light and a telephone in the shed when let, this being taken into consideration in the price. Duckworth, however, knew of no runway. If one had been there Rice must have had it installed and removed on his own responsibility, a thing, Duckworth pointed out indignantly, which he had no right to do. Not only had the tie-beams been cut into and thereby weakened, but a weight might have been suspended from them which they had not been designed to carry, and the man might have brought down the entire roof. Scandalous!

Asked if he had any idea what Rice could have been doing with timber, cement and clay, Duckworth grew superior and said, 'Perhaps his business.' French let it go at that.

When he reached the Yard he found that three 'Rice, Bros., Builders & Contractors' had been located—in Stepney, Kennington, and Camden Town respectively. He and Carter spent the afternoon visiting one after another, but in each case a short investigation proved that not one of them could possibly have had any connection with the man who had stayed at the Kelvin. French returned to the Yard and got on to the men who had turned up these names.

'No, sir,' all of them declared in reply to his questions. 'There's no other firm of the name in London. No builder's yard had been taken under the name, and none has been given up. All sources of information have been covered, and if there had been such a firm we should have got to know.' And when French went in detail into what they had done, he was forced to the conclusion that they were right.

But, if so, it threw a very significant light on the whole affair. If this tale of Rice's about wanting the shed temporarily till his firm's yard was ready for occupation were a falsehood, the whole business immediately became definitely suspicious. Sutton's opinion became confirmed, and the matter would have to be probed to the bottom. French decided that for the present, at all events, he must carry on.

10

The Electric Runway

Next morning, no further information having come in to the Yard, French and Carter set off to the telephone exchange to which the shed was connected. French on the previous evening had made a list of all the enquiries he could think of which might conceivably throw light on the affair, and this visit to the telephone people was his first item.

His question here was a simple one. The installation numbered 4237 was in a certain shed in which the police were interested. Could he get a note of any numbers which had been in communication with this installation during the last eleven weeks?

The district manager said he was anxious to help the chief inspector in any way in his power, but he doubted whether the information was available. As the chief-inspector doubtless knew the individual numbers of subscribers using the service were noted only in the case of trunk calls. These were kept until the accounts were made up and were then destroyed. There was therefore a chance that a record of trunk calls to or from the yard might be in existence. In the case of local calls the individual numbers of the subscribers involved were not noted, and no information could be given.

As he spoke the manager pressed a button, and a young woman appeared. She, it seemed, was in charge of the account in question, and he asked her to produce all details she had for the required period.

French, however, was out of luck on this occasion. After a short delay the girl reappeared to say that for the last three months there had not been a single trunk call to or from the number. There had not, in fact, been many calls of any kind, though there had been a few local ones.

Another of the routine lines of approach had petered out! Though he hadn't expected much, French was disappointed. He looked up his book, ticked off the first item, and noted the second. This was a visit to the electricity station serving the area containing the shed.

Here he had slightly more success, though the information he received was not of great value. Like his predecessor in the telephone exchange, the manager rang up for an assistant as soon as he understood what was required. This time the summons was answered by a young man.

'I think, Parkington, you dealt with that man Rice, who wanted the power point in his shed in Redliff Lane? This is a chief inspector of police, and he would like to hear all about it.'

The young fellow, obviously thrilled, said that he could give all details.

'This man Rice called here in person,' the manager went on, 'and asked to see someone in authority. I saw him myself. He said he had rented a shed in Redliff Lane for three months, and he wanted to install a temporary travelling lifting apparatus. He thought a pair of electrically-operated blocks on a runway would suit, and he wanted a point put in from which he could get the power. I discussed the simple business formalities required, to the terms of which he agreed. I then called Mr Parkington here, and he went down to the shed with Rice. Tell them, Parkington, what took place.'

'I went down to the shed with him, sir, and he showed me where he wanted the runway. It was to go right round the shed in a sort of oval. I thought a single power point in the centre, connected with the motor by a flexible cable, would suit. Mr Rice agreed, and we had a plug put in. The flex, he said, would be supplied with the motor, so we had nothing to do with that.'

'Can you tell me the capacity and the maker of the runway?' French asked.

'Mr Rice said it was to lift a ton, but he didn't say where he was getting it. He said he only wanted a temporary job, as it was not his own shed, and it would be coming down in two or three months when he moved to his own premises.'

'Then,' the manager continued, 'we had a letter from Rice saying he was giving up the shed. The current was cut off, a bill was sent Rice, he paid it, and the transaction closed.'

'Did he pay by cheque?'

'No, he called and paid cash.'

'On what date was the matter closed?'

'Tuesday week, the 15th instant.'

This seemed to be all the information obtainable, and after asking for a description of Rice and finding he was undoubtedly the man he had heard of elsewhere, French took his leave.

The next item on his list was 'More intensive search of shed', and he decided he would go on with this. Stopping at a street telephone booth, he put through a call to the Yard. First he wanted all the firms who sold runways to be circularized, in the hope of finding the one who supplied Rice. Secondly, he required Boyle and Cooper, fingerprint and photographic experts respectively, to meet him at the Redliff shed immediately.

'You stay by the door and let them in, Carter,' he directed, when they themselves reached the place. 'I'm going ahead in the office.'

Reaching the hut, French began a meticulous search. There were more old newspapers than he had realized, and lifting them out to the carpenters' bench, he began to go through them one by one.

Painstakingly he turned over each page, only to find that if any old letters, accounts, or other documents had slipped in between them, they had been carefully removed. The papers consisted of *Daily Telegraphs* and *Evening Standards*, about a dozen or more of each, of varying dates within the last couple of months, but they bore no marks to give them an individual interest.

Before French had finished with the newspapers, the men arrived from the Yard. He set them to work at the office, to get all the fingerprints they could. There were not many available, as most of the woodwork was too rough to take impressions, but they got about a dozen clear prints. These were duly photographed.

'That's all right,' French said when Cooper indicated they had finished. 'Then get on to the rest of the shed.'

Having completed his newspapers, French turned back to the office. There were scraps of paper in the desk and in some of the drawers, but nothing in the slightest degree helpful. Most of these papers were leaves torn from catalogues, principally of building materials. There was no writing on any of them, except some cabalistic figures, apparently dimensions. French kept all such, though he doubted they would be helpful.

When he had completed the office he stood for a moment in the doorway, wondering if there could be anything he had overlooked. Then he noticed that the desk, though a fixture, did not fit close to the wall. There was a narrow space along the top.

With scant consideration for Messrs Duckworth & Crozier's client's property, French seized a piece of wood and levered the desk clear. Behind it was a piece of crumpled paper. He smoothed it out.

It was a label, dirty and covered with cobwebs, but new and unwritten on. It contained a modernistic representation of a factory in green and crimson, and the words, 'From the Corona Engineering Company, Ltd., Claygate, Surrey, England.' The back was gummed and its size was about four inches by six.

French heaved a sigh of relief. Here at long last was a clue! To get an unused label from this Claygate firm betokened a certain amount of intimacy with them. An application to them would surely lead him to Rice.

He put the label away and continued his search. But he could find nothing else in the slightest degree promising. Nor could Boyle, the fingerprint man. Nowhere about the shed was there any surface smooth enough to retain clear impressions.

As the telephone in the shed was not in use, French went out to the nearest street booth. He would fix up an appointment with these Corona people and go down to see them at once.

But when he asked for the name from Directory Enquiry he was told that none such was on the register. He therefore rang up the Claygate police station instead.

'The Corona Engineering Company, sir?' replied the sergeant in charge. 'I never heard of it.'

'It's probably a new firm,' French explained. 'Are you sure there's none of that name just opened or about to open?'

'I'm sure there's not, sir. I never heard of it, at all events.'

French suddenly became much more interested. 'Well, sergeant,' he said, 'that's curious, because I have their label here. I wish you'd make a few enquiries for me, will you? Slip round to the various house agents, and so on, and find out if any ground has been sold to these people for building. Also find out if there is a firm in the neighbourhood named Rice Brothers. Do what you can for me.'

The Corona Engineering Company, French imagined, was a new name for Rice Brothers, and the new premises Rice had spoken of were at Claygate. If so, it would account for his not having been able to trace the place. He had not counted on a change of title. And, if the alteration was quite recent, the Corona name would not yet be generally known.

At the same time it was obvious that another and more sinister explanation was possible. Suppose Sutton were right, and that Rice Brothers were up to no good? In this case there might easily be no Corona Engineering Company, and the title would simply be required to help on whatever crime or fraud was in progress.

This was a plausible suggestion enough, but when French tried to go a step further he found it a good deal less easy. Was this assumed evil-doing connected with the loss of the *Jane Vosper*? Was the crime to sink the ship, and the fraud to obtain insurance money which was not due? If so, where would a bogus Corona Engineering firm come in? French could not form any idea.

On the other hand, if the crime were not connected with the *Jane Vosper*, then he, French, was more completely at a loss than ever.

However, the matter was not entirely exhausted. One further enquiry still remained.

In small type at the bottom of the label was the printer's name—Hale & Hardy of Angel Street. Angel Street, French knew, was near St Paul's, and in a short time he and Carter were at the place. It was a small establishment with old and dilapidated premises. And the owner whom they saw was old and dilapidated also. The firm was clearly a survival, and one which looked as if it would not survive very much longer.

Mr Hardy, however, was willing to tell all he knew. It appeared that some couple of months earlier a Mr Rice called to say that his firm required some labels and that he would like to see one or two designs. Rice gave the wording he wanted, and explained that some kind of factory illustration was to be worked in with it. He gave the address of the Kelvin Hotel, Commercial Road, and said he would call again in three or four days.

'What was Mr Rice like in appearance?' French asked.

From Hardy's description there could be no doubt that his client was the same elusive individual who had been behind all these manifestations.

'We got out two or three designs,' Hardy continued, 'and in three days Mr Rice turned up again. He approved one of the designs, that which you have there. He said his firm was not yet actually manufacturing, but the premises were complete and they would soon start. He would take, he said, five hundred labels to begin with, and if they were generally approved he would come back for a larger supply. We printed off the labels, and after a couple more days he came back. He paid for them, and took them away. That was the last we heard of him.'

'He never came back for the larger quantity?'

'No, never.'

All these details, French thought, were suspicious. So far there had been no indication of any member of the Rice firm other than this one individual. The whole affair might be a one-man show. Rice might have no brothers, and the Corona Engineering Company might be simply James Rice—if it existed at all.

On the other hand, everything might still be in order. So far there was no actual proof that anything was wrong. It would be necessary to wait for the Claygate sergeant's report before a conclusion could be reached.

In accordance with French's practice of keeping in touch with the Yard, he rang up when the interview with Hardy was over. On this occasion his care was rewarded. Two pieces of information had come in.

First there was a further report from the sergeant at Claygate. There were not many house agents in the place, and he had got in touch with all of them. The result was a complete confirmation of his earlier statement. There was no 'Corona Engineering Company' at Claygate, and no land had been let to such a firm. He had accounted for all the vacant ground in the neighbourhood, and none of the owners or agents concerned had ever heard of the company. Nor was there any firm called Rice Bros. in the district.

Here at last, French thought, was something final. It seemed impossible to believe that he was not on to some fraud, some crime upon which Sutton had blundered, with the result that he lost his life. French wondered intensely what could have drawn the man's attention to the affair. The suggestion was that it was something he had heard or discovered at Waterloo, but so far no connection between Waterloo and Rice had appeared. Unless it was that the factory site at Claygate was really projected: because Waterloo was the station for Claygate. Perhaps Sutton had been to Claygate. Perhaps the factory was a reality, and for some unknown reason it was being run under another name.

French decided that it might be worth while running down himself to Claygate and having a word with the sergeant. However, for the moment that could wait. A second piece of news had come in.

It appeared that the firm who supplied Rice with the runway had been discovered. It was a well-known engineering firm, Messrs Turner & Entwhistle of Huddersfield, whose London office and showrooms were in Victoria Street.

'Victoria Street,' said French, emerging from the booth. 'They've found the runway people.'

Carter thought that was pretty good, considering how short a time there had been for enquiries, but French said nonsense, that Turner & Entwhistle were about the first people you would ring up. 'I hope we'll get there before they close,' he went on, looking at his watch. 'We spent more time in that blessed shed than I realized.'

On this occasion, however, their luck held. The representative who had dealt with the Rice affair was still on duty. It proved to have been carried out in much the same way as the rest of Rice's activities.

Some three months earlier a man who gave his name as James Rice, and his address as the Kelvin Hotel, Commercial Road, called and said that he wished to purchase an electric hoist or pair of blocks travelling on a runway. The runway was to be hung from the tie-beams of a shed roof, and was to be a complete ring, consisting of two semicircles of 15 feet in diameter, joined by two straight sections 15 feet long. The blocks were to be operated by a motor, and were to lift one ton. It was important that they should work quickly, that was, in the lifting and lowering. No motor was required to pull the blocks along the runway, as this, Rice said, could be done by hand. The apparatus was required for moving reinforced concrete beams and slabs about his builder's yard.

The representative had suggested that he should visit the shed so as to inspect the roof trusses to enable him to supply suitable suspension arrangements. But Rice said this was unnecessary. He gave a drawing of the principals, and said the suspension clips must be made to attach to the runway at any point. He explained that he had mechanics in his employment who would do the erection.

The representative was doubtful that a good job could be made in this way. However Rice was insistent, and his orders were of course carried out. The runway was got out in sections to bolt up together, and they then asked where they should send it. Rice surprised them by saying he would call for it. He paid the price in notes, the runway was duly sent from Huddersfield, and Rice called for it at the railway. His signature for it at the goods depot closed the transaction so far as they were concerned.

One other point the representative mentioned. Rice had stated that he only required the runway temporarily, and asked if they would take it back later at a valuation. The firm had not agreed to this—it did not deal in second-hand stuff—but they had given Rice the name of Cleaver Hooper, Ltd., who did that sort of business, and he had said he would get in touch with them.

Asked for the address of Cleaver Hooper, Ltd., the young man said, 'Waterloo Road, just beyond the station.'

Waterloo! Could this be at last the connection French had so long been seeking? Sutton had left Hislop to go to Waterloo. Was it to call on Cleaver Hooper?

On reaching the street French rang up Cleaver Hooper from the first booth he came to. But there was no reply. The establishment had evidently closed for the night.

As he thought over the situation that evening, French grew less optimistic about what he was likely to learn from Cleaver Hooper. If Sutton had visited them on the day of his disappearance, he could surely at most have only learnt about the second-hand runway. What could this have conveyed to him, which would have made him dangerous to those concerned in the fraud?

On the other hand, here was a likely suggestion of where Sutton might have been going on that fatal afternoon. Even if the dangerous secret were not learnt through Cleaver Hooper, Sutton, had he visited them, might have dropped a hint of where he was going next.

It was therefore with some eagerness that French set off

with Carter next morning to pay the call. On sending in his card he was received by the senior partner, Mr Cleaver. He explained shortly what he wanted.

'Yes,' replied Cleaver, 'you're quite correct. We did that piece of business with Mr Rice. He called here first, and I saw him. He asked me if we would be disposed to buy a set of electric blocks and runway which he had had in his shop for a couple of months, and which were new and in perfect order. He showed me the invoice and specifications from Messrs Turner & Entwhistle, and explained that the runway had been for use in a temporary shed which he had occupied while his own premises were being completed. I agreed to take the stuff, subject to its being in the good order he described. I then asked where we could inspect it, but he said he had taken it down and that it was now loaded in his van, and that he would run it to us here, where we could inspect it at our leisure. I agreed. He went away and returned shortly, driving a 30-cwt. Ford van, containing the runway. It proved to be in perfect order as he had said, and we therefore paid for it. He left, and the transaction ended.'

'You've not heard from him since?'

'No, he simply took the money and went off.'

'Did you pay by cheque?'

'No, he made a special point about that. He said his banking account was in the country, and he'd rather have cash.'

'Did he give you any hint as to what the runway had been used for?'

'Yes, he said he was a builder, and it was for lifting ferroconcrete slabs and beams from where they were cast to where they were stored, and out of store when they were required for use.'

French nodded. 'One other question and I've finished. Did a Mr Sutton, a private detective acting for certain insurance companies, call on you within the last fortnight? I should explain that this Sutton has disappeared, and I am trying to trace him.'

About this Cleaver was sure. Sutton had not called. Before leaving, however, French made it his business to interview the rest of the staff, and made quite certain that Sutton had not applied to anyone connected with the firm.

With the exception of what it really had been used for, the history of the runway had now been established. French wondered could Rice's statement as to its purpose have been true? In the shed were traces of ceement, sand, stones, and marks of where these had been mixed to make concrete. For reinforced concrete work forms are required, and forms are made with timber by carpenters. In the shed was a carpenters' bench and traces of sawdust and shavings. Was Rice really making concrete castings? The contents of the shed certainly tended to confirm his statement, and it was definitely a builder's job.

In fact, there was still nothing suspicious about the shed except the two points: the fact that Sutton had expressed doubts about it, and the matter of the name of the firm. Sutton's ideas were weighty because of his disappearance, but, of course, there was nothing to show that the Rice shed had anything to do with his fate. Nor was the matter of the name of serious significance. Rice Bros. might be working under another name, and, if so, this would probably account for French's failure to find them. No, while the affair was admittedly suspicious, there was no actual proof that anything was wrong.

Of course, this line of reasoning did not help French.

Sutton had disappeared, and he had to find out where he had gone to. The Rice shed, so far, had been his only line of enquiry. It was still his only line of enquiry. He could only assume that the solution of his problem lay along it, and act accordingly.

What remained to be done? Only, so far as he could see, the completion of the detailed search of the shed. He had broken that off on discovering the Claygate label. He supposed there was nothing for it but to go back and finish it.

As he returned with Carter to the Yard it occurred to him that one routine avenue of enquiry had so far been overlooked. Had Rice ever obtained a passport? If so, and if it could be traced, information about him should be forthcoming.

While not hopeful of a result, he sent a man to the passport office to make enquiries. Then, having instructed Carter to bring the apparatus for testing paper ashes, the two men set off again for Redliff Lane.

11

Scraps of Paper

On arrival at the shed Carter produced a somewhat unusual collection of objects. There was first a small saucepan, a flat sieve which fitted across its top, a domed lid to go above the sieve, and a spirit lamp with a frame on which the saucepan could be heated. There were some small flat bits of wood, a small drawing board with pins, a roll of very transparent tracing paper, a bottle of colourless gum arabic, and a couple of spoons.

While French began to examine the ashes in the fireplace, Carter drew the carpenters' bench over and laid out his apparatus. The saucepan he partially filled with water and lit the lamp beneath it. He put on the lid, but left the sieve out. Then he cut a piece of tracing paper and fastened it down with the pins on to the board. He cut some other scraps of tracing paper of various sizes.

French, meantime, had begun very carefully to remove the burnt fragments of wood from the top of the ashes. He could see that beneath these was paper. It was completely burnt, but he thought that some small flakes might remain, which might bear a word or words.

Slowly he worked, removing what he could with his fingers and as gently as possible picking up with the spoons what was already in dust. Under the dust the paper was in powder, but where the sheets had been protected by bits of charred wood a few tiny flakes remained. These French could see, bore writing. To get them out unbroken was the difficulty.

Taking one of the scraps of paper cut by Carter, he pushed it gently under one of the larger fragments. Then, raising it as one would a spade, he was able to lift the fragment out. He tried again with another scrap of tracing paper, continuing till he had removed all the fragments he could find.

It was not a large bag. Seven tiny pieces of charred paper lay on seven bits of tracing paper on the bench. Most of the pieces he had seen had crumbled into dust on the touch of the tracing paper spades, and of the seven bits he had secured, not one was more than an inch across.

French now paused for a moment to take photographs of his treasure trove, so that if in his further operations he destroyed any of it, a record should remain.

The next step was to mount the pieces, so that they could be handled and, if necessary, used as evidence. Where such scraps are fairly flat this is not a difficult job, but these bits were badly twisted and warped, and it was therefore necessary to flatten them out before mounting could be attempted.

Taking the sieve, he laid the seven bits of tracing paper on it, each bearing its bit of distorted ash. Then he placed the sieve on the saucepan, which by this time had grown fairly hot, covering it with the lid. As most charred paper is hydroscopic, the scraps were likely to take up sufficient moisture from the steam to become soft, and so flatten by their own weight.

This expedient worked on the whole fairly well. When French considered his mixture was sufficiently cooked and removed the sieve, most of the pieces had flattened down well enough. Then he came to the most difficult part of the work. Pinning a piece of tracing paper down on a tiny scrap of wood, he brushed it over with the gum. Then he laid the gummed paper down on the top of the first charred fragment, and left it to dry. This he repeated in the case of the other six bits.

As the drying would take some time, French now left this part of the work, and resumed his general inspection of the shed. He was meticulously painstaking and careful, but he did not learn a great deal that he hadn't known before.

In fact, he learned three things only. The first was that the timber worked was white deal or spruce, and that at least some of it was $1\frac{1}{8}$ inches thick. This was shown by the width of some of the shavings left by the planes. The second was that wire nails, inches and 2½ inches long had been used, as well as $\frac{5}{8}$-inch tacks and flat-headed 1-inch nails. The third point was that the clay had been deposited recently and for a short time only. It had covered a few bits of grass and weeds growing between the cobbles, and these remained as green as the adjoining untouched roots.

While he could think of no explanation of the presence of the clay, French had to admit to himself that the nails and timber worked in well with Rice's statement that he had been making reinforced concrete forms. Spruce of the thickness in question would just work in for the purpose, as would also the 2-inch and 2½-inch nails. The stones and sand, which he had observed on his first visit, were also such as would have been used for concrete.

Having exhausted all the possibilities of the shed, French began with Carter to work on a fresh line: an interrogation of all those who lived close by.

This was a tedious and unpleasant enquiry, and very unprofitable it proved also. Persons had been seen entering and leaving, but no one who had seen them could describe them or seemed to have noticed anything whatever about them. The same applied to the vehicles. One woman who lived opposite had observed a Ford truck going in and out, but she hadn't remarked the driver, and of course had not noted its registration number. She had seen other trucks and lorries going in and out, some of them quite large, but she didn't know to whom they belonged, or anything individual about them.

Of course, in a way, there was no reason why anyone should have taken the necessary interest in the shed to cause him to observe and remember its visitors. Working men, Ford trucks, and vans and lorries are not so uncommon in East London as to arouse curiosity. Still, to a man like French, trained to continuous observation, it seemed strange that not one of all the people who must have seen arrivals and departures could tell him anything about them.

Tired and disappointed, French returned to the shed for the mounted fragments, which by this time were hard and dry. They had struck satisfactorily on the whole, and either side could be read, either directly or through the tracing paper. Packing them carefully, he returned to the Yard and began a preliminary examination of them before passing them over to the technical department which dealt with such matters.

French knew he wasn't an expert, at the same time he tried to learn all he could from the blackened scraps. And first it seemed fairly obvious that he was dealing with three different documents or kinds of documents. Four of the scraps were of a very thin and poor-class paper, two others, though still of poor paper, were of a better type, while one was of a superior quality still. Again, on the first four, all the writing consisted of figures and x's, with 's and "s, the signs for feet and inches. These four bits seemed parts of invoices or bills for timber.

French sat thinking. He wondered if the timber had been bought in sufficiently large quantities to enable him to trace the sale. If he could do so, the amount and scantling might give some clue to its purpose. Further, the timber salesmen might have noticed something about Rice, or whoever bought the stuff, which would enable him to be traced.

He decided that it might be worth while advertising in journals read by those in the timber trade. Having noted the point, he turned back to the papers.

Of the two pieces of medium quality, the first was little bigger than a sixpence and bore only four letters: 'arm c'. They were in handwriting, and the paper was torn immediately in front of the 'a' and after the 'c'. The second was larger and seemed to be the heading of a letter or bill. There were fragments of two lines. The upper was in script and read: 'on, W.C.2.', and the lower in small capitals, 'TEL'. Whether these two scraps were parts of one and the same document French could not say, but, judging from the quality of the paper, they might well have been so.

202

The piece of superior quality bore parts of two words printed in capital letters. They were: 'KE & NEW'. As in the previous case, the paper was torn close enough before the 'K' and after the 'W' for both of these to be internal letters of words. From the kind of type, as well as the ampersand, French imagined this might be part of the name of a firm, on the heading of a letter or bill.

French looked from scrap to scrap, then concentrated on the 'arm c'. Arm chair seemed the obvious suggestion, though he couldn't see how this would fit in with anything that could have gone on in the shed.

As this 'arm c' didn't seem promising, he set to work on the other clues. First he put a man on to make a list from the directory of all the timber yards within a reasonable distance of the shed, with instructions to call at these and try to trace the sale.

Then he turned to the 'KE & NEW'. If his idea were correct, the 'KE' must be the end of a proper name. He began by trying to think of as many names ending in 'KE' as he could. At once a number occurred to him: Macke, Noake, Parke, Peake, Lake, Blake, Tuke, Romeike, Yorke, and many more.

With some men he began to go through the telephone directories of London, in the hope of finding one of these names followed by one beginning with 'NEW'. They worked at it late that evening, several of them. When they knocked off about ten o'clock they had finished all the names that they had been able to think of, with the result that five possibles had been found. There were Warke & Newcome, Clarke & Newlands, Blake & Newington, O'Rorke & Newton, and Hooke & Newlands.

French had hoped that one of these would have proved

a timber merchant's, or a furniture or upholsterer's—if the 'arm c' stood for 'arm chair'. But none of them was represented. Of the five, one was a bookseller, one a house agent, one a tailor, one a solicitor, and one a grocer. Not, French thought, a very promising selection. None of them, moreover, could be the firm which had 'on, W.C.2.' on its paper, as not one of the five was in this division of London.

Obviously nothing more could be done that night, but next morning French set off with Carter to visit the five firms. His procedure with each was the same. He began by asking if they had had any dealings with the firm of Rice Bros. of Redliff Lane, and when each, with monotonous regularity, said they had not, he went on to describe Rice, and ask if they knew such a man under a different name. None of them, however, recognized the description, and French at last had bitterly to admit that this clue, from which he had hoped for so much, had also petered out.

Fortunately for him, this was Saturday, and when he had finished with the five firms it was lunch time. There was nothing more that he could do for the moment, and he decided to take a full weekend, in the hope that on Monday morning a fresh attack on the problem with a rested mind might give him a result.

On Monday morning two pieces of news had come in, one positive, the other negative. The negative did not disappoint French, as he had not really hoped for anything from it. The passport department reported that a passport had not been issued to anyone of the name of James Rice.

This meant nothing, except that still another line of research was closed. With a shrug French turned from it to the other message.

It was from one of his men and stated that he had found

204

the timber merchants with whom Rice had dealt. It was the firm of Morgan & Trusett, of Cable Street, at the back of the London Docks. French at once rang them up and made an appointment with their manager, Mr Armstrong. Half an hour later he and Carter were at the place.

It was a large and busy yard, just the sort of yard which would be chosen by a man who did not wish his own particular transaction to bulk too big in the minds of those who dealt with it. Armstrong, to whose office they were shown, was a sharp-looking man who had the facts at his fingers' ends and gave his information concisely.

It seemed that Rice had called in person—and the description showed that it was the man in question—and had given a large order for timber. The main item was for no less than 33,700 lineal feet of 5 inches by $1\frac{1}{8}$ inches tongued and grooved spruce of good quality, cut into lengths. There were 3500 pieces of 24 inches and double that of something under 46 inches. There was other timber as well, but in much smaller quantities. It was all roughly machine-cleaned. It was not to be delivered, as Rice said he would call for it himself. This was agreed to. Rice paid a deposit, the timber was cut, and he did call with a Ford 30-cwt. truck, and took it away.

'That stuff would run into a good many loads, wouldn't it?' French asked.

'Yes, between thirty and forty, I should say. We can turn up the exact number if you want to know, for there was a separate invoice for each. It took four or five days, I remember, to get it all away.'

'Did Rice drive the truck himself?'

'Yes, he and another man. The other man, I think, did most of it, but Rice came for several loads.'

Here, certainly, was some information at last. Another man! This was the first time French had heard of a second member of the firm.

'What was this second man like?' he asked.

He was, Armstrong said, of medium height and build, dark haired and clean shaven and with a swarthy skin. He had had very little to say for himself, simply getting the goods and driving them away, and Armstrong had not heard his name. This, of course, would be on the dockets he signed, and could be ascertained if French so desired.

French thought he would like to have it. It proved to be J. Matthews.

French then produced his mounted paper fragments. Armstrong thought the four-figured pieces on the poor paper were possibly his firm's invoices for the timber in question. He set some men on the job, and after considerable trouble they were able to produce carbon blocks which exactly corresponded. These, after all concerned had signed them, French took over as exhibits for a possible future trial.

The other three burnt fragments were then shown, but Armstrong declared they had no connection with his firm. Some other clue, therefore, lay in the 'KE & NEW' and the 'W.C.2.', if only French could find it.

The information he was gaining still tended to support Rice's statement that he was making reinforced concrete articles in the shed. Pieces of timber of the sizes purchased might very well have been used for forms. They would be just what was wanted for such things as lintels, steps, column bases, slabs, and such like. Alternatively the boards would suit admirably for timbering cuts for drains or other small excavations. The long pieces would have done for facing the sides and the short for the cross struts.

As he returned to the Yard French wondered whether there could be anything in this latter idea: that the stuff had been used for timbering a drain or other excavation. At once the clay occurred to him. That surely suggested an excavation? Not perhaps in the shed. More likely where building was going on.

Then French got a sudden idea and he came to an abrupt halt to think it over. One of the Sherlock Holmes tales which he had so eagerly devoured when a boy recurred to him. *The Adventure of the Red-Headed League*. In this story the pawnbroker's assistant had been driving a tunnel! A tunnel! Could Rice Bros. have been driving a tunnel?

A tunnel to where?

French remembered how, after leaving the pawnbroker's door, Sherlock Holmes had stood at the corner of the street, and on the ground that an exact knowledge of London was a hobby of his, had noted the various buildings in the block. There was, if French's memory were correct, a small newsagent's, another shop, the branch of a bank, a restaurant, and so on. Holmes, on seeing these, had said that his work was done, and had dragged the long-suffering Watson off to a concert.

It was no disgrace, French thought, for any detective to take a leaf out of Holmes's book. He bored Carter very much by hurrying back to Redliff Lane, and there walking round to improve his exact knowledge of London and to see the buildings in the adjoining streets.

Then suddenly he could have kicked himself. What was the one great building which dominated all this area?

Standing practically beside Redliff Lane and the shed? What but the Royal Mint itself?

Was this the solution of his problem? A tunnel to the Mint! Was it possible?

Were there no cellars in the Mint into which an approach other than by the door might be invaluable to a man short both of money and scruples? Were there no cellars, moreover, which might remain unvisited in the orthodox way during long periods? Cellars from which their silver stores might be removed—if otherwise than through the door—without the loss becoming known for a considerable time? French could not but believe that there were. A tunnel from the shed, lined and shored by these boards and stiffened by concrete, might easily prove the means of transferring a vast quantity of the nation's wealth into Rice Brothers' coffers.

The construction of such a tunnel would unquestionably be within the power of a few skilful and determined men, provided with some knowledge of engineering and of the layout of the Mint. Such things had been done before, many and many a time. Achievements of War prisoners who escaped from Germany recurred to him. If tunnels could be driven as they had driven them, when handicapped by every conceivable obstacle that could be put in their way, how much more could it have been done by Rice Brothers, with all the appliances of science to help them?

The boards, moreover, would exactly suit. Something less than four feet high by two feet wide was exactly the size such a tunnel would be made. Moreover, the extra number of the longer boards would undoubtedly be due to doubling them to meet the additional strength required for the sides.

French grew more and more excited as he considered the idea. Of course, if he were correct, the theft would already have been committed; the money or bullion would be gone. All the same, it would be something more than a feather in his cap if he were to discover the affair before the Mint authorities themselves.

Then, as usual under such circumstances, doubts began to assail him. Three difficulties, indeed, occurred to him, and grew more and more formidable the further he considered them.

The first was the simplest to deal with. Had Rice got enough timber to line so long a tunnel?

French thought he could determine this immediately. Redliff Lane ran south from Great Prescott Street, passing under the railway. The shed was, in fact, close to Royal Mint Street. And across the street was the Mint. Within, French imagined, after pacing what he could of the distance, 600 or 700 feet.

3500 pieces of wood 2 feet long and 5 inches wide had been bought by Rice. These would have been wanted for top and bottom. They would have therefore done a length of 1750 boards, each 5 inches, or over 700 feet. This was just about the length required.

The first of the three difficulties was no difficulty at all. What about the second?

This was that Rice would not have had sufficient time to drive so long a tunnel in the eleven weeks during which he had rented the shed. This was a point, however, that French could not answer to his own satisfaction. He didn't know enough about engineering. It would be easy, however, to get an expert opinion. The point would have to wait over.

The third difficulty was that he scarcely believed Rice could have so completely made good the floor of the shed where the mouth of the tunnel had been. He, French, had looked over the floor, not indeed with microscopic care, but still fairly closely, and he had seen no traces of it having been broken. Had the concrete or stable bricks been lifted and re-set, fresh cement should show. If the entrance had been in the cobbled area, the earth should have appeared disturbed.

This, however, was a point which could easily be settled by further inspection. Nothing like the present! French walked round to the shed again and, with Carter's help, set to work.

He began by tracing on the ground the area which had been covered by the clay. This was not difficult, in spite of the obvious efforts which had been made to sweep the place clean. French's idea was that if the floor had been opened it would be near the heap.

He knelt down and with his torch began to examine the joints between the bricks. For a time he searched, his eagerness dying gradually down and his doubts becoming stronger. These joints looked as if they had not been disturbed for a hundred years! No opening had been made through them.

Indeed, he now began to think the whole tunnel idea a bit far fetched. Would Rice know the Mint well enough to enable him to drive a tunnel to the particular cellar in which was stored coin or bullion? Without accurate plans would the thing be possible? French didn't know. Then he thought that a vertical photograph taken from an aeroplane plus a knowledge of the building might enable it to be done. This, again, was a matter for an expert.

Suddenly French stopped and stared at a mark on a joint he had just reached. With a slowly-rising excitement he took a lens from his pocket and examined more closely. He passed on to the next, and as he did so his excitement grew. Was this mark not a join between old and new cement? And these next joints? Were they not also new?

He was a little puzzled. Sharp-angled smears of cement were to be found on the smooth V-shaped corners of the bricks at each side of the joints. With old work such would surely have been rubbed off long since. In point of fact, there were no such marks on the obviously old portion.

But what was bothering French was that the cement was black, or rather a sort of grey, purplish black. Fresh cement was light grey.

'Here, Carter, what do you make of that joint?' he called.

Carter came over and made an examination. Then he looked up with something very nearly approaching excitement in his manner.

'You've got it right enough, sir,' he declared. 'Those bricks have been re-set recently.'

'But the cement's black.'

Carter nodded. 'That's right, sir, but it's fresh, for all that. You can do that with cinders. There was a builder's yard near us when I was a kid, and I've seen it done again and again. A lot of people like black mortar with red bricks. That's how it's made.'

'With cinders?'

'With cinders or ashes. You grind them in with the sand in the mortar mill. The stuff comes out just that blue-black colour.'

French's excitement was now scarcely to be hidden. 'That

accounts for the pile of cinders,' he declared joyously. What a *coup* this would be!

For a moment rosy thoughts filled his mind and then he got back to business. 'Help me to mark all these fresh joints,' he directed. 'Got a bit of chalk?'

Carter had two pieces, and they began to draw a white chalk line along the bricks which showed signs of having been re-set. As they worked French grew more and more certain that he was on the right track. A definite area of about five feet by two had been moved, and this was just about the size that the entrance to the tunnel would have been.

'See,' he said presently, 'here are some new bricks. They must have broken some of the old ones in raising them.'

'Yes, sir, that would be where they started the hole, where they couldn't get them from below.'

'We must have these up again,' French went on. 'The tunnel may be partly filled in, but its lining will remain. I wonder shall we have to get a warrant or will that Duckworth let us do it without?'

'Why not do it without asking him?'

'Carter, I'm ashamed of you. I feel very much inclined to, but I think we'd better not. No, we'll go back to the Yard and I'll have a word with the A.C. We'd have to go back in any case to get the men to lift the floor.'

Once more full of eager optimism, the two men returned to Westminster to make arrangements for the next step in the investigation.

12

The Tunnel

Sir Mortimer Ellison was impressed by French's report. He did not express approval of what French had done, nor did he state his agreement with his theory, but French knew from his manner that he considered the discovery of importance. The Assistant Commissioner rarely disclosed his thoughts, though when he did so action on the part of his subordinates usually became somewhat hectic. On the other hand, he seldom turned down his men's suggestions. Where possible he preferred to let them do their job in their own way. If they succeeded he never withheld the credit that he considered their due, and if they failed he never rubbed in their failure unless he doubted that they had done their best.

In this case he did express the opinion that the floor of the shed must be taken up. 'If you're satisfied it has been recently lifted, and if the agents know nothing about it, you must lift it again. I imagine if you give them a written undertaking to leave everything as you found it, they'll raise no objection. They may have to consult the owner, but that will probably be a matter of form. If you find them unreasonable I'll of course get you authority to go ahead in spite of them.'

'I'll go and see the agents now, sir. If they raise no objection we ought to get the thing cleared up this evening.'

'I shall be interested to hear what you find.'

Before leaving the Yard French made some arrangements. A bricklayer and helper and two labourers upon whom the police were in the habit of calling in such emergencies were warned to be in readiness. They were to accompany Carter to the City when French gave the word. Certain tools were to be taken, and as the electric current was cut off from the shed lamps were to be included to enable the necessary work to proceed after dark.

Everything being in order at headquarters, French returned once again to Fenchurch Street and called at Duckworth & Crozier's. This time he was not kept waiting. Mr Duckworth seemed to have forgotten a good deal of his own importance, and listened in a quite human way to French's request.

'But you know, chief inspector,' he said when French had finished, 'it's not our shed. We're only the agents. I don't see that we have the power to give you this authorization.'

'Then can you get in touch with the owner?'

'Unfortunately we can't. He's abroad.'

French smiled. 'I'm afraid we can't wait for his return,' he said pleasantly. 'You understand that while we're not at present making any charges, there's reason to suspect a serious crime has been committed. An immediate investigation must, therefore, be made. We can, of course, get the necessary authority, but that means delay, and we'd rather go ahead at once. We can't do any harm, Mr Duckworth.

I'm prepared now to sign an undertaking that we'll leave everything as we find it, and if we prevent you letting it, we'll pay fair compensation.'

Duckworth shrugged. 'If you'll put that in writing I'll give you the permission. As a matter of fact,' he went on in a burst of confidence, 'the owner told us he didn't want to be bothered with business, and left us free to do what we thought best about his property.'

A short guarantee was soon drawn up, and this French signed in the presence of two of the clerks. He was extremely pleased. There would now be no delay through red tape, and the job would be pushed ahead as quickly as was humanly possible.

He borrowed Duckworth's telephone and instructed Carter to go down to the shed as soon as he was ready. Then he walked on to Redliff Lane, opened the large entrance gates, and stood waiting inside them.

He had not a long vigil. Scarcely ten minutes had passed when a light van drove up and turned into the shed. French closed and locked the gates and, following down the laneway, saw his men dismounting.

It was half-past four, getting dusk in the streets and almost dark in the shed. 'We'll have those lamps lighted before you start,' French directed, and soon two small portable acetylene flares shone out. French had a look round to make sure their operations were invisible from the adjoining buildings. Then he gave the word to begin.

A sledge hammer, some sets, a pickaxe, shovel and other tools had by this time been unloaded, and the men had taken off their coats and were getting to work. 'That area where you see the chalk marks,' French explained, 'and you needn't break more of the bricks than you can help.'

Some strenuous work with hammer and set cleared away a few bricks, leaving exposed the concrete on which they had rested. The bricklayer examined this with a professional air.

'Fresh concrete, sir,' he said. 'Not been here many days.'

'Good,' French returned. 'You may cut through it.'

The operations were slow, and French covered his impatience as best he could. Cold chisels were driven under the remaining bricks, in the attempt to raise them undamaged from their bed. This was accomplished in most cases, and at last the whole chalked area was stripped.

Then followed the removal of the concrete. It was not very hard and was smashed up by blows of the hammer and the pieces lifted out.

French could hardly contain himself as he watched these operations. There was something exciting about an excavation, an excavation, that is, which was expected to reveal hidden mysteries. It was not the first time by many that he had been present at such an operation. Usually it had been out of doors and, by some strange coincidence, usually it had been in bad weather. He remembered that awful night of rain and storm on the slopes of Cave Hill above Belfast, when he and the Belfast police had watched four suspects digging for the black box they so much wanted. And that excavation in the filling of the new Guildford-Godalming By-pass, with the ghastly finds that were there unearthed! Other more orthodox diggings he had also been responsible for, mostly in cemeteries: the exhumation of bodies. For French work with pick and shovel had grim and sinister memories.

The bricklayer and his helper, as good trade unionists, knocked off when the concrete was all out. The attack was shifted to the clay and the labourers had their innings. The clay came out easily, practically without the use of the pickaxe, showing it had been but lately placed in position. French noted with growing doubts that so far there were no signs of the timbering, though he realized that at the end of the tunnel there would be a large space for working in, and the timbering was probably set back beneath the overhanging brickwork. As the hole deepened his eagerness increased till he could no longer stand still. He paced jerkily up and down while the labourers took spells at the work.

Gradually the level of the clay fell. He needn't be impatient, French reminded himself. The tunnel would have to be pretty far down below ground level. Otherwise the traffic of the railway and of Royal Mint Street would crush down all Rice's timbering.

Probably, he thought, they would not get down to anything of interest that night, and he began to consider how long they would work, and whether he would have some food sent in for the men. He didn't think it would be fair to keep them later than about ten or eleven o'clock, but—

A hoarse exclamation from one of the labourers broke into his train of thought. He hurried over to where the man was standing in the hole, which was now about three feet deep.

'What is it?' he asked testily.

But before the men replied, he saw. There, just beginning to show at the bottom of the excavation, was a little hump, a small rounded projection sticking up above the general level. At one edge the clay had fallen away from it, and its surface showed clean. It was covered with grey serge! After a sudden sharp exclamation French stood as if turned to stone. Grey serge! Grey serge with a tiny check pattern! How often in this case had he not read and written the words, 'Grey serge with a tiny check pattern?'

Slowly and automatically he took off his hat and wiped the perspiration from his forehead, as he stood staring at the grey covered object. Paralysis seemed to have smitten the others also. The man who had made the discovery climbed awkwardly out of the hole, and joined the others as they stood round, looking down.

Then French pulled himself together. 'Get it uncovered,' he said in a low tone.

The labourer climbed down again and began very carefully to remove the clay from about the remains. Soon its form began to reveal itself. The body was lying on its side, and the hump that had first come into sight was the shoulder. It was lying with the knees drawn up to the chest, so placed, French imagined, to reduce to a minimum the excavation required.

'Don't move it,' he went on. 'Clear it as much as you can, then we'll have it photographed before we get it out. Here, Carter, you know what I want. Carry on while I go and phone.'

French rang up the Yard, reporting briefly to Sir Mortimer Ellison, and giving instructions for a photographer to come at once to the shed. Then he informed Superintendent Nairn of Leman Street of his discovery. 'The body's in your division, super, so I suppose you'll deal with it,' he went on. 'Your doctor, and so on?'

'I suppose I must,' Nairn agreed, 'though I'd much rather leave it to you. Right. I'll get the doctor and a stretcher and come round at once.'

French wondered if he were growing callous when he

found that his feeling of satisfaction at this step forward in his case far outweighed any regrets for Sutton's fate. Sutton he had believed to be dead from the first; indeed, he had never had much doubt that he had been murdered. From the point of view of Sutton, therefore, the discovery made little difference to his outlook. But to his investigation it made all the difference in the world. It meant probably the difference between success and failure. And success, apart from the advantage it would be to French personally, would enable him to perform the only service for Sutton that was left—to avenge his death. Success would mean that Sutton's murderer would hang.

French had scarcely returned to the shed when those he had called began to arrive. First came Superintendent Nairn and the men with the stretcher. The superintendent was filled with interest, but declared that the case was French's and that he would only interfere where his duty demanded. Then the photographer appeared and was set to photograph the body from different angles. Before he had finished the doctor arrived. This latter was a small talkative man with a perennial twinkle in his eye.

'Hallo, Nairn, you ghoul,' he began breezily. 'What horror are you battening on now?'

'Evening, doctor,' Nairn returned. 'Do you know Chief Inspector French of Scotland Yard?' And when the two men had shaken hands went on: 'This is the chief inspector's case. He's found this body and he wanted you to see it before he moved it.'

'Sorry to have called you out, doctor,' French said pleasantly. 'I wasn't absolutely sure it was necessary, but thought it better to be on the safe side.'

'What he means by that,' Dr Caldwell said in a loud

aside to Nairn, 'is that if he's seen anything he makes the most of it, but if it's missed it'll be my fault. As full of tricks as a circus monkey.' He glanced at French, and the suspicion of a wink floated over his left eye. 'They're all the same, police officers. Aren't they, super?'

'They can't cover their mistakes so easily as doctors,' Nairn rejoined with obvious pride at his powers of repartee.

'Older than the hills,' retorted Caldwell with cheery scorn. 'Here, chief inspector, do you expect me to get down into that blessed hole? For if you do, you never made a bigger mistake in your life.'

'Then we may get the body out?'

'Of course you may. Put it on to the stretcher and lift it on to that bench. Do you know whose it is?'

'Yes, but I'll wait and see before I speak.'

'Profoundly wise and profoundly justified remark of old Asquith's that,' the doctor went on. 'The sort of answer these meddlesome, questioning people should always get, eh?' He grinned at French and went on: 'Some day you can do better than what I asked: you can tell me how you came to find it.'

'I'll do that with pleasure,' French promised, 'but not, if you'll excuse me, just at the moment. Carefully, now,' he went on to the men, who were engaged in lifting their ghastly burden on to the stretcher.

As they put it down French moved round and looked at the face. It had been covered with a handkerchief, but this had slipped off, and he could see the features. Decomposition had already set in, but they were still perfectly recognizable. French saw that his suspicion was correct. The body was Sutton's.

Operations now rapidly became routine. After a short

preliminary examination of the remains, the doctor decided he would do nothing more till they were removed to the mortuary. Nairn thereupon arranged the necessary transport. The doctor, who had come in his own car, drove off at the same time, promising to proceed with the examination at once.

'What about the inquest?' went on Nairn. 'I suppose I shall have to fix it up with the coroner?'

'I imagine so, super. Your division, you know.'

'Quite. But you'll supply the evidence?'

'I can supply some. Evidence of identity and of the discovery of the body; but that's all.'

'How you came to search in the shed?'

French grinned. '"Information received" rather suggests itself.'

'You don't want to bring in this shipping affair?'

'No, and I couldn't if I did. I've not proved any connection.'

Some further details settled, Nairn drove off, and French turned to his men. 'I don't want you to do any more tonight,' he explained, 'except one thing. I want you to see whether the earth below the body has been recently disturbed?'

A short examination supplied the answer to this question. The ground in question was hard. All four workmen were positive that it had not been opened for many years.

If so, all French's elaborate theory about the tunnel to the Mint vanished from the realms of the actual and became a dream which had merely wasted a good deal of his time. There was no tunnel. There never had been a tunnel. Probably such a thing had never been thought of by the men he was seeking. The opening in the floor was for a grave, and for a grave only.

But, satisfactory as the discovery of the body was from the point of view of his enquiry, it did not clear up the case as a whole. It left it in fact more mysterious than ever. It seemed clear that Sutton had got on to whatever game Rice had been playing, but it did not suggest what that game was. The problem of what Sutton had learned, and of how he had learnt it, remained just as far from solution as ever. French told himself that what Sutton had discovered, he should be able to discover. But this, though the only comfort he had, did not take him very far.

He sent the workmen home, having arranged for them to return in the morning. Then, having asked Nairn to have the shed watched during the night, he took his leave. Stepping into a telephone booth, he rang up Mrs Sutton to say that he was going down to see her by the first train.

His interview with the widow—the daughters were out— was very painful to him. He hated to be the bearer of bad news and to see people in trouble. In this case, of course, what he had to tell did not come as a surprise. Almost from the first Mrs Sutton had believed her husband to be dead, and French's story only confirmed what her own inner consciousness had told her all along. All the same, the news came as a cruel shock. French minimized it as far as he could, pointing out that the deceased's features were calm and had shown no signs of suffering. But he was glad when the visit was over and he had left the unfortunate woman in the charge of a kindly neighbour.

In the morning he was early back at the shed. There he set his men to sift every grain of the clay which had been removed from the grave, in the chance of finding some small object which the murderer might have dropped.

Leaving these in charge of Carter, he went on to the Leman Street station and saw Superintendent Nairn.

'The doctor's examining the remains,' said the latter. 'Would you like to have a word with him?'

French chatted for a few moments and then a constable showed him to the mortuary.

'Morning, chief,' cried the doctor cheerily as he caught sight of him. 'Looking for information, I suppose? Well, I can tell you nothing. Must have a P.M.'

'What does it seem like, doctor?' French returned, having met this attitude before.

The doctor straightened up from his work. 'It seems like a crack on the back of his head with something blunt but heavy. The skin's not broken, but the skull's fractured. Enough to kill him instantaneously.'

'That sounds clear enough. What more do you want?'

'That's unofficial, as you know very well. If I'm to say there's no poison there, for example, I must have the P.M.' He grinned.

'Well, it's not suicide and it's not accident, at all events, I take it?'

'It's not suicide,' agreed the doctor, 'but how you know it's not accident beats me.'

'I think we may take it it's murder,' said French.

'Only unofficially.' The doctor gave the suspicion of a wink. 'Officially you can't say what hit him.'

'I'll take the risk.' French grinned in his turn. 'Where'd you leave the clothes, doctor?'

With a nod of his head Dr Caldwell indicated an adjoining room, and French, passing through, set to work on his examination.

First he took the objects in the pockets. With one

exception all the objects were there which a man in Sutton's position might naturally be expected to carry. There was a wrist watch, money, keys, fountain pen, pencil, rubber, and such like. The exception was paper. There was not one scrap of paper anywhere. The notebook which a detective would certainly have carried was gone, and so were all letters or other documents which the man might have had at the time of his death. Quite obviously the body had been searched, and as a safeguard these had been removed.

French swore. The hope of finding out from the note-book what Sutton had learnt, upon which he, French, had been building, was now dashed. He was as far from solving his problem as ever.

Nor did he, again with one exception, learn anything from the clothes. But, though he didn't realize it at the time, that exception was to prove one of the most vital discoveries of the case. With his accustomed thoroughness he subjected each garment to the severest scrutiny, but without result. There were no marks, tears, stains or other helpful indications.

Until he came to the shoes.

The shoes, he found, were quite new. Moreover, the insides of both, particularly at the heels, were clean and free from clay. The feet, he remembered, were close together in the grave, and where they had touched each had protected the other from the earth.

It occurred to French that to lift the body into the grave and place the feet as they had been placed, would probably have involved lifting the feet together. He went through the movements in imagination. Was there a chance that, if this had been done, the actual shoes might have been held and fingerprints might remain on the smooth and hard surface of the heels?

It was unlikely, he thought, but it was worth a test. He got out his grey powder and dusted it over the leather. And then to his delight he found that this very long shot had reached a bull's eye.

Both heels bore fingerprints. They were on the inside edges and pointed towards the toes. They looked, and French was certain they were, prints of the little fingers of a right and a left hand.

Of course, in a way and at the moment, they were no use to him. He had no prints of little fingers with which to compare them. But they might become quite invaluable if he were lucky enough to arrest a suspect. With the utmost care he packed the shoes for transport to Scotland Yard.

Presently he returned to Leman Street and told Nairn of his find. The superintendent was impressed, and they discussed the affair for some time. Then French said he must go. 'You've arranged the inquest, I suppose?' he asked as he stood up.

'Tomorrow at half-past ten. Will you let everything come out, or do you want an adjournment?'

French considered. The finding of the body could not be kept a secret, and the murderer would therefore be warned that to this extent the police were on his track. The further particulars gained were so trifling that he did not see how they could give anything away.

'I don't want an adjournment. The only thing that I should like kept dark is the possible connection with the loss of the *Jane Vosper*, and as that's only theory it won't be mentioned.'

Nairn nodded. 'I'll warn the coroner, in any case.'

Freeman Wills Crofts

Leaving the police station, French returned to Redliff Lane. There he found that his men had completed their detailed examination of the clay, unfortunately without finding anything of interest.

French was more than ever disappointed. A profoundly important discovery had been made, and yet the solution of his problem seemed no nearer than before. Of course, from one point of view he was further on. Without a corpse there could have been no charge of murder. Things were to the good in so far that if and when evidence came he would be able to use it to make an arrest. But he was afraid that the question of an arrest was one for the far distant future.

Next morning he attended the inquest. The proceedings were formal and dull. French was the first witness. In reply to the coroner's questions he said that, acting on information received, he proceeded to a shed at 29 Redliff Lane, and there made a search of the floor. He saw that a certain area looked as if it had been recently taken up, and this he had opened. He there found the remains on which the inquest was being held.

The coroner had been impressed by Nairn's warning and accepted this statement as adequate. Briefly asking his jurors if any of them wished to put a question, he gave them little opportunity to do so, adding immediately, 'Thank you, chief inspector, that's all. Now, Dr Caldwell, if you please.'

The doctor had but little to add to the statement he had already made to French. The cause of death was the blow on the back of the head, delivered, he was of opinion, with some soft, heavy, yielding object, such as a sandbag. He had made a post mortem and had found no other cause of death. The organs were all healthy and there was nothing deleterious in the stomach.

Mrs Sutton was the next witness. She formally identified the remains as those of her husband, and told of his business affairs and of the last time she had seen him alive. Her evidence was skilfully extracted, for it did not suggest that her husband's death was connected with his cases.

Hislop, the assistant in the export department of the Weaver Bannister Company, described his journey with the deceased from Watford to Baker Street, and repeated the latter's remark that he must now part company, as he had business at Waterloo.

Jeffrey was called, as the deceased's principal employer, to give evidence as to the man's professional position. Here also the questions were so framed that no question of his having been on a dangerous job was raised. Jeffrey spoke warmly of Sutton's industry and capability, and said the firm held him in high esteem.

If all this left the position somewhat obscure, it did not seem to worry the coroner. In his short address to the jury he pointed out that their duty was to find the cause of death, not to conduct criminal proceedings against any person or persons. In this case two outstanding facts seemed to give them all the information they could possibly require to reach a conclusion. First there was the evidence of the doctor that death had been caused by a blow on the back of the head, and his further professional opinion that that blow could not have been self-inflicted. Secondly, they had the fact that the body had been buried with every evidence of a desire to keep the death secret. Here was, in his opinion, overwhelming evidence of premeditation. He thought the conclusion that wilful murder had been

227

committed was unavoidable, but, of course, this was a question for the jury, and for them alone. He thought, also, the jury would agree that no evidence as to the identity of a possible criminal had been put before them. But, as he had pointed out, the question of responsibility for the crime was not a matter with which they had to do. If they agreed with him they would return a verdict of wilful murder by some person or persons unknown. But, of course, as he had said, this was entirely a matter for themselves.

Needless to say, the suggested verdict was returned, and that without a retirement.

That afternoon French gave orders that he was not to be disturbed, and settled down to struggle very seriously with his case. It was now no vague instance of disappearance, which, however unlikely, might always have been deliberate. Now it was murder, and murder must be followed up with all the energy and all the resources at the investigating officer's command. He, French, *must* succeed! The case was too important to permit of failure. Apart from the fact that the murdered man was a friend of his own, apart from the sympathy he felt for the widow, apart from all his feelings on the matter, his professional existence was to a considerable extent at stake. A chief inspector who failed in his cases wouldn't be a chief inspector long.

For the hundredth time he got out his notes and worked slowly through them. At each item he stopped and thought. Had this fact no bearing that he had missed? Could no deduction be made from it which up to now he had overlooked? He had obtained an immense amount of material. Surely he should be able to make more of it than he had?

He sat pondering, comparing, sifting his facts, trying to

reconstruct his theories. But he could get no further. Every avenue he tried seemed to lead to a dead end. Sutton had been on to what Rice was doing. How did he get on to it? What *was* Rice doing? Both questions seemed to be unanswerable.

How tired he, French, was of the whole business! Not only mentally tired, but actually physically weary. He had gone over the facts, over them again and again, till he was sick of the thought of them. He had gone stale to the whole problem. He would put the blessed thing aside and do some other work. When he came back to it fresh he might do better. A wave of discouragement flowed over him.

But it happened that as he thus luxuriated in pessimism he was automatically fingering the two scraps of burnt paper whose origin had up to the present eluded him. That 'arm c', he thought dully. What could armchairs have to do with the affair? Did it really refer to armchairs?

Then suddenly an idea flashed into his mind. 'Arm c' didn't only stand for armchairs! What about alarm clocks?

Alarm clocks! And the *Jane Vosper* was blown up—must have been blown up—by time bombs! Alarm clocks! Most time bombs were operated by clocks.

And of all kinds of clocks, alarm clocks were the most suitable for the purpose. Alarm clocks! Yes, that was something to think about.

Instantaneously French's weariness vanished. He was suddenly fresh and rested, optimistic, capable and as energetic as ever. Alarm clocks! Yes, it was an idea. He would follow it up without any loss of time.

If the 'W.C.2.' scrap were part of the same sheet as the 'arm c' piece, as from their quality seemed not unlikely, the enquiry should be short. He had only to send to all the watchmakers in the area and show them the 'W.C.2.' and the 'TEL' printing and spacing to find the one in question. And, of course, lest the 'W.C.2.' scrap did not apply, enquiries as to the sale of alarm clocks would be made at the same time. He decided to concentrate on the W.C.2. area first. If he got nothing there he could try elsewhere.

Late though it was, he began work immediately. He sent for a number of men, explained what was required, furnished them with photographs of the lettering, and started them off on their rounds. They were to work till the shops closed and begin again as soon as they reopened next morning.

French was more impressed by this alarm clock idea than he had been by any other of his theories of the case. For this, if it proved true, would bring the investigation back to what it had been long divorced from: the connection between Sutton's death and the blowing up of the *Jane Vosper*. French was satisfied that in that direction and no other lay the solution of his problem. If Rice had bought alarm clocks it would not prove that he had caused the explosions, but it would make it much more likely.

In bed that night aea ethoughts reverted to the subject. There had been four explosions. If four alarm clocks had been purchased, the presumption of a connection would be strengthened. How he wished he could prove it!

Then a devastating consideration flashed into his mind. Was he not on the wrong track altogether? Would alarm clocks have been any use for the *Jane Vosper* outrage?

An alarm clock went off within, at latest, about ten hours of its being set. Under no circumstances could the functioning of the alarm mechanism be delayed beyond this period. But in the case of the *Jane Vosper* the mechanism didn't operate for more than a week. Alarm clocks would have been no use here. If they had been used, they would have blown the ship up before she left the dock.

Here was a bitter disappointment. The first really hopeful idea he had reached had proved a wash-out! His depression suddenly returned. Again he felt physically weary. Thoughts of failure filled his mind. His comfortable satisfied feeling passed and he grew restless and on edge. Once again he began to go over the evidence . . .

When he reached the Yard next morning he considered calling off the men who were working the watchmakers' shops. They had, however, gone out, and for the moment he was out of touch with them. As they rang up to report progress he would recall them.

He was, therefore, the more astonished when shortly before eleven he had a telephone message from one of them. Messrs Attenborough of Dentite Street, off the Strand, who specialized in alarm clocks, had invoices lettered as was the burnt scrap. The constable suggested that perhaps French could see his way to call over.

French, though still sceptical of result, felt he must do so. He told the man to wait for him in Dentite Street, put aside his correspondence and left the Yard.

13

The 'ARM C' Scrap

Though the purchase of an alarm clock by Rice no longer greatly interested him, French felt that if the man really had had dealings with the Attenborough firm he, French, should know all about it. He was glad, therefore, when shown into Mr Attenborough's private office, to find that gentleman ready to do anything in his power to assist.

First French was shown the firm's letter heading, which was believed to correspond with that found in the shed fireplace. For economy's sake the same lettering was used for letter paper, bills, invoices, and sales dockets, those forms of which one is handed to the customer or enclosed in his parcel at the termination of his purchase and which is at once his record of the transaction and his receipt for the money paid.

French carefully compared the two printings, using a powerful lens and a transparent gauge ruled into tiny squares. He was soon compelled to admit they were identical. Of course, this did not prove the burnt scrap had come from Attenborough's. The number of firms with

'London, W.C.2. Tel' on their paper was so great that the setting up might be identical in a number of cases. But at least the balance of probability was in French's favour.

French next asked whether the firm had had any dealings with Rice Bros. Here a short search supplied the answer. The name was unknown to them. It did not follow that no goods had been supplied, but no account had been run, and no correspondence had passed.

There remained the extremely long shot represented by the 'arm c' scrap of charred paper. Had the two scraps come from the same document? If so, could the document be traced by Messrs Attenborough?

When this was put to Mr Attenborough he shook his head. It was true, he agreed, that as Rice Bros.' name was not on their books, the only document dealing with a purchase by them would be a sales docket. But to search through their old docket books would be a colossal task. He really did not think they could undertake it. Besides, these docket books were not kept indefinitely. If the original of French's scrap had been in their books at all, it might well have been destroyed. What was the date of the scrap?

This was a question which French had expected and he had tried to work out an answer. The shed had been rented on 1st August, and it was unlikely that anything connected with the affair would have been purchased before that date. Again, the *Jane Vosper* had sailed on 21st of September, and it was equally improbable that such a sale would have taken place later than, say, a week previous to the start. The purchase then would be limited to the six weeks between the beginning of August and the middle of September.

Mr Attenborough rubbed his chin. If the 'arm c' referred to one of their alarm clocks, the matter would not be so overwhelming. The transaction would be recorded in the books of one salesman. If French liked, he would get this man in and French could question him?

French would be delighted to do so. He was sorry for the trouble he was giving, but in the case of murder every avenue must be explored . . .

Mr Attenborough murmured 'Quite', and called for Mr White. Immediately a young man with a chubby face appeared.

'This is a chief inspector from Scotland Yard, White,' the proprietor went on. 'He's enquiring into a sale he thinks we may have made. Will you help him in every way you can? Now, chief inspector, it's up to you.'

White proved much more intelligent than he looked and quite unexpectedly helpful. Shown the 'arm c', he said at once that he thought it was his writing. He couldn't be absolutely sure, for the loop of the 'a' was formed with some irregularity. Sometimes if he wrote quickly this defect did occur, but very seldom.

At French's request he produced his books and showed examples of the perfect and defective loops, and it spoke well for the young man's accuracy that they had to examine no less than twenty-four dockets to find one of the latter. French was delighted at this development for the obvious reason that if he could turn up the carbon block the defect might prove invaluable as an identification.

But could he turn up the carbon block?

White was not enthusiastic. 'Can you tell me the date, sir?' he asked. 'If I knew that I could quickly find out whether my book is still existing.'

French repeated his estimate.

'I think some of the books for that period are destroyed, sir,' White remarked to Attenborough. 'But if you approve I could get a search made through the ledger records of the period which would show what alarm clocks were sold. This would show where to look for the dockets.'

Attenborough nodded. 'Do so,' he directed, 'and let me know if you find anything.'

'Smart young man,' said French when White had disappeared.

'Yes, he's not too bad,' the proprietor admitted. 'I don't think, chief inspector, there's any use in your waiting. We'll let you know if we find anything. Then if you want to make further enquiries, our books are open to you.'

This seemed sound advice, and French took it. He returned to the Yard and picked up his abandoned correspondence.

But he had scarcely begun work when there was a call from Attenborough's. Mr Attenborough believed they had found the docket. If the chief inspector would care to call back, they would show it to him.

Quarter of an hour later French once again entered the little office. White was sent for and laid an open docket book before French. When the latter saw it he gave an involuntary gasp.

The sale was dated for the 8th August, and read:

'4 best Invictor alarm clocks @ 21/- £4 4s. 0d.'

French stared. Alarm clocks! And four! Four explosions! Could it be? What about the ten-hour limit?

There was, of course, no proof that these had been

bought by Rice. Even though the defective 'a' looked the same, it did not follow that it was so. It would be necessary to go through all the dockets for the period to ascertain whether another showed the same peculiarity.

French, however, did not wait for this to be done, but busied himself with his lens and bit of squared celluloid. He was more careful than ever, and the result of his examination showed that either the two copies were the same, or a very unusual coincidence had occurred. Then he shook his head. Coincidences like that didn't occur. The papers were the same.

'Can you remember any of the circumstances of that sale?' he asked White. 'Surely alarm clocks are usually bought singly. Can the fact that four were required bring back anything to your mind?'

White said that he had been thinking over it and that he did remember the transaction. He recalled it because it had no less than four unusual features. The first was the point French had raised about four clocks having been bought. The second was that they were bought by a man of good position. He was elderly and well dressed, and White remembered thinking that alarm clocks are usually bought by poorly-dressed people or women. Then thirdly, this man was very urgent that the clocks should be reliable. He wanted the best quality—the price was secondary. He wanted them to stand any amount of abuse as well as to go in any position.

At this French felt a sudden thrill of excitement. Was there here a reference to the stowing of cases and the pitching of ships? If not, what could the requirements have meant?

The four clocks made a fair-sized parcel and White had

asked should he send them. To this the man replied no, that he would carry them. He did so, and this was the fourth unusual feature of the case. The sales docket was packed in the parcel.

And, French thought, as part of this docket had almost certainly been found in Rice's shed, it followed that the alarm clocks had gone there, too. And if they had gone there, for what purpose other than the blowing up of the *Jane Vosper* could they have been used?

'Tell me, Mr Attenborough,' he asked, 'could those clocks have been altered by a skilful mechanic to alarm after eight or ten days, instead of hours?'

Attenborough looked at him curiously, as if wondering what lay behind the question. 'I'm afraid not, chief-inspector,' he answered. 'The clocks were twenty-four-hour clocks, which means they would go for thirty to forty hours. If they could by some means be wound each day, another wheel could no doubt be added to the alarm train, which would delay the alarm acting for the time you say. But if they were not wound it would be impossible. I do not think there would be any way of reducing the speed of the escapement so as to make one winding keep them going for that time.'

French swore internally. If this were true, the clocks could not have been used for igniting the bombs. Had they, then, not been bought by Rice? Or, as this seemed demonstrated, had they been bought for some purpose not connected with the *Jane Vosper*?

Lest there might be some misunderstanding in Attenborough's mind as to what exactly he had meant by his question, French pledged him to secrecy, and explained the whole matter at issue. But the result was only to make the man more certain of his ground. Quite definitely the clocks could not have been kept running for several days unless they had been wound each day, though had they thus been kept running the alarm action could have been altered to operate at the end of days instead of hours.

French then concentrated on the appearance of the purchaser. Here White had not been so observant as in the matter of the clocks themselves. He could not give a clear description of the man. All the same, such details as he did remember were certainly consistent with the view that he was Rice.

French left the shop in a very puzzled frame of mind. Here was what looked like an entirely convincing clue, and it had, so to speak, turned to dust in his hand. He wondered if Attenborough's view were correct, and presently he thought that another opinion was desirable. He therefore called on Mr Wilbraham of St James's Street, an expert consulted by the Yard on clock and watch matters.

But Wilbraham completely substantiated all that Attenborough had said. The escapement of slow-action clocks, such as those which run for a year without re-winding, was totally different to that of the alarms sold, and the latter could not be altered in any way to make them go for several days with one winding.

It was clear, then, that whatever the clocks had been used for, it was not for bombs to sink the *Jane Vosper*. French saw that he might wipe out the whole affair from his mind.

He found it less easy to do in practice. That Rice had bought the clocks, he was satisfied. What had he wanted them for?

Then a further idea occurred to him, a simple idea which

should, with any luck, give him his proof. How he had come to miss so obvious a line of research he couldn't think. The more he considered the matter the more incomprehensible his failure seemed.

If Rice had blown up the *Jane Vosper*, he would have required some explosives with which to construct his bombs. Explosives are not easy to come by, and their acquirement is, therefore, correspondingly easy to trace. Could French prove that explosives had been obtained?

He saw now that it was an investigation which should have been put in hand days ago. What if it were connected with the loss of the ship rather than the death of Sutton? He had long since come to the conclusion that these affairs could not be separated.

He returned to his room and set to work. Suppose Rice had required explosives, how would he have obtained them?

There seemed to be four possible ways: Either he could have bought them direct, somehow getting the necessary licence, or he could have obtained them from some recognized source by a trick of some kind, or he could have stolen them, or he could have made them in a laboratory.

The first way French thought extremely difficult—so difficult as for practical purposes to be out of the question. A genuine certificate would not be granted by the police without such an enquiry as Rice could not have borne, and a forged one would present even greater obstacles still. To get the form alone would be next thing to impossible. French did not think he need waste time over this idea.

To have obtained explosives by a trick did not seem feasible either. Of course, it depended on the trick; but French could think of none which would be likely to succeed. This heading he thought he might also dismiss, at least for the present.

To steal the stuff seemed a more promising proposition, as, given careful preparation and ordinary luck, it should not be a difficult matter to break into some isolated magazine. French put the idea on one side till he should consider the fourth possibility—the making of the explosive in a laboratory.

Here the difficulties were of another kind. It would be easy to make an explosive, but very hard to obtain the necessary chemicals secretly. French did not believe that Rice would have risked buying them, and he could see no other way in which they could have been obtained.

On the whole, then, the third method, that of direct theft, seemed the most likely. It would be best, at all events, to try it first.

French began by inserting a notice in next day's *Police Gazette*. He was anxious to know of any thefts of explosives which had taken place during the critical six weeks. To sink a ship by explosions in the hold would take a considerable amount of stuff. Therefore trifling cases need not be taken into account.

Soon the answers began to come in. Of major thefts there were three. The first was a burglary at a gunsmith's at Leeds. A quantity of both arms and ammunition was stolen. The police, however, had a clue to the thief, and though they could not prove that their suspect was guilty, there was not very much doubt about it.

In the second case a quantity of gelignite and detonators was stolen from a quarry near Bangor. Here there was no clue whatever.

The third instance was that of blasting powder and fuse

missing from a road contractor's store near Penrith. Here again there was no clue.

French considered these three cases. On the face of it the second was the most likely from his point of view, as gelignite and detonators were far more suitable for ship destruction than either gun ammunition or blasting powder. The date of No. 2 was also more promising, No. 1 being a little early and No. 3 a little late. French decided he would concentrate on the Bangor quarry.

He began by ringing up the Bangor police to ask if they had any further information on the case. They replied that they had not, and that the matter remained a complete mystery. French then said he might possibly be interested, and a meeting at Bangor police station was arranged.

Next morning he and Carter left Euston by the Irish Mail and shortly after two o'clock reached Bangor. It was many years since French had been along that strip of Welsh coast, and he enjoyed every foot of the way. He had forgotten how fine the scenery was, and, as was usual when he travelled anywhere he admired, he decided he would spend his next holiday in the district.

At the police station Superintendent Evans greeted him with cordiality. He hoped, he said, that French was going to help them to clear up what had been a puzzling case. He needn't say that all their information and resources were at his, French's disposal.

French explained enough about the *Jane Vosper* to enable Evans to appreciate the object of his enquiries. The super was extremely interested and said that such a possibility had not occurred to him. The most he had visualized was an attempt to do some legitimate blasting without the formality of a licence.

'I suggest you come out and see the place,' went on Evans. 'I'll go with you if you like, and we'll take Inspector Griffiths, who was in charge of the case.'

Nothing could have pleased French more. In five minutes they were in the super's car, bowling along the Carnarvon road. A mile or so outside the town they turned left up towards the higher ground, and soon came to Llandelly, the townland containing the quarry.

The next half-hour reminded French vividly of the Joymount-Chayle case he had had a year or two earlier down on Southampton Water. There the question of a theft of explosives had arisen, and there he had also visited a quarry, very similar to this one, and for a very similar purpose. There it was to see whether explosives could have been stolen, not to clear up an actual case of theft. But, apart from this, the two visits were practically identical.

Here, as at Joymount, was the great face from which the stone was taken, with its benches and precipices and faults, the noisy chuffing drills, the heaps of fallen stone, the Decauville tramways, and the men posted like flies here and there on the rock. There was the pit containing the crushers at the base of the towering stone bins, the elevators carrying up the crushed material, and the usual office and power sheds. And, what interested French even more, there was, quarter of a mile away, the small stone-built explosives store.

Superintendent Evans saw the foreman, and, through him, the charge hand whose business it was to attend to the explosives. As at Joymount, this proved to be a workman of a superior type. He was responsible for the working of the store. He held the only key kept at the quarry, and no one else was allowed into the store. He gave out all the explosives and was responsible for keeping a tally of what was in stock.

He had not, however, a great deal to tell about the theft. On Monday morning, 2nd September, he had gone as usual to the store to count out the explosive required for the dinner hour blasts. He had found the door closed, but unfastened. It had been forced with something like a small bar or jemmy. Inside there was no sign of anything having been interfered with, but he had immediately counted his stores and found that both gelignite and detonators had disappeared. Some 40 sticks of gelignite were gone, and he thought about a dozen detonators, though as the latter were so small, he could not be sure of the exact number. He had at once reported the matter to his foreman, who had sent for the police.

Inspector Griffiths then took up the tale. He had made an examination of the site. He had searched most carefully for footprints and fingerprints, but without finding either. Nor had he been able to find any small article which the thief might have dropped. He had, however, found one object which he had hoped might prove a clue, though unhappily it had not done so. This was a tiny fragment of wool or frieze or serge, which had caught in a splinter of one of the shelves. It was at the police station, and he would hand it over to French. The super had had it examined by an expert, who said it was tweed of a certain type. He, the sergeant, had then made the obvious enquiries, but had not been able to find anyone who wore this sort of tweed. The suggestion, therefore, was that it was the thief's, and that he was a stranger in the district. He should perhaps have mentioned that during the search for fingerprints he had found clear traces of gloves.

Enquiries as to anyone having been seen about the quarry had yielded nothing.

Superintendent Evans then described how he had had general enquiries made in the neighbourhood with the same object. No stranger had been observed anywhere in the district during the whole of that weekend. On Saturday night, however, a Ford van had been seen parked in a deserted lane some half-mile from the quarry. The farm hand who had observed it lived close by, and if French would care to see him he had only to say the word.

French thought that, when he had come so far, he might as well see all that was to be seen. The superintendent accordingly led the way back to his car.

'Here,' he said, after a couple of minutes' drive, 'is where the car was seen. You will notice that it's a very secluded place, hidden from casual observation by those trees, and a vehicle might well stand here for hours without being seen.'

'I can understand that,' French answered, looking about him. 'Why should a vehicle be hidden here if not in connection with the theft?'

'Quite; we appreciated the point. The sergeant went into it and could find no reason whatever. Nor could he find anyone who could explain it. No one had been called on, or anything of that sort.

'The man who saw it lives up this lane,' the super went on. 'We might walk up.'

As they walked French could not keep out of his mind the point that the van was a Ford. Was it the van which had carried the timber and other materials to the Redliff Lane shed? The affair was certainly promising.

The farm hand, when eventually they ran him to earth, had not a great deal to tell. On the Saturday night in question he had been at a dance at a neighbouring farm house. He had gone about eight, and it was while on his way that he had seen the van. The night was dark, but he had passed close beside it. It was an ordinary 30-cwt. Ford covered van, but he had not observed the number. No, there was nothing remarkable about it whatever. He had returned home about two in the morning, and the van was then gone.

At the police station, on their return to Bangor, French was handed a tiny splinter of wood, cut from the explosive store shelf, and containing in a crack the little bit of tweed. It was so small—a few woolly hairs—as to be barely visible, and French's congratulations of the sergeant's observation was no mere formal politeness.

French was considerably interested to notice that the tweed was grey in colour. On the few occasions when Rice had been seen in cold weather, he had been wearing a grey overcoat. French grew more and more eager as he thought that here was cumulative evidence. That a Ford van should enter into both enquiries meant little. That the same should be true of a grey overcoat was of slight importance. But that both a Ford van and a grey overcoat should be common to each was a quite different proposition. It made distinctly probable the idea that there really was a connection.

It was dark when they returned to the police station, which greatly disappointed French, as he had hoped to have had time to go down to the Strait to see the bridges. However, he had to be content with inviting Evans to dinner, before catching a train for Town.

On reaching the Yard, he sent the bit of tweed over to their technical adviser for further examination. Then, with Carter, he set off once again to the Redliff Lane shed.

'We *might* somewhere have missed a bit of this stuff,' he urged, though he did not think it very likely. 'We'll go over every scrap of wood that Rice might have come up against when wearing his overcoat. If we could get a bit of the same stuff in the shed it would give us a big lift forward.'

They searched all the morning with meticulous care, but without success. French was disappointed in spite of his previous pessimism.

'Come along to that hotel,' he went on doggedly. 'The coat might have been hung up somewhere in that bedroom, and, if so, we might get a few hairs there.'

If perseverance and thoroughness could have achieved success, French would have succeeded. But neither of these qualities, admirable though they were, could find non-existent objects. There was no wool in the bedroom either, and at last the two men returned to the Yard.

There he found that a complete specification of the cloth from which the wool had been torn had been received from the expert. He reported that, should the tweed be found, it should be easy to identify.

But could the tweed be found? For some time French sat thinking at his desk, then he drafted a paragraph for insertion into all journals likely to be read by the cloth manufacturers of the Midlands and elsewhere. He said that Yard officers had found a scrap of the tweed on the site of a serious crime, and that they were anxious to trace its manufacture in the hope of finding the coat from which the scrap had been torn. Would any manufacturer who had made such a material kindly advise the Yard in confidence? Then followed the technical specification.

French realized the extremely tenuous nature of the clue. Conceivably the manufacturer might be found, though this, of course, was very far, indeed, from being certain. But if he were found, the real difficulty would only begin. The tweed might have been sent to scores of tailors, and each of those tailors might have made scores of coats from it. Unless Rice had bought the coat in his own name, it would probably be impossible to trace it to him. Of course, in such investigations there was always the chance of some supplementary evidence coming out which would give the necessary lead. It would not do to neglect the possibility, at all events. French felt that he must do all that he could, and then hope for the best.

Having sent out his paragraph, he went wearily home.

14

Mute Witness

The next three days proved to be the most disappointing and unproductive that French had experienced since the case began. He worked as hard as ever, but he accomplished nothing. None of his enquiries led to a result. Every line he tried petered out or reached a point from which he was unable to carry it further.

He grew steadily more and more discouraged. It wasn't that he was short of facts. There were plenty of facts, but he couldn't connect them up. He was at a complete stand-still, not only as to the death of Sutton, but equally as to the blowing up of the *Jane Vosper*. And nowhere could he see a line of research which he had overlooked, or which promised to give him what he wanted.

And it was small comfort to think, as he sometimes did, that he had been up against things to an equal extent many times in the past. Again and again in his cases he had reached a dreadful and exasperating position from which he could visualize no further progress. Again and again failure had stared him in the face. And in many of these self-same cases he had ultimately succeeded. Many an investigation which had ended triumphantly for him had looked as badly as this one during at least some part of its progress. But he hadn't always pulled off his cases. These deadlocks hadn't invariably freed themselves. Until he got a fresh start, he knew that the fear of failure would grow more and more insistent.

It was, therefore, enormously to his relief that on the fourth morning he found on arrival at the Yard that news had come in. It was not the news he wanted, but it was news, and better than nothing. The manufacturer of the tweed had been found.

At least if that was not quite proven, it was probable. Mr Blott, the managing director of the Huxtable Wheatley Weaving Company of Bradford, wrote to say that during the last six years his company had made a tweed which seemed to conform in all respects with that specified. He enclosed a sample which would enable the Yard experts to say whether or not it was what they sought.

For several hours French remained on tenterhooks while the experts made tests and looked through microscopes. Then in the afternoon came the reply he had expected. The sample was in every respect like that found at Llandelly, but there was not a sufficient quantity of the latter to set the matter beyond doubt. Though probable, it was therefore not certain that Mr Blott's firm was that required.

French swore disgustedly. More possibilities! Could he nowhere in this darned case find anything that was definite?

There was, however, only one thing to be done. He must assume the samples were the same and see if it led anywhere. Perhaps similar notices from other manufacturers might come in later, and, between them all, he might get what he wanted.

He rang up Mr Blott and asked him to let him have a note of all the firms to whom he had sold his tweed. Blott replied that he would post the information on that night.

In due course the letter arrived. At first glance French's heart fell as he saw that list contained some sixty-five names. Could they ever go over sixty-five firms and in each find all those men for whom overcoats had been made? It seemed an almost hopeless job.

But when French began to read down the list his mood quickly changed. At the sight of one of the names his exasperation and disappointment passed as if they had never been and in the twinkling of an eye he was once more eager and optimistic. Blake & Newington! Something familiar about that! Blake & Newington was one of the five names he had deduced from the 'KE & NEW' scrap of burnt paper he had rescued from the fireplace in Rice's shed. Was there here the connection he had so long sought?

Full of energy and in the highest spirits, he called Carter, and together they set off for Blake & Newington's establishment in Oxford Street. It was a good-sized concern, which, if French had been in a normal condition of mind, would have considerably dashed his enthusiasm, representing, as it did, so much the larger a clientele to be interrogated. However, the reaction from despondency was upon him, and he enquired for the manager with a feeling that he was approaching the end of his troubles.

Mr Domlio was a dry-mannered man with a careworn expression. He heard what French had to say, then shook his head.

'I'm afraid what you've asked won't be easy to answer,'

he said. 'This material was popular when it first came on the market some five or six years ago—indeed, it still sells—but I may tell you we've made a good many overcoats of it.'

'I'm sorry for giving you the trouble,' French apologized, 'but I'm afraid nothing but a complete list would be any use.'

The manager saw this for himself, and said that the search would mean a considerable amount of work, though it could be done. French asked how soon he could get the results.

'Well, we'll start at once,' Domlio replied without enthusiasm. 'I'll ring up the Yard when we've finished.'

There was nothing for it but to leave the matter to him, though French would much have preferred setting to work on the job himself. But should Domlio's clerks fail to supply information leading to Rice, he decided he would have a look over the firm's books with his own staff.

Next morning, however, there came a return from Domlio which from its business-like appearance suggested that the search had been well and truly made. In the last six years twenty-nine overcoats had been made of the tweed, nearly all in the first two years.

French pondered each name and address as he came to it, and as he did so his hopes faded. Not a single one, so far as he could see, could possibly belong to Rice. The districts in which the purchasers lived indicated men of a better social standing than the builder. Of course, this was far from conclusive, but the suggestion was not encouraging.

But a discouraging prospect did not mean that French could relax his efforts. Every one of the twenty-nine men must be interviewed, and before he gave up the investigation he must be satisfied that none of them was in any way connected with Rice. It meant a lot of work, but he couldn't help that. It was the only line which held any possibilities at all.

He began by drafting a circular, to be sent to the police of the areas in which the twenty-nine men lived. In each case he would be obliged for a confidential description of the personal appearance of Mr Blank Blank, of Blank Terrace, Blank, and if possible a note of whether he was at home between the previous 1st August and 15th October.

This enquiry involved another delay, and French found his temper wearing thin as he tried to busy himself with other work. But next morning the answers began to come in, and in dealing with them he recovered his poise.

First taking up the descriptions, he speedily eliminated twenty-two men out of the twenty-nine. One of the seven remaining might or might not be Rice. He made a list of the seven names.

Then he turned to the question of those who had been living at home during the critical period. On this point the returns were not complete, the police of some areas having replied that the information could not be obtained secretly.

As far as the reports went, however, French saw that all but four men had been at home. The information had been obtained from railway ticket collectors, police on beat, and maids. He made a second list of the four.

The next step was obviously to compare the lists. Only one name was common to both—that of Mark Cruttenden, of 27 Holywell Crescent, Pinner.

This man, it seemed, was a bachelor and lived with a

housekeeper in a small house in one of the best parts of the district. He had been from home, off and on, during most of the period mentioned, and indeed was still away. He was believed to be something in the City, but it was not known what. In normal times he went in most days by rail, and had a first-class season ticket.

All of this except the two points of appearance and absence from home was exceedingly unpromising. This did not seem to be the type of man who would rent a shed in the East End and drive a lorry, personally loading up into it timber and other heavy objects.

As French was considering the point another possible test occurred to him. The paper burnt in the shed, if it had come from Blake & Newington at all, had certainly come from them recently. When did Cruttenden buy his coat? If a long time ago, he could scarcely be the wanted man.

A telephone call to Domlio soon brought the answer to this question. Cruttenden was one of the first to buy a coat of the given tweed. His account was five years and four months old.

French swore. So that was that! He had been wasting his time. He was being too clever and finding clues and connections where none existed. He must start again somewhere else.

But, try as he would, he couldn't see where else to start. And, try as he would, his thoughts still returned to Cruttenden. Cumulative evidence again! Cruttenden was something like Rice in appearance: in itself, nothing whatever. Cruttenden and the man who had stolen the explosives—Rice by hypothesis—had overcoats of the same tweed and had probably dealt with the same tailor: again nothing whatever. Cruttenden was away from home at intervals during the period Rice was at the Kelvin Hotel, also at intervals. Here again the facts proved nothing.

But was it not somewhat different when these three sets of facts were put together?

French felt he could not dismiss Cruttenden from the enquiry without further investigation. It would not do to depend on probabilities. He must be sure.

Then a further idea flashed into his mind. The coat had been purchased over five years earlier, and the bill for it could not, therefore, have been furnished during the time Rice occupied the shed. But was that the only transaction Cruttenden had had with the tailors? Had a bill or other document been recently sent him?

To obtain an answer to this question was again only the work of a few moments. On ringing up Domlio French learnt that Cruttenden was a regular customer, that he had bought a new suit a short time previously, and that the bill had been sent him early in September. On the 16th September he had paid by cheque, and the receipted bill had been returned on the following day.

This bill sent to Cruttenden might then have been that burnt in the shed. More firmly than ever French felt that he could not eliminate the man until all these doubts had been cleared up. Further, he must clear them up at once, so that his progress in the case should not be impeded.

The first thing was to get hold of someone who could identify Rice. After some thought he decided on Duckworth & Crozier's clerk, the man who had taken Rice to see various sheds before the letting was arranged.

For once leaving Carter behind, French went down to the house agents in Fenchurch Street. Mr Duckworth's manner had undergone a complete change since French's first visit, and he was now evidently anxious to help the police in every way possible. He at once agreed to give the necessary leave.

The clerk, Archibald, was obviously delighted at the prospect of a holiday and thrilled at the way in which it was to be spent. Anxious to put the expedition beyond doubt, he had earnestly assured French that if he saw Rice he would instantly recognize him.

In due course they reached Pinner and found their way to Holywell Crescent. No. 27 was small, as the local police had stated, but it looked well furnished and as if Cruttenden was comfortably off. It was detached and was surrounded by a tiny area of garden and shrubbery, rather convention-ally arranged, but tidily kept. In the rear was a small garage.

'I understand this Cruttenden is not at home,' French explained to his companion. 'I shall ask for him, and you listen to what you've got to do.'

Archibald nodded eagerly.

'If he turns out to be at home, you say to me, "Well, if you're going in, I'll be getting along," and you'll go to the railway station and wait for me there. If he's not at home I'll try and get into the house, and you come with me and keep your eyes open.'

The door was opened by an elderly woman with a peering air, very thick glasses and a rather stupid face. French took off his hat.

'Is Mr Cruttenden at home?' he asked politely.

Mr Cruttenden was not at home. He was in Paris, and the housekeeper didn't know when he would be back.

'That's unfortunate for me,' French went on. 'I was rather anxious to see him. But you might be able to tell me what

I want, and if not perhaps I might write a note and leave it for him?'

The woman hesitated. The invitation for which French was hoping did not seem to be materializing.

'I think,' he added, 'I should tell you who I am.' He produced his official card and handed it over. She held it up to her eyes while he explained that he was a police officer from Scotland Yard. 'I wanted to see Mr Cruttenden about an accident that we believe he saw, in the hope that he could give me some information about it. But perhaps you could help me?'

She seemed troubled by the suggestion, but otherwise reacted admirably.

'Won't you come in?' she invited. 'But I'm afraid I know nothing about any accident.'

'No,' said French, 'of course not. But you might be able to tell us if Mr Cruttenden was at home on the day it happened. If not, there is no use in our troubling him on the matter.' As he spoke he moved into the hall, adding, 'Thanks, it's easier to talk when one's sitting down.'

French had imagined she was going to keep them in the hall, but she could scarcely do otherwise than accede to his suggestion. To his delight he found himself leading the way into what was evidently Cruttenden's sitting room.

It was plainly but comfortably furnished, with a small rolltop desk in one corner, a well-stocked bookcase along the wall beside it and two deep armchairs before the fireplace. A small table with books and papers stood in the centre, and in the corner behind the door was a fair-sized safe. One or two not very interesting pictures hung on the walls, and on the chimney piece were some photographs in frames.

But though French took in these details, he was more interested in the reactions of Archibald than in the room. The clerk, throwing himself wholeheartedly into the role of Dr Watson, gave a sharp look round the room on entry. His gaze passed systematically over the furniture, and in due time reached the.chimney piece. There it halted. He stared at one of the photographs, while expressions of doubt, surprise, satisfaction and excitement followed one another in rapid succession across his face. Finally he got behind the old lady, who was indicating chairs, pointed to the photograph, and nodded with deep meaning.

French was very nearly as excited himself. The photograph depicted a group of bowling men surrounding a silver cup. One of the members was an elderly man with heavy features, clean shaven but for a small moustache. French leaned over towards the clerk. 'Sure?' he breathed *sotto voce* as he thanked his hostess for the chair. Archibald nodded emphatically.

In spite of himself French grew still more excited. To have traced Rice thus far could only mean that he would shortly get the man himself. And if he had the man himself . . . Did that mean the end of his case? Could he actually prove that Rice was guilty of the murder . . .?

Well,this was not the time to consider these questions. What he must do now was to see that no suspicion of his real business penetrated to the mind of the housekeeper, so that if and when Cruttenden returned he would not guess that the authorities were on his track.

'We have a lot of trouble about street accidents,' French went on when they were seated, 'and, as you can understand, we're always glad to find anyone who has seen one happen, so as to get first-hand information as to what

really did take place. Now we understand Mr Cruttenden
was passing when an accident took place down near the
station. Our informant was not certain that it was Mr
Cruttenden, and we came up to find out. Perhaps you
could tell us when Mr Cruttenden was here and when
away, as, if he was away when it happened, of course, it
must be someone else that we're looking for.'

French was banking on the fact that the housekeeper
was stupid looking. And he was justified. She did not ask
when the alleged accident had taken place, as any wide-
awake person would have done. Instead, she began to
answer his question.

French, indeed, found himself in greater luck than he
could possibly have expected. She found she could not
remember the dates, and excused herself to go for a diary
from which she could ascertain them.

She was scarcely out of the door when French had the
photograph frame on the table and was deftly opening
the back. Fortunately for him—he was having an almost
terrifying streak of luck—the photograph was held by
four tiny brads, not by a sheet of pasted paper. In less time
than it takes to tell it French had the brads out and the
wooden backing removed, and had noted the photographer's name. With equal haste he replaced the fittings,
and when the old lady returned he was seated as before in
his chair and the photograph stood unaltered in its place.

'A good photograph of Mr Cruttenden in that group,'
he remarked conversationally as she reseated herself.

'It's an old one, but it's not bad,' she agreed, in a pre-
occupied tone, producing her book and beginning to point
to certain items.

French now settled down to find out in detail when in August and September Cruttenden had been at home and when away. The housekeeper did not appear to notice the strange way in which the accident altered its date, nor did she question its connection with Cruttenden's friends and callers, and other details of his activities. French was careful to end his conversation on the question of dates, which made it easy to get up and profess disappointment. It was evident that Mr Cruttenden had been in France on the day of the accident and therefore it could not have been he who saw it. His, French's, informant must have been deceived by a casual likeness. He was extremely sorry to have troubled the housekeeper to no purpose.

His first action when he left the house was to compare the two lists of Cruttenden's movements he had received, this one which the housekeeper had just given him, and that of the manager of the Kelvin Hotel in Whitechapel Road. And then at last the doubts which had been worrying him were dispelled! The two series almost exactly dovetailed. When Cruttenden had been at Pinner Rice had been absent from the hotel, and when Rice had been at the hotel Cruttenden was away from Pinner. With one outstanding and magnificent exception! On the night on which the explosives had been stolen from the Llandelly quarries, both Rice and Cruttenden were from home!

Moreover, certain slight differences between the two men's descriptions now became highly suggestive. Cruttenden wore no glasses; Rice wore dark-rimmed spectacles. Cruttenden's small moustache was brushed neatly sideways, Rice's untidily downwards. Cruttenden was always well dressed, clean shaven and natty, Rice unshaven, slovenly and badly dressed. If these variations did not denote a disguise, French declared that he would eat his hat.

Obvious routine steps had now to be taken, and French set about them without delay. He called at the photographers and obtained some copies of the Pinner photograph. Then, returning to the Yard, he selected a dozen other photographs of people as like Cruttenden as he could find. With these he placed one of the man in question. Then he went round to certain persons who had seen Rice—Duckworth, Morgan & Trusett, the timber merchants, the manager of the Kelvin Hotel, and Mr Hardy, who had printed the Claygate label. All of these at once picked out Cruttenden's photograph and stated unhesitatingly that it was that of Rice.

Here, then, was certainty at last! Cruttenden was the man he wanted! Or at least one of the men. The major difficulty in the case was overcome. Once he had his hands on Cruttenden—and that should be a speedy matter—the back of the case was broken.

And with the information Cruttenden's arrest should bring him, it shouldn't take long to find the others concerned. Nor should it be a big job to get the complete proof he still wanted. No! At last his difficulties were breaking down, and he was on a fair way to success.

15

The Timber

The discovery of the identity of Rice of the Redliff Lane shed with Cruttenden of Pinner broke the deadlock in the Sutton case. No longer was French at a loss as to his next step: rather was he overwhelmed with all that had to be done. Here was a criminal about whom little was known. Obviously his life history must be investigated, with all its ramifications of family, friends, business, pleasure, and activities of all kinds. Cruttenden was, as it were, handed over to French and his staff as a liquid is handed over to an analytical chemist: so that what was once an unknown quantity might be resolved into something familiar and well understood.

This meant work—detailed, tedious, meticulous work. It meant the making of scores, perhaps hundreds of enquiries, with profound satisfaction if not more than ninety-nine per cent of them proved useless. One per cent result on his efforts would mean success. He would be thankful for half of it.

French began by a report to Sir Mortimer Ellison. The

A.C. did not attempt to hide his surprise at the news. To him also it seemed unthinkable that this quiet and apparently worthy citizen should be connected with crimes such as were being investigated. But he saw that the proof that such was the case was overwhelming, and he raised no objection to French's request for a search warrant to go through the Pinner house.

The document having been obtained, French returned to Holywell Crescent, taking with him Carter, as well as Boyle, the fingerprint man, and Cooper, the photographer. The housekeeper was obviously puzzled and uneasy when she saw the quartet, but French was fatherly with her and very polite. He produced his warrant, explained it to her, and pointed out that he thought Mr Cruttenden must, after all, have the information he required, and that, as they must get it, and as Mr Cruttenden was not at home, there was nothing for it but to look among his papers in the hope of finding it. He assured Mrs Sandford that she would not be inconvenienced in any way and that everything would be left as it was found.

Then ensued the usual meticulous search. The desk was taken first. It was locked, but a few minutes' manipulation with a bunch of skeleton keys sufficed to shoot back the bolt. It was then gone over for fingerprints, and these were photographed. Then, while the fingerprint man and the photographer were engaged elsewhere, French went through the papers.

It was evident that Cruttenden was a man of tidy habits. The papers were neatly arranged and docketed, and were, as French had imagined they would be, entirely innocent. They were just the papers that a suburban dweller like Cruttenden would naturally have in his desk. There were bills for gas, water, provisions, and so on, mostly receipted, as well as a number of letters of a private and quite innocuous type. Clamped together was a neat little bundle of motor manufacturers' advertisements, suggesting that Cruttenden might have been contemplating buying a new car. In fact, with two exceptions, there was nothing which interested French in the slightest degree.

Of these exceptions the first was negative. On no single scrap of paper was there a hint of the nature of Cruttenden's business. There was nothing to account for the income the man must have had to live as he did. This did seem to French a little remarkable. He could understand that business papers would be kept in the office—Cruttenden must have had some business, as he had gone up most days to Town—but he could not understand how every reference to business had been avoided in the private papers. It was certainly suggestive.

The second exception was more definite. In a pocket in the desk was Cruttenden's bank book. To French's surprise it showed four unexpected facts. Firstly, Cruttenden was evidently extremely hard up. He was overdrawn to quite a considerable extent. Secondly, some fairly large sums had been drawn out recently, leaving this debit balance. And what interested French about these withdrawals was that they corresponded exceedingly closely to certain estimated costs of hiring and furnishing the shed, which he, French, had worked out. There were items for which he could not account, but those that he knew, such as the rent of the shed and the price of the timber, he believed he could trace.

The third fact was also suggestive. None of the names of the recipients was given. All the withdrawals had been in the form of cash to self.

But to French the fourth fact was by far the most interesting of the lot. Practically all Cruttenden's income, lodged in sums, many of which were comparatively large, had the same peculiarity. None of the payees was named; all the sums had been paid in cash.

For some moments French sat motionless at the desk considering these points. Where do systematic cash payments—he was going to use the word 'usually', but he substituted 'often' for it in his mind—where do systematic cash payments often come from, particularly to a man who is hard up? The nasty word blackmail suggested itself. If Cruttenden were a blackmailer it would explain a good many things.

It would explain the cash deposits, the absence of information as to the man's business, the character which would turn to ship wrecking and to murder, the willingness to do anything to carry through an illegal deal, provided it were profitable, as well as the safe to conceal dangerous papers. And, conversely, if Cruttenden were the out-and-out bad hat that now seemed likely, what more probable than that he would turn to blackmail to replenish his emptying coffers?

It was obvious to French that he must open the safe, though equally obvious that he couldn't do it on that visit.

The search dragged on wearily, but without revealing anything else of interest. Then French had another interview with the housekeeper, Mrs Sandford. By this time even she had grasped the fact that the story of the 'accident' was not to be taken too literally, and an intense perturbation showed in her manner. French tacitly dropped any attempt to explain his questions, simply asking them as if such an interrogation were an everyday affair to which no exception could be taken.

From Mrs Sandford he learned a good deal about Cruttenden's home life, though only one point raised his interest to fever heat. Cruttenden, it seemed, lived very quietly. He went out but little in the neighbourhood, though his business frequently kept him late in Town, often indeed until after the last train, when he returned by car. He entertained very little—practically not at all—though two or three men did come in occasionally to sit with him, usually on a Sunday evening. French naturally asked for a description of these men, and it was the housekeeper's word portrait of one of them which so keenly aroused his interest.

For, as far as description could go, this man was the partner of the shed! He was exactly like, at all events, the man who took turns with Rice to transport the timber from Messrs Morgan & Trusett!

But what his name or his business was or where he lived Mrs Sandford had no idea. Nor could she give any more information about any of the other callers. All she could say of them was that they were also quiet. They smoked and had a few drinks and talked in low tones and left early in the evening: model callers, from her point of view. And, what she seemed to appreciate even more, all the callers were men.

About the end of July, Mrs Sandford went on in answer to further questions, Cruttenden had told her that he was taking over a temporary business in Paris and would have to stay over there a good deal for some three months. He would come back at intervals, but would always let her know beforehand. And so he had. Sometimes she had a card from Paris, but usually Cruttenden had telephoned on arrival in London. She had had no information recently, and didn't know when he would be back.

This seemed all that French was likely to obtain, and, as Boyle and Cooper had also finished, the four men left. French, sending the others back to the Yard, went to the local police station. There he arranged for the house to be watched, so that he might learn without delay if Cruttenden appeared. If the man were seen, he was not to be allowed to escape, though, as French would prefer to make the arrest, he was not to be detained by the local force unless this became necessary.

From the police station French went on to Cruttenden's bank. There he saw the manager, and, explaining his business, asked for any confidential information about the man's finances which the manager could give him.

But Mr Clotworthy evidently considered his first duty was to his client. His thin-lipped mouth closed like a trap and he politely intimated that if French required such information he must first obtain the necessary authority to demand it, when it would be handed over. Until then, nothing was doing.

On returning to the Yard French found that the last possible shred of doubt that Cruttenden and Rice were one and the same person had been removed. The finger-prints on the inside of Cruttenden's desk were the same as those in the office in the Redliff Lane shed. Definitely, then, he was not pursuing a will-o'-the-wisp, but was on the right track.

But though this knowledge was so satisfactory in one way, a dreadful feeling of doubt on another point was growing up in his mind. Conclusive as the evidence connecting Cruttenden with the *Jane Vosper* affair seemed to be, must there not be in it some hideous mistake? Because what could the man have possibly gained by such a crime?

He had not insured either ship or cargo. It seemed to French that he couldn't possibly have gained in any way whatever. And if he didn't gain, why should he have done such a thing?

The more French considered this point, the more overwhelming it seemed to grow. Nothing criminal is done without motive. What could have been the motive here? So far as French could see, there could have been none.

But if there were none, did it not mean that Cruttenden could not have sunk the *Jane Vosper*? But if so, what about the explosives and the alarm clocks? Perhaps not the alarm clocks—he had not been able to see how they could have been used. But the wool from the coat practically proved that Cruttenden had stolen the explosives. If not to blow up the *Jane Vosper*, what was this for?

French swore. It was confoundedly puzzling. It looked as if the man must have been acting as an agent for somebody else. If so, there must surely be a whole side of the affair to which he, French, had not as yet tumbled. For the life of him, he could not see what this might be.

But, disquieting as these considerations were, they did not in any way affect his next step. Obviously he must find Cruttenden. How was he to set about it?

The man had told his housekeeper that he was going to Paris. French wondered had he gone?

He went round to the passport office and put some questions. There a short search revealed the fact that Cruttenden possessed a passport, which included France among the countries covered. French noted its number, intending to advise the coastal passport officers to indicate the holder to the police.

'By the way,' the young man who was attending to French said suddenly, 'this name Cruttenden is familiar to me. I dealt with it quite recently. Let's see. So many of these applications pass through our hands that it's not easy to remember all of them. But I remember specially noting this name. Yes, Mark Cruttenden of Pinner. I got one of those silly ideas one does get—about pinning something to the mark. Imbecile, but if anything like that occurs to you, you remember the names.'

'That's interesting,' French approved. 'If you dealt with the man recently you'll have a record, I suppose?'

'Oh, yes, I'll be able to turn it up. I should remember, though.' He paused for a moment, then made a sudden gesture. 'I've got it! We had an application from him asking that the passport be made to include Russia. That's it. Perhaps, if you're interested, I'd better turn the papers up and make sure?'

'I wish you would,' said French.

A reference to the files showed that the young man's recollection was accurate. Some couple of months earlier Cruttenden had sent in his passport, saying he wished to travel to Russia. The passport had been amended accordingly.

When French once again reached his room at the Yard his first act was to put through a call to the Sûreté in Paris, asking if the presence of Cruttenden in Paris was known. This, of course, was a long shot, but owing to the French system of hotel registration such knowledge was not impossible. Then, having warned the police and passport men at all sea and air ports, he turned his attention to the question of Russia.

Rice was in London on 17th October, because on that

day he called at the agents and gave up the keys of the shed. If he had gone to Russia, therefore, it must have been since that date. Could his movements be traced?

The easiest way to go would, of course, be by air or sea. The journey across Europe was long and tiring. But if the visit were to be kept from the English police, overland would be the way chosen, because of its comparative secrecy. French thought that his enquiries should be first about direct sea. Air could be taken next, and rail if both these failed.

He rang up Lloyd's, asking for a list of all steamers which had left for Russian ports during the period in question. There were twenty-seven, of which four had sailed from London. Of the latter, two were Russian and two British. French decided to try the Russian first.

But by sea he drew a blank. The most careful enquiries failed to reveal any trace of Cruttenden's journey. Next he tried air. He put several men on the job, but without success. If the man had gone, he had done so by the ordinary rail and cross-Channel steamer route.

For a time he considered applying to the Soviet police, then he thought he would postpone this enquiry until he had something further to go on. A more immediate matter, he considered, was the safe in the Pinner house. He would have that opened and go through the contents before deciding on his next step.

Accordingly next morning, with Carter and a couple of experts armed with drills, an oxy-acetylene plant and other strange tools, he went out once again to Holywell Crescent. There a period of intensive activity ensued, resulting in the door of the safe swinging open. French pounced on the contents like a terrier on a rat.

A glance assured him that the neatly stacked papers were indeed treasure trove. Quite apart from the sinking of the *Jane Vosper* and the murder of John Sutton, to have obtained these papers alone would have been well worth all the labour he had put into the case.

His suspicions had been correct. Cruttenden was a systematic blackmailer. There was enough information here to get him a life sentence. French almost gasped as he saw some of the names on the man's sinister list.

This was extraordinarily satisfactory. Even if the ship and the murder part of the affair should not work out so well as he hoped, this discovery was still a personal triumph for himself. Blackmailers were a pest whom the authorities were naturally anxious to exterminate, and this case would undoubtedly prove to be one of the most important dealt with for many years.

But the discovery would help on the *Jane Vosper* and Sutton affairs also. Cruttenden was now an outlaw, a criminal to be hunted down and arrested at sight. The blackmailing charge would give all the opportunity which was required to investigate the man's life. Now the bank manager could be made to disclose his books. And the same would apply to everyone with whom Cruttenden had had dealings.

Also enquiries might now be put through to Moscow. In fact, in every way the investigation had taken a most happy turn.

After reporting his discovery to Sir Mortimer, French drafted his Russian message.

But though French was delighted with his progress, he remained profoundly troubled by his inability to find a motive for Cruttenden in the *Jane Vosper* case. What the man hoped to make out of it he could not imagine. His bank account showed that so far he had not done so, or, if he had, he was holding the money elsewhere. Obviously he was acting for someone else. But for whom? French could think only of the Southern Ocean Steam Navigation Company, but he simply could not see a company of the standing of this one putting themselves in the power of a man like Cruttenden. But then, again, if they had not done so, why had Cruttenden acted?

French was walking along the corridors at New Scotland Yard on his way to his room while these thoughts were passing through his mind. Suddenly, to the astonishment of a sergeant who was following him, he stopped dead in his tracks, an expression of incredulous amazement printed on his features.

The timber! Was it possible that in the timber lay the explanation of the whole confounded puzzle?

Staggered for a moment by the immensity of the vista this idea opened up, his body presently began to function once more and he resumed his walk to his room. There, throwing himself into his chair, he began to consider the matter with some degree of coherence.

The timber! What was the timber for? He had at first supposed it was for making forms for reinforced concrete work, then he had believed it was for shoring a tunnel, then once again he had thought of concrete forms. But was it for any of these things? No, it was for something quite different! And the concrete! Yes, he saw what that was for now!

What a fool he had been! How blind, how utterly blind! There for all these days, these weeks, almost, the clue to the affair had been in his hands, and he had failed to see

271

it! Ah, yes, the timber was the crucial feature. For the first time he obtained a coherent view of what had unquestionably been done.

Like a man in a dream he picked up his notebook and turned over the leaves till he came to certain measurements. Then he looked in another place and found his note of the quantity of the timber which had been purchased. Lastly he began to calculate.

Mathematics was not French's long suit, and he had to make three shots before he solved his problem. But when he did obtain the answer it was worth all his trouble.

Yes, the amount of timber ordered was just what would have been required for the job. It worked in so well that all doubt as to the correctness of his new theory vanished. At last he was down on bedrock fact! He knew!

At once the theory began to offer fresh lines of investigation. If Cruttenden and his friend who had helped with the carting were both skilful carpenters and had worked from morning to night all the time they had had the shed, they could never have done all the work which was required. They must have had help.

Then French remembered that workmen had been spoken of by various witnesses. These workmen! French saw that he had overlooked them in a disgraceful way. Any one of them could at any time have handed him the solution of his puzzle.

For the moment the problem of finding Cruttenden receded into the background and that of finding the tradesmen took its place. This at least should offer no serious difficulty. Enquiries at the neighbouring labour exchanges as to carpenters or joiners engaged by Rice Bros. of Redliff Lane should obtain the required information.

To ring up the labour exchanges of the Redliff Lane district was a matter of a few minutes only. The first six calls produced no result, but at the seventh he received the information he wanted.

At this exchange, it seemed, Mr Rice of Rice Bros. of the address mentioned, had called in person and had asked for six joiners for two or three weeks to do a special job. The men had been supplied. As soon as they had finished Mr Rice had taken six others, three concrete placers and three labourers. These he had kept about ten days. There had been nothing in any way out of the common about the transaction.

The next step was automatic. French asked for a list of the names and addresses of the twelve men.

'Any of them working now?' he went on.

It appeared that eight were working, but two joiners and a concrete placer and his labourer were out of a job. These latter French determined to interview.

The first man he called on was at home. He was a joiner called Blenkinsop, and he was only too willing to tell all he knew about Cruttenden, the shed, and indeed any other subject to which French would listen. French did listen and with sympathy, realizing that the garrulousness came only from the desperate boredom of unemployment.

Apart from this, however, French felt that what he presently heard had been well worth waiting for. For the first essential question, 'What was the job he set you to do?'

brought complete confirmation of French's new theory of the crime, and showed him that at last definitely he was on the right track.

'We was making boxes, sir,' the joiner answered to this fundamental question. 'There was a box there, a crate or case, you might call it reely, and we 'ad to make a lot of others the same.'

'How many others?' French went on, striving manfully to hide his delight.

'I don't know for sure, but I did 'ear there was three 'undred and forty-nine.'

It was the number French had in his mind. Three hundred and forty-nine copies and one original made three hundred and fifty. Three and fifty cases! French rubbed his hands. This was something like! At last he was getting his proof! He asked another question, knowing the answer he would receive.

''Ow big? Why, just four foot by two by two. Outside measurements.'

Yes, that was the size. It was 350 4 feet by 2 feet by 2 feet cases that the Weaver Bannister Engineering Company of Watford had filled with petrol sets and sent to the *Jane Vosper*. 350 cases!

Leaving the joiner, to the latter's evident disappointment, French went on to the address of the concrete placer. But this man, unfortunately, was out. However, at his next call, he had better luck. The last man's labourer was sitting disconsolately over the fire, reading a two-day-old newspaper.

This man was also glad to see French. As soon as he realized that the call did not herald unpleasant consequences for himself, he showed enthusiasm. He had certainly worked for ten days for Rice Bros., and he would he glad to tell the chief inspector anything he wanted to know about the job.

It was, as French had foreseen, the filling of wooden boxes with a weak mix of concrete—or, rather, the partial filling of them, for the concrete did not come up to the lid. The mix was one in twenty, good enough for the purpose, but not strong enough to make beams or other articles from which the timber would be stripped.

'How many did you fill?' French went on, profoundly satisfied with what he was hearing.

Like his colleague the joiner, this man did not know for sure. But he also had heard. Three hundred and forty-six, he had heard Mr Rice say.

Three hundred and forty-six? For a moment French was dashed. He had been expecting to hear three hundred and fifty. Then he could have kicked himself. Of course, it must have been three hundred and forty-six! Four would be filled by Cruttenden and his friend in secret. The labourers would scarcely be trusted with the placing of gelignite.

After the evidence of these workmen no doubt as to the main outline of the plot could remain. In the Redliff Lane shed Rice and his partner had prepared 350 cases, doubtless identical with those of the Weaver Bannister Company. They had filled them with concrete until they contained just the weight of the petrol-electric set. In four of them they had buried explosives with some means of detonating them. All these dummy cases had gone aboard the *Jane Vosper*. The gelignite had exploded and the ship had sunk, so that the dummy cases should go to the bottom and the trick should remain undiscovered.

French wondered that Cruttenden should have dared to employ workmen on such a job. The least hint from one of them after the ship sank would have given away the whole affair.

'What were these boxes of concrete for?' he asked the labourer with an air of intelligent interest.

'For a sea protection round a new sewage outfall,' the man answered. 'The boys was asking that very question and Mr Rice, 'e 'eard them, and that's wot 'e said. They was to throw on the sea side of the new work, to break the waves till the concrete 'ad set 'ard. They was wanted in wooden boxes so's they could be lifted out again with a crane and used over and over again as the outfall was pushed forward.'

So that was it! Here was exhibited the same thought as was to be found elsewhere in this extraordinary case. An old but effective scheme had been adopted to disarm suspicion. As the real explanation of the work could not be given, another was dished up instead. Provided it was plausible, it would serve its purpose. It had indeed served its purpose. To these workmen it seemed so complete that it robbed the subject of any further interest.

And how plausible it was! How more than plausible! Darned good, French thought. Cubical blocks of concrete were normally used to protect sea works from wave damage. It was entirely reasonable that setting concrete should have a temporary cover of this kind, and it was equal common sense that the same blocks should be used several times over as new work was placed and as the old hardened. And if so much be granted, the retaining of the timber covering followed almost as a matter of course. If it were removed, the blocks might go to pieces. No wonder the men were satisfied!

French was more than delighted with his progress. With what he had now learned, the clearing up of the few points which were still obscure would be a matter of only a very short time.

He returned to the Yard to work out his plans for the next day.

16

The Weak Link

If 350 dummy cases were sent on board the *Jane Vosper*, as now seemed certain, two fundamental questions stood out among the dozens which immediately arose. These were, first: How had the substitution of the dummy for the genuine cases been made? And second: What had been done with the genuine ones? There was a third, of course: Why had the substitution been made at all? But French thought he knew the answer to this.

However, the first thing to do was to answer the two main questions, and to this French now set himself. First, how had the substitution been made?

He turned up his notes on the tracing of the cases from the Weaver Bannister works to the ship. The sets had been packed in the sheds of the Watford works and had there been loaded into railway wagons. They had been run from the works siding to the goods depot at Haydon Square by L.M.S. goods train. From the goods depot to the wharf they had been carted by Messrs Waterer & Reade, and the loading had been done under the supervision of the ship's own first officer.

The whole journey certainly seemed straightforward and in order, and when French had gone into it he had been satisfied that nothing crooked had taken place. Now it appeared he had been wrong. At some point the substitution had been made. At what point?

About this there could be but little doubt. On the face of it nothing could have been done before the cases left the works, or during the journey to Haydon Square. Nor again after they reached the wharf. Obviously the weak link was that of the cartage between the goods depot and the docks.

This was confirmed by another point. Not only from the point of transport was the cartage link the weak one, but geographically it was the only one possible. Redliff Lane, stretching between Great Prescott Street and Royal Mint Street, was actually on a direct line between the depot and the dock. Doubtless had the shed not been there, cartage would have kept to the wider street; but in point of distance via Redliff Lane was as short a route as any.

French seemed to see the lorries from Haydon Square turning into Rice Bros.' mysterious shed, stopping beneath the runway, changing their loads, and emerging again to complete the trip to the docks.

The electric runway! Here at last was the reason why so costly a piece of apparatus should have been installed, though the occupancy of the shed was temporary and short at that! It was necessary that the genuine cases should be removed from the lorries and be replaced by the dummies

279

in as short a time as possible. The lorries must make a reasonable number of runs per day, or Waterer's people might smell a rat. If hand loading were in force, this could not be done. Hence the runway.

The further French went in his surmisings, the further evidences of design he brought out. The purpose of the shed, its site and its fittings were now all accounted for. And the design was good. Grimly he thought it ought to have succeeded. He didn't like to think how nearly it had succeeded.

Another point now seemed to him fairly clear: Sutton had obviously discovered the substitution, and had been unwise enough to mention his suspicions to someone in the conspiracy. He had penetrated to the shed, or been lured there, and had so fallen into the conspirators' power.

If so, how sharp Sutton had been! How had he got on so quickly to the fraud, when he, French, with all the resources of the Yard behind him, was only now tumbling to it?

But all this, though he believed it to be the truth, still remained mere theory. Beyond the general probability, he had no proof for any of it. That must be his next care. Somehow, by hook or by crook, he must get his proof.

Where should he seek it? So far as he could see, there was only one place possible. He must go again to Waterer & Reade's, the carriers. If he were right so far, their lorrymen must have been privy to the affair. He must get hold of the lorrymen.

Then he remembered a significant fact: Both these men had left Waterer's, and without giving an address. It might not be so easy to find them. Cruttenden & Co. would probably see to that.

Ringing up to make an appointment with the manager, Keene, French called Carter and went down to the Otwell Street firm.

Keene saw them at once. He seemed slightly bored by another call on an old subject, but was polite, if a trifle dry, as he asked what he could do for them.

French began by pledging the man to secrecy. 'It's about the carriage of those cases from the Haydon Square depot to the London Docks,' he went on, and, as Keene nodded impatiently, added, 'We think that during that journey the cases containing the Weaver Bannister sets were changed for others containing concrete. We want your help in getting to the bottom of the affair.'

Keene put down the papers he had been toying with and stared motionless. 'What on earth are you talking about, chief inspector?' he said at last, evidently overcome by astonishment which rapidly changed to indignation. 'Do you mean to suggest that my firm has been party to some crooked trick?'

French shook his head. 'Of course not, sir,' he answered easily. 'But I'm afraid your firm has been the victim of a trick, as Messrs Weaver Bannister have been, though, fortunately for you, with much less serious consequences.'

Keene seemed considerably moved. 'Good God!' he exclaimed. 'I hope you are wrong. I feel sure you are wrong. What are the details?'

'We think—' French shrugged. 'Well, put it this way: We're not satisfied about the cartage of the cases from station to docks. In a word, I want to find those two carters who did the work. You told me they had left you?'

'That is so.'

'And without leaving an address?'

'That is so, too. I told you before. I don't know where they have gone.'

'You said they weren't with you long, sir?'

'No, they weren't. Only a week or so before that job.' Keene was looking more and more uneasy. 'I'll give you all the details.' He sent for a file.

'It happened that we got rather a rush of work just about the time this job came on. We had plenty of lorries, but our staff of drivers had been rather heavily reduced during the bad time. I decided to take on a couple of temporary men to get us through the rush, which I couldn't believe was more than temporary. We had a number of applications, and I looked through these and selected what seemed to me from the testimonials to be the two best men. They started with us, and it happened that these were the men who were put on to the job in question. They did it, as well as all their other work, very satisfactorily, as I thought. Then they left. They were not dismissed, but left at their own request. They both gave as their reason that they had got a permanent job.'

'I don't think when I was here before that I got a description of them. One I saw, a man called'—French glanced at his book—'William Henty. The other had left. What was he like, if you please?'

'I did see him on different occasions,' Keene replied, 'but I don't know that I looked at him very carefully. Probably you could get a better description from the foreman. According to my recollection, he was a big man with a heavy face and a little moustache. Rather untidy looking, but a good lorryman.'

It was now French's turn to stare in amazement. Slowly he put his hands into his pocket and drew out his collection of photographs. 'He's not among those, by any chance?' he asked, handing them over.

Keene sat slowly turning them over. When he came to Cruttenden's he stopped. He looked at it more closely, his head bent, while French sat thrilling with the excitement of a fisherman whose float has suddenly bobbed. But Keene presently passed on the next. He went through the whole collection, then he turned back to Cruttenden's. At it he stared for a few moments longer. Then he handed it over.

'I believe that's the man,' he declared, 'though I'm not absolutely sure. He was unshaven, our man, and much less tidy. But it's certainly like him.'

'You wouldn't be prepared to swear to him?'

Again Keene hesitated. 'No, but I suggest you show this to the foreman,' he said. 'He could probably give you definite information.'

French nodded. Here was a tremendously valuable piece of information. If Cruttenden had got a job as lorryman, it explained how the exchange of the crates had been kept secret. Cruttenden! Of course! Here was the same excellence of design as he had found elsewhere in the affair.

Then French got a further idea, and for a moment he sat in silence, oblivious of his surroundings, as he turned it over in his mind.

If one of those two lorrymen were Cruttenden, what about the other? The other he had seen himself. Hastily he turned up Mr Armstrong's description of the second lorryman who had called for the timber from his firm. Why, of course! What a fool he, French, had been! The second lorryman was undoubtedly Henty. There could be no doubt that these two beauties had somehow got billets with Waterer & Reade to enable them to carry out their evil plans. How had they done it?

'You spoke of testimonials, sir. Have you still got them?'

The manager shook his head. 'I'm afraid not. The men asked for and were given them before they left. That's usual, you know.'

'Of course, sir. You haven't a note of who gave them?'

'Yes, we have, I think.' Keene looked up his file. 'Yes, here are the names. You see, they're good people.'

On the staff card for Joseph Grey was written in the 'Reference' space, Sibley Greer & Co., and on that of William Henty, Harrison Bros. These were both carriers of excellent reputation.

'Did you take up the references?' French asked.

'No, I didn't. They were written on their respective firms' paper and I knew the signatures. Both are firms with which we do business. No. I sent the men out with a lorry and an observer. He reported both were good drivers, and I let it go at that.'

'Well,' said French, 'we can soon settle the point. Perhaps, sir, you would ring up those firms and ask if the references are OK?'

Keene did so at once. The replies distressed him and delighted French. Neither of the men had ever been heard of and no testimonials had been given.

'Just one other point, sir,' French went on, striving to hide his deep satisfaction. 'How did it come that these two men were chosen for that particular job?'

Keene shrugged. 'That was a matter for our shed foreman,' he declared. 'But what doubtless weighed with him was that these two men were taken on to deal with special jobs outside our usual contracts. We have a large number of what I may call standard jobs, which go on regularly from week to week. For instance, we do all the carting for Lambson's Brewery, and the same for other firms. But the carrying of these cases was a special job, one of the very jobs to cope with which we had taken on the men. It would be natural to send our own men to the jobs they knew and the new men to the special non-recurring job.'

'Scarcely sufficiently sure for my men to bank on,' French answered. 'Because if they hadn't been put on that job, their whole scheme was lost.'

Keene shrugged again and a thin smile curved his lips. 'I expect you know as much about that as I, chief inspector,' he said.

His suggestion was obvious. The foreman had been squared. But, if so, there would be little use in asking him the question, as he would undoubtedly deny it.

However, the point was not of immediate importance; other matters were more urgent. It could, and of course would, be gone into later. The main outlines of the fraud were becoming clearer and clearer with every question French asked, and he was content, though keener than ever to reach the end of the enquiry and get his men.

He wished he could obtain definite proof that the Weaver Bannister cases had been taken into the shed. It was progress to be certain that they had. But to be certain was not enough: he must prove it. Was there no way in which he could do so?

The only possibility seemed to be to go over once again that journey between the rail depot and the dock. It was true that he had already done it thoroughly, but as there was no other way in which he could hope to get his information, it would be worth repeating. If no one at either end could help, someone surely must have noticed one of the Waterer lorries entering or leaving the shed. They must have entered and left not far short of a hundred times; and it would indeed be strange if not one of all those movements had been observed.

He therefore left the carriers, and, returning with Carter to the Haydon Square depot, began a second enquiry over the same ground as the first. But this time he was even more thorough. Also he made it a point to see everyone in the place, instead of only those who had actually been concerned with the cases.

It proved a wearisome and thankless job. Those whom he had questioned before took up the line that they had already told all they knew, and they didn't see why they should have to repeat the same thing all over again. The others said, 'What cases?' and then declared they had never heard of the affair at all.

But these attitudes were natural, and French expected to encounter them. He did not allow them to damp his ardour. In spite of veiled opposition and open sarcasm, he persevered. What did it matter if his job were unpleasant? It was all in the day's work.

His only fear, indeed his expectation, was that all this unpleasant work would go for nothing. It was unlikely that he could have missed anything really important on his first visit.

He was therefore the more delighted when a chance question to one of the goods porters whom he had not previously interrogated brought him a wholly magnificent and disproportionate return.

Shown Sutton's photograph, this man at once recognized the deceased as a detective who had questioned him about the cases. He had not himself been engaged with them, but he had been working at the next crane and he had seen them being taken out of the wagons and loaded up on the lorries.

It happened that at the dinner hour the porter had left the depot in advance of one of the lorries. He lived in Redliff Lane, and he had hurried there in order to have as much time at home as possible. On his way the lorry had passed him, but it had been held up in a traffic block and had not gone out of sight. He had been surprised to notice it turning into Redliff Lane. He had therefore watched it, and he had seen it enter Rice Bros.' shed.

'Did you tell that to Mr Sutton?' French asked, feeling that if the answer were yes, the mystery of Sutton's fate was solved.

The answer was yes. Sutton had appeared very much interested, but so far as the porter saw he had not gone to the shed. He had had its gate pointed out to him, but had then walked off in the direction of Mark Lane Station.

Here at last was the solution of one problem which had worried French almost from the beginning of the case. At last he knew how Sutton had come to meet his end. He had found the shed before the conspirators had given it up, and he was therefore a danger to them. Knowledge is not always power. Sometimes it is weakness and death. It was so with Sutton. He knew too much; therefore he died.

Asked why he had not come forward with his information, the porter became much aggrieved. How, he demanded, could he have known it had any value? He wasn't aware that the detective who had interrogated him was the Sutton of whose disappearance he had read. Nor that the cases were labelled for the docks, or that there was any reason why they should not have been taken into the shed. If French considered him a blooming thought reader, then, he pointed out, French had made a serious mistake.

The good fortune of discovering this porter had answered the first of French's two fundamental questions. How had the substitution of the dummy for the genuine cases been made? There still remained the second: What had been done with the genuine cases? To this problem French decided now to turn his attention.

It was probable, he thought, though of course not certain, that the genuine cases had been removed from the shed by Cruttenden himself with his Ford van. Other things being equal, he would wish to keep the knowledge of their origin from outsiders.

But if so, they could not in the nature of things have been taken very far. A long haul would have meant spreading the operation over too long a time. If, therefore, they had been taken a comparatively short distance only, to where could it have been?

The obvious suggestion was a railway goods station or a ship.

If he were right in this, the problem should be an easy one. He had only to enquire at the various adjoining goods yards and docks to get what he wanted.

He was about to start on this when a further idea occurred to him. Russia! Cruttenden's Russian passport. Had the man sold the 350 sets in Russia?

Here might be a tremendous narrowing of his investigation. His first step at all events must be to find out if any steamer to Russia had recently taken with her 350 4 feet by 2 feet by 2 feet cases.

A telephone call to Lloyd's soon supplied him with a note of all ships which had sailed for Russian ports within the period during which the sets must have been dispatched. Of these two at once attracted his attention. They had sailed from the north riverside wharf between London Bridge and the Tower. This was exceedingly close to Redliff Lane. Moreover, they were Russian ships. Further, no other vessel had sailed to Russia from anywhere nearer the shed than the Surrey Commercial Docks.

Lloyd's people had given the owners or agents of each of the boats on their list, and in less than an hour French was at the office of the agents of the promising two.

The manager was not at first inclined to give away information, but on being assured that the matter did not affect him or his steamers, but only the senders of the consignment, he thawed. Yes, there had been such a consignment. It had gone on the steamer *Chernigov*.

'Who sent it and to whom was it invoiced?' French asked in high delight.

Books were sent for, and in a few moments the information was available. The 350 crates were brought to the wharf by a private carrier, and they were invoiced from the Corona Engineering Company of Claygate, Surrey, to the Commissar for Agriculture of the Soviet Government.

French's satisfaction now knew no bounds. Here at last was the essential link that he had so long sought! At last the entire scheme was clear. It was not for the insurance money on ship or cargo that Cruttenden and Henty had laboured and schemed; it was to steal the sets! The sinking of the ship was a mere incident—a precaution designed to prevent the theft becoming known.

French took out his notebook and began to figure. The sets were sold by the Weaver Bannister Company at £350 apiece. Suppose Cruttenden and Henty had got £300 from the Soviet Government. It would have brought in £105,000! Knock off £5000 for expenses, and there remained a profit of £100,000. One hundred thousand pounds!

No wonder the men had taken trouble and undergone risks to carry out their plans! There was here an amply sufficient reward.

But, French once again told himself, personal belief, however well founded, was not enough. Before he could say with certainty that what he suspected had been done, he must get a lot more proof.

Well, it should not be hard to get.

Returning to the Yard, he put his newly-obtained information before Sir Mortimer Ellison. That that astute gentleman was delighted he could see at a glance. The A.C. even allowed himself a brief word of compliment.

'And what do you want next?' he went on.

'An application to the Russian Embassy, I suggest, sir,' French returned. 'If the Soviet Government have bought the sets, the Embassy people will know something about it. I suggest that if our facts were put before them they would react suitably.'

'A good phrase,' Sir Mortimer said dryly. 'Then let us leave no stone unturned to get them to do so. With the help of the Home Office we shall explore every avenue. I'll arrange for someone to call. You'd better go with him.'

French, slightly confused, agreed that this would meet the case, and withdrew.

At the interview which was afterwards arranged the representatives of the Soviet Government proved entirely helpful. They were horrified to learn that the sets which they had bought were stolen, and assured their visitors that they had taken all reasonable precautions against fraud. They produced documents and laid the whole of the facts as they knew them before French and his companion.

From these it seemed that in the previous June the Soviet Government had advertised for 500 petrol-electric sets of a special type. They were to be larger than such are usually made, and were for the purpose of lighting the groups of buildings which were coming into being on the Soviet collective farms. The English manufacturers, however, had proved somewhat disappointing, and, though the matter was discussed with some of them, the price quoted was not considered satisfactory, and no contract had been placed. The matter had dragged on for some weeks, and then they received a visit from a man giving the name of James Rice. He was, he said, agent for the Corona Engineering Company, which was about to build large works near Claygate in Surrey. At the moment he had rented a small shed near the Tower, but his small firm was being incorporated in the Corona Company, and he would be moving to Claygate when the new works were ready.

He had, he went on, a number of sets which, though not absolutely what the Soviet Government had specified, were, he believed, equally suitable. He was not going to sing their praises, but he asked that a representative might be sent down to the shed to inspect a sample. If it proved not up to requirements no harm was done, but if it gave satisfaction negotiations might be entered upon. He said that unhappily he couldn't supply 500, he had only 350. These, however, he could hand over within a comparatively few days.

Here the story was taken up by the engineer representative who had acted for the Soviet Government. This man, a big six-footer named Chmielinski, said he had fixed up an appointment with Cruttenden and they had met at the shed. On his remarking on the nature of the premises, Cruttenden had told him the story of their being only a makeshift until the works at Claygate should be finished.

This seemed reasonable to Chmielinski, though he did not give the matter a great deal of thought. What interested him was the set, which he examined and tested thoroughly. It was a beautiful piece of work, entirely suitable for their requirements. But there was only one. Cruttenden said the others were still at the Corona factory, but that that need not affect the matter. He proposed that this set should be marked by both parties, and that it should then be taken by the Russians as a sample to which all the remainder must conform. These others would be subject to inspection and test, and payment would not be expected unless they were found to be similar.

Chmielinski reported accordingly and in due course a firm agreement was entered into between the Government and Cruttenden. Nothing was heard of the matter for some time, then on the 8th October they were asked to send a representative to the shed to examine the 350 sets. Chmielinski had gone down again and had found them in opened cases. He had not actually unpacked them, but as all seemed of the same excellent quality as the sample, he had passed them for export. As it was impossible to test each one under load in the shed, it was arranged that this would be done at Leningrad, before the Soviet representatives there took them over. Cruttenden undertook to go to Leningrad for this purpose. He had done so, and, so far as they knew, the tests were in progress. It was part of the bargain that if the sets proved satisfactory the money should be paid in English pound notes. They had not considered this suspicious, owing to the difficulties connected with currency and exchange.

'What was the agreed price?' French asked when Chmielinski had finished.

'Rice asked £325 each, but after further negotiations he agreed to take £295, provided we met him on some points of detail. These were of no importance, and we were glad to do so.'

So French's estimate was correct, and the scoundrels had netted just about £100,000 as the result of their scheme.

French was not interested in the question which was then discussed, what was to be done to square up between Messrs Weaver Bannister, the Land and Sea Insurance Company, and the Soviet Government. What mattered to him was the whereabouts of Cruttenden. He waited till a favourable break in the conversation, then asked the question.

The Embassy representatives did not know. But they would find out. There was obviously personal feeling in their reply. French felt that they would do their utmost to help him to get his hands on those hundred thousand one-pound notes. The subject had evidently become a sore one.

Deeply satisfied with his progress, French returned to the Yard to lay his plans for the tracking down of his two criminals.

17

Fire Alarm

French had not much more than settled down to work when he was rung up from the Russian Embassy. A reply had come in from Leningrad. Cruttenden had been there for some days while the sets were being tested. The tests had been completed, the sets found satisfactory, and the money paid. Cruttenden had left for London on the Russian steamer *Kursk*, due in the Thames on the following morning.

Nothing could have pleased French better. He set to work at once to ensure that Cruttenden should be suitably greeted on his arrival.

Not immediately on his arrival. There still lurked in the background the shadowy individual known as Henty. It was but just that the welcome to be prepared for Cruttenden should be extended also to Henty. Now Henty's whereabouts was unknown. Could it not be arranged that Cruttenden's last service to his King and country should be the clearing up of this essential point? French thought it could.

For the remainder of the day French sat in his office, first considering his plans, and then interviewing those concerned to ensure that his arrangements should be carried out without a hitch. Then, supremely pleased with himself, he went home.

The *Kursk* was due to pass Gravesend about midday, and well before that time French had reached the riverside town and introduced himself to Dr Busby, one of the port health officers. The doctor was a big man with a hearty manner and a loud voice.

'Ha,' he greeted French with a twinkle in his eye, 'my new clerk, are you? I hope you can write better than the last, or you'll not hold your job long.'

'Have I much writing to do?' French asked meekly.

'Now how do I know?' the doctor queried. 'I suppose you scarcely expect me to teach you your work?'

'No,' said French, 'I don't suppose you could do that. I think I'd better have a lot of writing to do. Keep my face out of the limelight, you know.'

'Righto, I'll fix it. What's this Johnny been up to that you want to get your claws into?'

'In confidence?'

'Sure.'

'Then I'll tell you. The *Jane Vosper*.'

'Holy smoke! You mean he sank her?'

'He was the ringleader. There was another man in it, too.'

The doctor shrugged. 'Then he deserves all that's coming to him. I'm glad to have a finger in the pie.'

A man put his head into the room. 'Steamer's just coming up, sir,' he declared. 'Boat'll be starting in two or three minutes.'

'Good. Will you come along, clerk?'

The *Kursk* was a raised quarter-deck vessel of about 2000 tons register. French followed the doctor aboard a launch containing some other port officials, and in a few moments they were out in the river and transferring to the Russian. French was curious apart from his quest. It was the first time he had been on a Soviet vessel, and he had somehow expected to see something different from what might normally be expected. He had read tales of the strange equality that obtains between officers and men, and hoped that some interesting scenes would take place for his entertainment.

However, the men of the *Kursk* did not seem very different from other seamen. He thought they were a mild, kindly-looking crowd, not perhaps of a superlative intelligence, though he reminded himself that he had yet to see the ship's company which exhibited the latter trait in a marked degree. He noted with some surprise the good terms on which Dr Busby seemed to be with the Russians. The same, indeed, applied to all the port officials.

After various formalities had been gone through the crew lined up on the deck and Dr Busby passed from one to another, looking at their tongues and asking them questions. As he did so he barked out cryptic utterances to French, who dutifully made a show of writing them down.

At the first glance French saw Cruttenden. There was no mistaking him, as the photograph was a good likeness. French was careful neither to stare nor to avoid looking at him. He contented himself with a mere glance, passing on at once to the next man.

This was half of what French wanted: to satisfy himself that Cruttenden really was on board. The second half was to see that he didn't leave the ship before the proper point of disembarkation, at which Inspector Tanner and Constable Shaw would be prepared to welcome him. As soon, therefore, as the doctor had finished, French faded away to the captain's cabin, where, owing to a note sent from the Embassy, he was received as an honoured guest.

The port officials having left in their launch, the *Kursk* went on up the river. It was a dull day with a cold wind blowing in from the east. The river showed the colour of lead, mottled with the lights and shades of waves and relieved with occasional flecks of white. The banks were low and the buildings drab and uninspired looking. French, staring along the deserted deck from the captain's porthole, was glad of the warm shelter.

They passed through the Tower Bridge as dusk was falling and drew in to the wharf on the south side of the Upper Pool. From his retreat French watched the berthing. So far his man was all right, for the *Kursk* had not stopped since leaving Gravesend. But now a critical time was approaching. Cruttenden must neither be allowed to get out of sight nor to obtain a glimpse of his bodyguard. French could now see him on deck, shooting little suspicious glances around, and from the shelter of a boat spying out on those on the wharf.

He had more cause for suspicion than he knew of. Taking cover behind a shed was Tanner, and at the entrance, chatting with a stevedore, was Shaw. French held up his handkerchief at the porthole and was glad to see that each of the other men took his handkerchief from his pocket and gave it a slight wave before putting it to its predestined use.

Then suddenly French felt a thrill of pure satisfaction.

A middle-aged man of medium height, with a firm jaw and an intelligent expression, had strolled on to the wharf and had stopped in a casual way to light a cigarette. One glance at him was sufficient. It was Henty, the lorryman of Morgan & Trusett's, and almost certainly the man who had helped to cart the timber to the shed and Cruttenden's most frequent caller at the house at Pinner!

French was at once faced with a problem which clamoured for immediate settlement. Here were his two suspects. Should he make sure of them while he could? He had sufficient force to do it.

For a moment he was tempted to act, then wiser counsels prevailed. He did not know that only these two men were in the thing. It behoved him to make sure. If he moved now, he would probably never know. Besides, Tanner and Shaw might misunderstand his change of plan, and there might be a hitch in the arrests. No, for better or worse, he would stick to his programme.

The *Kursk* was a purely cargo ship, and Cruttenden was the only passenger. He had, as a matter of fact, signed on as steward to keep within the letter of the law. As soon as the gangway was in place he went ashore, carrying two small suitcases. In them, French was certain, were somewhere about 100,000 one-pound Bank of England notes.

As the man passed down the gangway, French again fluttered his handkerchief. Shaw nodded to his acquaintance and left the wharf in advance of the quarry, while Tanner came to life and moved round the corner of his shed. Henty had also gone towards the exit. Soon all four had disappeared, Cruttenden, obviously unconscious of his position, between the others.

Directly the coast was clear French hurried off the ship,

and in the Borough High Street was just in time to see
Tanner hailing a taxi. By a stroke of luck another was
coasting past at the moment, and French jumped in and
told the man to follow Tanner's.

The chase led through the High Street and Borough
Road into Waterloo Road, and up to the station. There,
discreetly shadowed by their two satellites, Cruttenden and
Henty moved towards the booking office. Cruttenden
bought a ticket, and the two men disappeared into an
electric train.

Shaw, after a word with the ticket examiner, sprinted
for tickets, while French joined Tanner, and with platform
tickets both men went through the barrier, so that if the
quarry attempted any diversion, they should not be left
unattended. But they made no move. Shaw presently arrived
back with the tickets and, openly joining forces, the three
officers got into a compartment in the last coach.

The train was a local to Surbiton and stopped at every
station. At each halt Shaw cocked out an eye, but for a
considerable time there was no sign of the quarry. Then
at Raynes Park the two men got out and, without looking
round, left the platform.

The others were not far behind them, Shaw keeping to
the front and French, whom both men had seen, dropping
behind. In the open, however, there was not such need for
care, as it had grown practically dark.

On the approach to the station a private car was parked.
Cruttenden and Henty got in, started the engine, and
drove off towards the south. There was no other vehicle
in sight.

'Damn it,' cried French, 'we can't afford to lose them.'
He rushed out into the road and looked quickly up and

down. From the direction of Town a car was approaching, empty save for the driver. French hailed it.

'Officers from Scotland Yard,' he cried. 'We're after a man in that car—a murder case. A lift, please, as quick as you can.'

Whether the driver was aware that the police have the right to call on civilians for assistance in emergencies, or whether he was of sporting tendencies and the idea of a chase appealed to him, he nodded, and while the three men wrenched open the doors, he set his gears. As they leapt on the running board he let them in and the car bounded forward.

The other car had by this time disappeared round a bend, but when they swung round in their turn, French caught sight of its rear light far ahead.

'What about the speed limit?' queried the driver as he manoeuvred round a lorry.

'You needn't exceed,' said French. 'They'll go well within it so as not to risk being held up.'

Their assistant was a skilful driver, and the needle of his speedometer never rose above thirty nor fell below twenty-nine. Steadily they overhauled the other, whose speed seemed to be about twenty-four or twenty-five. The chase led towards such country as obtains in that district, and presently the car ahead turned into the drive of a small detached house.

'Splendid!' said French. 'Drive past and let us out at the corner.'

French took their good Samaritan's name, so that an official letter of thanks for his services should be written him, then, bidding him a cordial goodnight, saw that he drove away. The three officers crept slowly back to the house.

It was a square-built structure standing in small grounds thickly planted over with shrubs. These made it wonderfully private, considering how close were its neighbours on either side. The drive had a wide sweep and the shrubs blocked the view of the door from the road. A light shone through the fanlight of this door, but all the front windows were in darkness.

The three men advanced up the drive, keeping as much in the shadow of the bushes as possible. It was now so dark that there was very little chance of their being seen, unless someone actually left the house. However, French did not want to run any risks, and they took cover as if it were broad daylight.

The wind had died down and the sky had cleared. Luckily there was no moon, though the stars were shining brightly. It was bitterly cold; if it was not actually freezing it would do so before long. The men shivered as they huddled uncomfortably behind the bushes. All devoutly hoped their vigil would not last long.

They had waited only a very few minutes when a light sprang up in a window on the left side of the house.

Motioning the others to remain where they were, French crept forward to investigate. But he was immediately disappointed. The window was fitted with a blind, which was drawn down so fully as to prevent any view into the room. The window, moreover, was tightly shut, and no sound could be heard.

French saw that to remain where he was would be simply to waste his time. He therefore tiptoed back to the others, warned them to keep a sharp look-out and let no one get away, and explained that he was going to ring up for help to rush the place.

302

He had noticed a telephone booth at a corner not long before they reached the house, and hurrying back, he called up the local police station. Explaining what he proposed to do, he obtained the local superintendent's blessing, and asked for a local man in uniform to be sent to work under his instructions. Then he got on to the Yard and demanded reinforcements.

Till these forces arrived there was nothing to be done but watch. The local man was the first to put in an appearance, and him French stationed behind a bush where he could be called on when required. The others could not turn up for another fifteen or twenty minutes. Having adjured everyone to maintain complete silence, French took cover again.

His precautions proved themselves justified when, not five minutes later, a car turned into the drive and pulled up beside the other one in front of the door. Two men got out, rang, and were presently admitted. From his hiding place French could not see them clearly, being satisfied only that there were two, and that both went into the house.

This put another complexion on the affair, better in the sense that if there were a gang, all the members might be taken, worse because it would not be possible to take four men so easily as two. If the four were armed, an arrest might be a costly business enough. He wondered would he be wise to risk it with the force at his disposal.

A few seconds' reflection showed him that he would not. If any of the men got away he would be seriously to blame for having done so. With a word of explanation he returned to the telephone booth, and once again ringing up the local station, asked for four men to surround the house during his operations.

He was a good deal surprised by the arrival of the two visitors. So far as he had ascertained, only two had functioned—Cruttenden and Henty. If these other two had taken an active part in the affair, he could not imagine what they had done. And it was unlikely that they would be given a share in the proceeds if they had not had one in the work.

For a moment he thought they might be capitalists who had financed the scheme, but he soon remembered that Cruttenden's bank account showed that he had paid out what appeared to be the necessary sums for this purpose. No, this did not seem to be the explanation, and the development puzzled him.

However, this was not the time to try to think out puzzles. Or, rather, he had to solve a more pressing one of a different nature. How was he going to arrest four—or perhaps more—men, probably armed and certainly desperate, without getting some of his men shot?

He had a scheme in his mind, but he was not now sure that it was good enough. It was to help in it that he had sent for the local policeman. He tried to think of something better. But before he could do so the four local constables arrived, followed in a few seconds by two cars from the Yard, and it was too late to change his plans.

He had been watching out for the reinforcements, and, telling the constables to wait at the gate, he waved the drivers round the next corner, lest the sound of cars pulling up at the gate should be heard. Including the drivers, five fresh men had come, so that there were now thirteen available for the attempt.

French was not altogether happy about making the attempt with so few, particularly as according to his scheme seven would be employed outside the house, and therefore only six could enter. However, his scheme also provided for getting one of the enemy outside, so that the numbers of those within should be depleted to this extent. For some minutes he weighed the matter, then he decided to try his luck.

He began by placing the four local constables round the house, with instructions to hold anyone who might break away from the attackers. Then, calling the others together, he instructed them in their parts. When they had repeated the directions and he was sure that they understood what was expected of them, all but the single local constable crept forward and took cover behind some bushes just beside the door. Tanner then moved out to the left corner of the house, close to the lighted window, while another man hid round the corner to the right. French crept stealthily about, seeing that all were posted correctly, and making sure in particular that the little group of his immediate followers were out of sight of the door, though close enough to rush in at a moment's notice.

Though his heart was beating somewhat more rapidly than usual, French felt perfectly cool and sure of himself. There was a certain amount of danger in what they were undertaking, but personal danger did not greatly worry him. What he did fear was losing any of the others, either of the criminals or of his own men. If Cruttenden or Henty or their visitors got away or committed suicide, it would be a serious matter for him, while if one of his helpers were killed or injured he would never forgive himself.

It was profoundly still as he moved about, making sure that all was right for the attempt. The road was far removed from the main thoroughfares with their ceaseless roar of traffic. The wind had fallen completely, and for the moment no trains seemed to be passing on the railway. Save for a faint starlight, it was now pitch dark. There was no need to delay any longer.

Satisfied at last that everything was ready, he gave a whispered warning to be ready and flashed his torch three times in the direction of the gate. Then, setting his teeth, he waited, his nerves on edge with suspense.

This was the signal to the local constable to begin operations, and very well he responded. There came the sound of running footsteps, first on the footpath and then on the drive, and the man rushed up to the door, rang with one hand and thundered with the knocker with the other. Presently hurrying steps were heard within, and the door was thrown open. A man peered out. French could see from the light in the hall that it was Henty.

The constable gave him no time to look about him. 'Fire!' he shouted urgently. 'Your house, sir! At the back! Come round!'

He led the way to the right and Henty, taken by surprise, rushed after him. French, knowing that he would be held by the constable and the man waiting round the corner, stood still for a moment. Then as there was no further sign from the house, he hurriedly tiptoed into the hall, followed by all his men except Tanner.

He had rather expected this development. All the men might, of course, have rushed out, in which case he would have taken them at a disadvantage with his group. But he imagined they would remain silently in that room with the lighted window, so as not to betray their presence unnecessarily. Doubtless, if the alleged fire proved serious, they would slip away unnoticed in the confusion.

But this immobility involved using the second plan which French had prepared and which he was now about to put into operation.

The front door led into a smallish hall, with two doors on either side and the staircase rising from the back. All the doors were shut, but from the arrangement of the windows outside French realized the lighted room was reached by the second door to the left. He silently grasped the handle, while his followers crowded behind him. There for a breath they waited.

Then they got their signal. There was a tremendous crash from within. Tanner had carried out his orders and heaved a large flower pot through the window. Before the reverberations died away French threw open the door and dashed in, followed by his six officers.

There were three men in the room, and as he had hoped and expected, all were startled and looking at the window. Before they could make a move to defend themselves, almost, indeed, before they could swing round, each was clutched by two of the assailants.

In spite, however, of this initial advantage, victory was by no means obtained without a struggle. The men fought like devils, writhing and twisting and obviously trying to reach weapons. But the police had gripped hold, and nothing could shake them off. Round and round they went, banging into the furniture, and smashing all of it except a huge desk, so massive that it withstood the combined weight of six of the combatants as they crashed against it. Then as soon as Tanner saw that none of the criminals could escape by the window, he rushed in and lent his fifteen stone to the attackers. This quickly turned the scale. One by one the men were overcome, handcuffed, and led out to the waiting cars.

Then at last French was able to consider the identity of the other two men. They were Hislop, Weaver Bannister's assistant export manager, and Keene, the manager of Waterer & Reade's, the carriers!

As they sat in the cars, driving to police headquarters, French could have kicked himself. How under heaven had he missed realizing that in order to carry out the scheme there must have been internal help from these two sources? How could an outsider have known sufficient detail about the sending out of the crates to enable them to be met and intercepted as they had been? How could Cruttenden and Henty have obtained the job of carting the crates, unless there was a benevolent power on their side in Waterer & Reade's? Now when he knew what had happened, it was so easy to see that it must have happened! How the mutual arrangements had been made, and why these four men had joined in the conspiracy was still, of course, unknown. But that they had done so he felt he should have long since recognized.

And in each case he had had his clue, and in each case he had missed its significance! When testing Hislop's statement as to his journey to the docks on the day of Sutton's disappearance, he had realized that though the man might have called at the shed on his way, he could not have murdered Sutton, for the simple reason that he would not have had time. This conclusion was perfectly sound, but what he, French, had overlooked was that Hislop would not have had to commit the murder. All he would have had to do was to entice Sutton to the shed, and Cruttenden could have done the rest. And French now hadn't the slightest doubt that that was what had been done. The two men were in it, and perhaps Henty as well. The Baker

308

Street-Waterloo story was simply a red herring depending on Hislop's statement alone.

The clue to Keene was even clearer. He had come upon it in his recent interview with the man. He had even remarked on it, but he had allowed a skilful suggestion on Keene's part to put him off. How could Cruttenden and Henty have foreseen that they would have been put on to the job of carting the crates? The truth was that they couldn't have. They might have tried for it, but without help from above they couldn't have been sure of succeeding. And to succeed was so fundamental to their plans that they would never have undertaken them unless this point was prearranged.

French wondered at Keene's having admitted that he recognized Cruttenden's photograph. Probably, however, he thought that French either knew the lorryman's identity or would discover it when he went to see the foreman, and he was afraid, therefore, to seem to hide it.

Another point which for a time puzzled French was that while Cruttenden had left the cartage firm practically as soon as the transport of the crates was complete, Henty had remained on for some days longer, indeed so long that French had himself seen him there. Then French thought he saw the explanation. Considering the questions which might arise about that transport, it would have been unwise for the two strangers who had been taken on just before the job, and who had carried it out, to leave immediately it was completed. If one remained a few days longer it would tend to prevent a connection being suspected between the job and the engagement. French later found that he was correct in this assumption.

However, all these perplexing matters would soon be

cleared up. With the knowledge he had, he would have but little difficulty in discovering what was still hidden.

One point, however, remained about which he was so anxious that directly he had seen the men in the cells at the local police station he hurried back to the scene of the capture. He had left a couple of men there and everything remained unaltered. He hastened to the room in which the struggle had taken place. Yes, there were the two suitcases Cruttenden had brought ashore from the *Kursk*. To open them was the work of a second, and then—a final and overwhelming satisfaction—he saw that both were full of one-pound Bank of England notes!

18

The Story of the Crime

A routine investigation into the lives of Cruttenden, Henty, Hislop and Keene, together with an attempt by Henty to turn King's evidence, brought out in all its sordid detail the facts which had led up to the scheme for the theft of the petrol sets, culminating in the loss of the *Jane Vosper* and the murder of John Sutton. A sad tale it was of human unhappiness, thwarted endeavour and misdirected ingenuity.

Cruttenden was the prime mover. For many years he had lived by his wits. He was a thorough scoundrel. As a younger man he had been guilty of various swindles, and then after a period of card-sharping on the Atlantic liners had graduated to his more recent profession of systematic blackmailer. It was from blackmail that his principal income came, but as a side line he ran gambling rooms in a flat in Wardour Street. His apparatus, like himself, was crooked, and he could at will drop the pea into any compartment of the roulette wheel that he desired, or miraculously arrange that the winning card should be found in his partner's hand.

In these activities he was enthusiastically helped by his partner and jackal, Henty. Henty's real name was Snow and he lived in the house in Raynes Park. Snow—or Henty, to continue to give him the name known to French—was morally the worse of the two, but he had neither the initiative nor the ability to visualize and carry out any new or difficult scheme. But with someone else to do the thinking for him he would stick at nothing, provided only that there seemed to be a reasonable financial return for his trouble.

For some time the partners had been making a good enough thing out of their evil activities, but latterly, as in more reputable businesses, profits had been dwindling till some months before the *Jane Vosper* affair ruin had begun to stare them in the face. As time passed their shifts became more and more desperate, and at last it became evident that they could no longer carry on as they had been doing. Either they must bring off some important *coup*, or they would go under.

It was a chance remark of Hislop's that gave Cruttenden his idea.

Hislop was an acquaintance of Henty's and occasionally played at the Wardour Street flat. But he was very sharp, so much so that the conspirators never attempted anything crooked while he was there. Cruttenden had talked to him on different occasions and had sized him up as an utterly ruthless and unscrupulous man who would do anything for money and his own advancement. From an unguarded remark Cruttenden, who had a nose like a terrier's for such matters, learned that Hislop was fond of taking women for expensive weekends, and that as his salary did not run to this, he was on the lookout for other sources of income.

It happened that one evening the two men were chatting over spirits and tobacco before leaving for home after play. Hislop, who was lucky at cards, had won a fair sum and was in an expansive humour. Cruttenden had happened to ask how business was, and Hislop, while agreeing that it was looking up, had been strong in condemnation of a recent decision of his firm's. It appeared that the Soviet Government was in the market for 500 petrol sets of an unusually large design, for which they were willing to pay a good price. They were for use on the groups of buildings which they were putting up on their collective farms, to take the place of the old insanitary villages. Messrs Weaver Bannister, however, had decided not to tender. Whether they feared they would not be paid, Hislop didn't know, but he personally didn't believe there was any chance of that, and he grudged losing the extra work. 'And we're making the very things, too,' he went on indignantly, 'large sets for the haciendas of the Argentine and Brazil. 350 sets are being made, and they'll be going out to South America in two or three months. Why in hades, when we've got the plant and the jigs and everything set up, we couldn't go on and make a few more beats me.'

The conversation had passed on to other subjects, but afterwards Cruttenden had thought over what he had been told. 350 sets about to be sent to South America on the one hand, and on the other the Soviet Government on the market for similar sets.

It was not at once that Cruttenden's great idea came, but as he continued pondering the situation it suddenly flashed into his mind. If he could steal the South American sets and sell them to the Soviet people, there would be big money in it. As he thought of that money, the decision was made. He would look seriously into the idea and see whether anything could be made of it.

Almost immediately he realized that he could not possibly work it alone. However, there was Henty, who would no doubt jump at such a chance of easy money. But even Henty would not be enough.

However, nothing could be done till he had a plan. Cruttenden was extremely ingenious and a good deal of intensive thought did produce a scheme. He went over it and over it in his mind, improving here, simplifying there, making it safer in a third particular. At last he thought the plan would work, and he began seriously to consider helpers.

He saw that he would require three. One he would want to help himself to carry out the actual manual details. For that there was Henty. So far it was easy. But he wanted two others, one in touch with the Weaver Bannister Company, the other in authority in some firm of carriers.

As to the first of these others, there could be no doubt as to the man. If Hislop would join all would be well. On the other hand, if Hislop would not join, it meant giving up the scheme. If Hislop were unsuccessfully approached, and if anything then happened to the sets, Hislop would know where to look. No, everything depended on getting Hislop into the affair.

Cruttenden approached Henty, to find him, as he had expected, enthusiastic. But sounding Hislop was not so easy. Cruttenden did it at last as a joke, as by this method he would be able to back out of the offer should he be dissatisfied with its reception. But he was not dissatisfied. Hislop fell for it with an enthusiasm almost equal to Henty's. But Hislop made one condition which somewhat surprised his tempter. He would not have anything to do with the plan if the lives of any sailors were to be sacrificed. He drew the line at murder.

Cruttenden was anxious to avoid murder also, but he had not seen how this was to be done, his scheme being to sink whatever ship was supposed to be taking the sets without leaving a trace. Hislop, however, saw the way. He knew about the Southern Ocean Steam Navigation's boats, having frequently dispatched goods by them in the past. He could, he felt sure, use his position in the export department of Weaver Bannister's to ensure that the entire consignment should be sent by one of these steamers. She could then be sunk, not just anywhere in mid-ocean, but close to the Madeira group. The weather at the time of year would almost certainly be good, and the chances of the crew getting ashore safely were so good as almost to represent a certainty.

With considerable relief Cruttenden agreed to this modification, and the detailed working out of the scheme continued. Cruttenden's idea was that they should hire the yard, not as builders, but as carriers. Then they would themselves convey the cases from the station to the docks and could make the exchange at their leisure.

But Hislop turned this down for two reasons. First, he said he should never be able to give the cartage order to an unknown firm. His chief, Dornford, allowed him a pretty free hand, but not to such an extent as that. Besides, it would look suspicious afterwards. Secondly, the name of the proposed cartage firm would have to be painted on the lorries used, and if enquiry were afterwards made, this would bring the detectives to the shed immediately.

Cruttenden had realized the difficulty, though he had not

seen how it might be overcome. Here again Hislop supplied the suggestion which was afterwards adopted. He, Hislop, was fairly well acquainted with a man named Keene, the manager of Waterer & Reade's, the big firm of carriers. He had reason to believe that this Keene was hard up, though whether he would be prepared to assist in the scheme or not, Hislop couldn't say.

It was obvious that if this man could be brought in, practically all their remaining difficulties would be overcome. If he would use his position to start Cruttenden and Henty as temporary lorrymen and to give them the job of transporting the cases, only the most unforeseen accident could give the affair away. But would Keene come in?

Hislop thought that if the whole plan were put before him he would simply go to the police. But he wondered whether if it were suitably bowdlerized, it might not find acceptance. They would tell him that they were only going to steal and resell twenty-five sets, which would bring in about £7500. Of this he would get one quarter, or, say, close on £1900. No one, it would be pointed out, would be hurt by the proposal except the insurance company, which was well able to bear it. Keene would know nothing about what was done. His part would be confined to taking on the two lorrymen and seeing they were put on the job. Extra work would be given his firm which would justify his taking on a couple of temporary men, and Cruttenden and Henty would produce admirable testimonials. In other words, whatever afterwards happened, Keene would be able to justify his actions, so that nothing could possibly be proved against him. Then, though this part of the scheme was not to be passed on to Keene, if there were trouble or if Keene balked when he learnt the complete proposals, he would be easily brought to heel. He would be told he was in it up to the neck, and when he protested he would be asked who did he imagine would believe that tale?

This seemed a good enough scheme to Cruttenden, but Hislop was not satisfied with it. He thought they should have a stronger hold on Keene. In the end it was decided that he, Hislop, should try to get him to play at Cruttenden's flat. He would be dealt with in the time-honoured way. At first he would win, then when he was properly committed he would lose. His loss would be minimized and he would be told it did not matter, that there was plenty of time and that the luck would turn, all as per custom. Then Cruttenden would produce a maturing bill. He would be excessively sorry, but would explain that he was short of cash and therefore wanted his money to meet it. It would be terribly unfortunate, and he wouldn't for anything it had happened, but there it was: he simply must have the money. He would have to have it, even if it meant going to the Waterer directors about it. Then, when Keene was properly worked up, there would be the suggestion of this safe and easy way of raising, not only what was due, but far more. Hislop was sure Keene would then fall.

This abominable plan was put into operation and worked better even than Hislop had foreseen. Keene, told only the minor scheme, agreed to do his part readily enough, and all looked promising.

By this time the actual details had been worked out. Henty started the ball by buying in an assumed name a completed set from Messrs Weaver Bannister. The nameplate was taken off this, and another, which had meanwhile been procured, was put on in its place. This last bore the name: 'The Corona Engineering Works, Claygate, Surrey, England.'

This set was exhibited in the shed, which Cruttenden in the name of Rice had hired.

Cruttenden then persuaded the Soviet Embassy people to send a technical representative to the shed to examine the set. The representative was delighted with it, which was not to be wondered at, as it was a first-rate piece of work. Cruttenden made his explanation about the transitional condition of the Claygate firm, and put through the agreement that 350 more sets should be supplied and taken over, provided they were similar in all respects to the sample.

The next step was to provide the new cases, and here a terrible difficulty arose which for a time threatened to wreck the entire scheme. Cruttenden's idea had been to buy timber and engage carpenters to make 350 cases identical with those of the Weaver Bannister Company. Drawings for these were to be supplied by Hislop, and they were to be filled with concrete to make the necessary weight. These dummy cases would then be exchanged for the real ones during the journey from the railway to the steamer, the electric runway enabling this to be done in the time available. The sets would then be unpacked, and after the nameplates had been changed, would be repacked in their original cases and sent to Russia.

This seemed a watertight scheme, and it all worked admirably up to the last item. But there it failed. It was found impossible to use the original Weaver Bannister cases for sending the sets to Russia, for the simple reason that the Weaver Bannister name was stencilled in black on two opposite sides and the paint could not be removed. The difficulty, of course, was recognized before it actually arose, but it was not seen till the partners had gone so far as to be committed to the scheme. The ideal solution would have been to have had loose-fitting concrete blocks made, and to have lifted the sets out of the Weaver Bannister cases and put in the concrete on the way to the docks. Thus the original cases would have gone aboard the *Jane Vosper*. But for this there was no time. As it was, they found the mere changing of the cases only just possible, and it would have been out of the question also to open them, remove the sets, pack the concrete blocks and close the lids.

What they eventually did was to have the Weaver Bannister cases altered. The lettering was confined to two boards on opposite faces, and while Cruttenden was changing the nameplates on the sets Henty knocked the four boards in question out of the cases and burnt them in the shed fireplace. From a different timber merchant new boards were bought, and from a more distant labour exchange fresh carpenters were employed, and the damaged cases were repaired. This, of course, was a very small job compared with making new ones. Henty then made all sure by stencilling the Claygate name where the old lettering had been.

The method of blowing up the ship was thought out with the greatest care. Gelignite and electric detonators were chosen as the most suitable explosives. These were also the easiest to obtain, and Henty spent some time searching the country for a quarry suitable for burglary. He decided on that at Llandelly, bringing Cruttenden a description of the place with photographs, taken early on a Sunday morning. Henty did not return to Llandelly, but Hislop assisted Cruttenden with the actual theft. Cruttenden drove the Ford van down, while Hislop travelled to and from Shrewsbury by train, joining Cruttenden in the suburbs.

The gelignite and detonators—three of the latter to each case to make absolutely sure of the job—were enclosed in concrete in the four special cases, which, of course, Cruttenden and Henty themselves filled. These cases were labelled to Buenos Aires to ensure that they should be put at the bottom of the consignment. In them were also placed some dry batteries, both to supply current to operate the detonators, and also for another purpose.

The timing of the explosions proved an almost insuperable difficulty, but at last Cruttenden solved the problem in a very simple manner. Four alarm clocks of good quality were purchased and were altered by Henty, who had some mechanical knowledge. He arranged a contact so that the alarm, instead of operating a bell, closed an electric circuit. This allowed current from the batteries to flow and operated two pieces of mechanism. The first was a tiny electric motor, which rewound the clock, switching itself off when the winding was complete, and setting itself to wind again next time the alarm trigger moved. The clocks would thus continue running as long as the batteries remained active.

But in addition to starting the motor, the alarm trigger operated a second electro magnet. This moved a wheel one tooth forward. On this wheel another contact was arranged so that when it was closed current from the batteries passed through the detonators, igniting the charge. Careful estimates showed that the explosions were required sixteen days after the crates were sealed. This meant that the contact on the wheel was fixed 32 teeth ahead, or, in other words, the alarm trigger would have to operate 32 times before the explosion took place. The clocks were accurately set, so that all four explosions should occur as nearly as possible at the same time. The filling of cement over the apparatus not only increased the effect of the explosion, but rendered inaudible the ticking of the clocks.

The crime was carried out strictly according to plan. From the conspirators' point of view everything went exceedingly well. Hislop succeeded in convincing his chief that the best way of sending the sets was by the *Jane Vosper*. Keene called at the Weaver Bannister works and, with the help of Hislop, obtained the order to transport the stuff from the railway to the docks. Cruttenden and Henty were taken on by Keene and were put on the vital job without suspicion being aroused. The dummy cases were stowed on the *Jane Vosper*, and the vessel sailed—all perfectly in order. Then the sets were unpacked, the Weaver Bannister nameplates were removed, and new ones bearing 'The Corona Engineering Company, Claygate, Surrey, England', were mounted in their place. The sets were packed in the altered cases, the lids being left off for the Soviet representative's inspection. Finally the cases were dispatched to Russia, Cruttenden making arrangements to follow them so that the final test could be made in his presence. The tests were satisfactory and the money was paid in Leningrad as agreed. The notes were discovered when passing through the English customs, though not their amount; Cruttenden said it was £10,000. But nothing was done about it, as it was not illegal to bring money into England, and Cruttenden had his story pat. He had gone to Russia, he said, to buy timber, but the timber firm had tried to do him down and he had scored off them by clearing out of the country with his money intact while they were waiting for him to sign the iniquitous agreement.

Henty had learnt with something approaching horror of the police visits to Cruttenden's house at Pinner. He consulted Hislop and Keene, and their first impulse was to warn Cruttenden not to return to the country. But they thought that if they did so their share of the swag might be endangered. Indeed, from the first they had been up against the difficulty that Cruttenden might play them false and decamp with the entire £100,000. They had to chance it, however, as they could not have denounced Cruttenden without giving themselves away. But they were not going to take the further risk of letting Cruttenden remain abroad. Henty, therefore, met him on his return to warn him not to go to Pinner and to tell him their meeting had been transferred from there to his own house at Raynes Park.

One point gave Cruttenden a good deal of worry: Would the Soviet people, reading in the papers of the *Jane Vosper* affair, not smell a rat and mention their suspicions to the Home Office?

Eventually he decided that there was little fear of this. The fact that the vessel was blown up by explosives in the Weaver Bannister crates might never become known, or, if it did, the public would scarcely hear it before the Board of Trade enquiry. But by the time that this took place Cruttenden intended that the sets should be delivered and that 'Rice' and 'Henty' should have ceased to exist. Incidentally, this did not work out quite as he had hoped. His calculations were correct, but he had not reckoned on a test being required at Leningrad, and this had dragged out till long after the enquiry was over. The Soviet people, however, had suspected nothing, not connecting the two affairs and not having the slightest idea that the Weaver Bannister sets had not sunk with the ship.

The scheme had worked out better than the conspirators could have hoped, but when it was nearly completed the luck changed and disaster befell them. Sutton, enquiring as to the journey of the cases, learned that a porter at the Haydon Square Goods Depot had seen a lorry loaded with cases entering the Rice Bros.' shed. Sutton believed that he was on to something serious and did not risk giving away his knowledge by calling immediately at the shed. Perhaps he was afraid for his life. Instead he rang up his friend in the local police force, asking if anything were known of Rice Bros. Also, and this was where he made his fatal mistake, he called on Hislop to ask him if he knew anything of Rice Bros. or of the cases being taken there.

Hislop, suddenly alive to the danger, held Sutton in conversation while he cast about in his mind for some way of meeting the situation. Finally he rang up Cruttenden, and they arranged that Hislop should entice Sutton to the shed, when Cruttenden would slip up behind him and kill him with a blow over the head. Cruttenden would afterwards bury the body in the shed. (French shrewdly suspected that in this Henty had assisted, but Henty denied it, saying that he did not know anything about the affair till afterwards, and French could not disprove his statement.)

This plan was carried out. Hislop returned to Sutton, whom he had left waiting in his office, and said that he considered the news serious and that he thought Sutton and he should go immediately to the shed and make enquiries. To his clerks Hislop said that he was going down to see a certain shipping manager. This, as a matter of fact, was true, as he had to pay a call on this man, though not necessarily at that time. Hislop by tricks at each end caused

323

the times of his leaving his office and of arriving at the shippers to be noted, so that he was able to put up a reasonable alibi, the deviation necessary to pass the shed not occupying more than three or four minutes.

He and his victim then went to Redliff Lane and knocked on the door of the shed. Cruttenden admitted them, closed the door behind them, murdered Sutton by striking him on the head, and, while Hislop hurried off to complete his alibi, buried the body. The final proof of this part of the crime was that the fingerprints found on the heels of Sutton's shoes proved to be Cruttenden's.

At the trial all four men paid heavily for their crimes. Cruttenden and Hislop were sentenced to death for the murder of Sutton, and Henty, whose complicity in this could not be proved, received fourteen years' penal servitude. Keene, who was not considered to have been party to the more serious crime, got five years.

A financial settlement was made by agreement between the interested parties. The Soviet Government, who had acted in good faith throughout, now behaved handsomely. On the true facts being put before them, they offered to keep the sets and to pay Weaver Bannister £55 on each— that is, the difference between the Weaver Bannister price and the amount they had paid Cruttenden. This was naturally satisfactory to Messrs Weaver Bannister, who were thus adequately paid for their work, and made no claim against the Land and Sea Insurance Company. The South American agents agreed to accept another lot of sets, as soon as these could be made.

But loss fell on the other insurance companies, the Lloyd's underwriters who had covered the *Jane Vosper* and the firms which had insured the remainder of the cargo.

All these, however, paid up without demur, and the matter was considered at an end.

French was profoundly thankful the case had reached a satisfactory termination, though he was not entirely satisfied that he had reached his conclusion as quickly as he ought to have done. However, Sir Mortimer Ellison appeared satisfied, and indeed actually went so far as to compliment French on his achievement. It was with a little glow at his heart, therefore, that he sat down once more at his desk to read up the dossier of a cat burglar who was badly wanted out Hampstead way.

By the same author

Inspector French's Greatest Case

At the offices of the Hatton Garden diamond merchant *Duke & Peabody*, the body of old Mr Gething is discovered beside a now-empty safe. With multiple suspects, the robbery and murder is clearly the work of a master criminal, and requires a master detective to solve it. Meticulous as ever, Inspector Joseph French of Scotland Yard embarks on an investigation that takes him from the streets of London to Holland, France and Spain, and finally to a ship bound for South America . . .

'Because he is so austerely realistic, Freeman Wills Croft is deservedly a first favourite with all who want a real puzzle.'
TIMES LITERARY SUPPLEMENT

By the same author

Inspector French and the Cheyne Mystery

When young Maxwell Cheyne discovers that a series of mishaps are the result of unwelcome attention from a dangerous gang of criminals, he teams up with a young woman who is determined to help him outwit them. But when she disappears, he finally decides to go to Scotland Yard for help. Concerned by the developing situation, Inspector Joseph French takes charge of the investigation and applies his trademark methods to track down the kidnappers and thwart their intentions . . .

'*Freeman Wills Crofts is among the few muscular writers of detective fiction. He has never let me down.*'

DAILY EXPRESS

By the same author

Inspector French and the Starvel Hollow Tragedy

A chance invitation from friends saves Ruth Averill's life on the night her uncle's old house in Starvel Hollow is consumed by fire, killing him and incinerating the fortune he kept in cash. Dismissed at the inquest as a tragic accident, the case is closed—until Scotland Yard is alerted to the circulation of bank-notes supposedly destroyed in the inferno. Inspector Joseph French suspects that dark deeds were done in the Hollow that night and begins to uncover a brutal crime involving arson, murder and body snatching . . .

'*Freeman Wills Crofts is the only author who gives us intricate crime in fiction as it might really be, and not as the irreflective would like it to be.*'   *OBSERVER*